STORM RUNNERS

ALSO BY T. JEFFERSON PARKER

The Fallen

California Girl

Cold Pursuit

Black Water

Silent Joe

Red Light

The Blue Hour

Where Serpents Lie

The Triggerman's Dance

Summer of Fear

Pacific Beat

Little Saigon

Laguna Heat

STORM RUNNERS

T. Jefferson Parker

HARPER LUXE

An Imprint of HarperCollins*Publishers*

STORM RUNNERS. Copyright © 2007 by Ed Gorman. All rights reserved. Printed in the United States of America. No part of this book may be used or reproduced in any manner whatsoever without written permission except in the case of brief quotations embodied in critical articles and reviews. For information, address HarperCollins Publishers, 10 East 53rd Street, New York, NY 10022.

HarperCollins bookstext may be purchased for educational, business, or sales promotional use. For information, please write: Special Markets Department, HarperCollins Publishers, 10 East 53rd Street, New York, NY 10022.

FIRST EDITION

ISBN: 978-0-06-123313-5
ISBN-10: 0-06-123313-7

Printed in the U.S.A

10 9 8 7 6 5 4 3 2 1

FOR THOSE

who bring the water

Acknowledgments

Thanks to Bill Farrar, who led the band.

To Sherry Merryman, who sent the secret documents.

To Susan Gust, who laid down the law.

To certain individuals who got me into Pelican Bay State Prison and back again—we know who you are.

STORM RUNNERS

PART I

Marching Bands
and Arabian Nights

1

Stromsoe was in high school when he met the boy who would someday murder his wife and son. The boy's name was Mike Tavarez. Tavarez was shy and curly-haired and he stared as Stromsoe lay the mace on the cafeteria table. A mace is a stylized baton brandished by a drum major, which is what Matt Stromsoe had decided to become. Tavarez held his rented clarinet, which he hoped to play in the same marching band that Stromsoe hoped to lead, and which had prompted this conversation.

"Sweet," said Tavarez. He had a dimple and fawn eyes. He could play all of the woodwinds, cornet and sax, and pretty much any percussion instrument. He had joined the marching band to meet girls. He was impressed by Stromsoe's bold decision to try out for drum major now, in only his freshman year. But this was 1980 in Southern California, where drum majoring had long ago slipped down the list of high school cool.

A little crowd of students had stopped to look at the mace. It was not quite five feet long, black-handled, with a chrome chain winding down its length. At one end was an eagle ornament and at the other a black rubber tip.

"How much did it cost?" asked Tavarez.

"Ninety-nine dollars," said Stromsoe. "It's the All American model, the best one they had."

"Waste of money," said a football player.

"May I help you?" asked Stromsoe, regarding him with a level gaze. Though he was only a freshman and a drum major hopeful, Stromsoe was big at fourteen and there was something incontrovertible about him. He had expressive blue eyes and a chubby, rosy-cheeked face that looked as if he would soon outgrow it.

"Whatever," said the football player.

"Then move along."

Tavarez looked from the athlete to the drum-major-in-making. The football player shrugged and shuffled off, a red-and-leather Santa Ana Saints varsity jacket over baggy sweatpants, and outsize athletic shoes with the laces gone. Tavarez thought the guy might take Stromsoe in a fight, but he had also seen Stromsoe's look—what the boys in Delhi F Troop called *ojos de piedros*—eyes of stone. Delhi F Troop turf included the Tavarez family's small stucco home on Flora Street, and though Tavarez avoided the gangs, he liked their solidarity and colorful language. Tavarez figured that the football player must have seen the look too.

That Saturday Matt Stromsoe won the drum major tryouts. He was the only candidate. But his natural sense of rhythm was good and his summer months of solitary practice paid off. He had been accepted for summer clinics at the venerable Smith Walbridge Drum Major Camp in Illinois, but had not been able to come up with the money. His parents had thought it all would pass.

On Friday, one day before Stromsoe won the job of drum major, Mike Tavarez nailed the third b-flat clarinet spot, easily outplaying the other chairs and doing his best to seem humble for the band instructor and other musicians. He played his pieces then spent most of the day quietly loitering around the music rooms, smiling at the female musicians but failing to catch an eye. He was slender and angelic but showed no force of personality.

Stromsoe watched those Friday tryouts, noting the cool satisfaction on Tavarez's face as he played an animated version of "When the Saints Go Marching In."

The song was a Santa Ana High School staple. By the time Stromsoe retired his mace four years later he had heard the song, blaring behind him as he led the march, well over five hundred times.

He always liked the reckless joy of it. When his band was playing it aggressively it sounded like the whole happy melody was about to blow into chaos. Marching across the emerald grass of Santa Ana stadium on a warm fall night, his shako hat down low over his eyes and his eagle-headed All American mace flashing in the bright lights, Stromsoe had sometimes imagined the notes of the song bursting like fireworks into the night behind him.

The song was running through his mind twenty-one years later when the bomb went off.

2

Days after the blast he briefly wavered up from unconsciousness at the UC Irvine Medical Center, sensing that he had lost everything. Later—time was impossible to mark or estimate—he fought his way awake again and registered the lights and tubes and the grim faces of people above him, then folded into the welcome darkness one more time.

When he was slightly stronger he was told by his brother that his wife and son were dead, killed by the same blast that had landed him here almost three weeks ago. It looked like we would lose you, said his mother. He could barely understand them because his eardrums had ruptured and now roared. A doctor assured him that a membrane graft would help.

Stromsoe lost his left eye, the little finger of his left hand, most of his left breast, and had sixty-four tacks removed, mostly from the left side of his body. The bomb makers had used three-quarter-inch wood tacks for close-range destruction. His torso and legs were a dense constellation of wounds. His left femur, tibia, and fibula had been shattered. Just as the bomb went off, Stromsoe had turned to his right, away from the blast, so his left side—and Hallie and Billy, who were two steps ahead of him—bore the fury.

A doctor called him "beyond lucky to be alive." His mother cried rivers. One day his father stared down at him with eyes like campfires smoldering behind a waterfall. Later Stromsoe deduced that his dad's eyes had been reflecting a red monitor indicator.

"They got him," his father said. "*El* fucking *Jefe* Tavarez is now behind bars."

Stromsoe managed a nod before the immensity of his loss washed over him again—Hallie whom he loved and Billy whom he adored both gone and gone forever. The tears would have poured from his eyes but the empty left socket was wet-packed with gauze and saline in preparation for a glass implant scheduled for later that week, and the right eyelid was scorched so badly that the tear duct had yet to reroute itself through the burned flesh.

A month later he was released with one functioning eye and a German-made cryolite glass one, a four-fingered left hand, a surgically reconstructed left breast, seven pins in his leg, sixty-four wounds where tacks had been removed, and two tympanic membrane grafts. He had lost ten pounds and most of his color.

He rode the wheelchair to the curbside, which was hospital release policy. His old friend Dan Birch pushed the chair while a covey of reporters asked Matt hopeful, respectful questions. He recognized some of them from the endless hours of television news he'd watched in the last month. Motor drives clattered and video cameras whirred.

"How are you feeling, Deputy Stromsoe?"

"Good to be on my feet again. Well, kind of on my feet."

"Do you feel vindicated that El Jefe Tavarez was arrested and charged so quickly?"

"Sure."

"You *finally* got him," said Susan Doss of the *Orange County Register.*

"That's nice of you to say, Susan."

He rolled along in the lambent April sunshine. Iceland poppies bloomed in the planters. His ears were ringing but he had never in his thirty-five years been more aware of the magnificence of nature's colors.

"Do you look forward to testifying against Tavarez?"

"I look forward to justice."

"What's next for Matt Stromsoe?"

"I honestly don't know."

When they reached the car Stromsoe shooed away Dan and his father, and got himself into Birch's Mercedes without much difficulty. Stromsoe pulled the door shut and Susan Doss leaned in the open window. He flinched because his peripheral vision was bad, then flushed with embarrassment because Susan was a reporter—young and pretty and intelligent—not someone about to kill him.

"You went to high school with him, didn't you?" she asked.

Stromsoe had kept his relationship to Mike Tavarez a private thing, but not a secret.

"He played clarinet in my marching band."

"He and your wife were an item back then."

"That came a little later."

"Will you talk to me about it? All of it?"

She gave him a business card and asked him for his home and cell numbers. He gave her his home but not his cell.

"I can't pay you for the interview," she said. "But I'd appreciate it if you don't talk to other media. You'll have offers from TV—real dollars."

"I turned them down."

She smiled. "I'll call you this afternoon, after you've had time to settle in and get some rest. You're going to need rest, Matt."

"Give me a few days."

"Absolutely."

3

It took Stromsoe a full month to find the strength to talk to the reporter. At first he couldn't say anything to anybody, could hardly order a combo at the drive-through window.

Two weeks after coming home he had scattered the ashes of his wife and son at sea, as Hallie had requested in a living will. The Neptune Society ship was filled with friends and family, and dipped and rolled noticeably in the big swells off of Newport while the minister spoke. Several people became sick. It was the worst two hours of Stromsoe's life.

He continued to drink on top of the Vicodin, a little more each night. He thought about the big sleep, saw some advantages to it. He thought about a lot of things he'd never thought about before.

Among them was the idea that the only way to save his sanity was to tell the story of his wife and son, staying his execution like Scheherazade.

"We got to be friends our freshman year," he said to Susan.

They faced each other at a picnic table in the small courtyard of his Newport Beach home. Susan's tape recorder sat between them, next to a cobalt-blue vase filled with cut wildflowers. She also had a pen and notebook.

Across the courtyard from where he now sat, Stromsoe's garage was still under reconstruction. His parents had begun the project weeks ago as a way of doing something optimistic but there had been some trouble with the original contractor. Around the partially rebuilt garage, trampled yellow crime scene tape had been replaced by very similar construction site tape. The muffled blasts of a nail gun popped intermittently in the cool afternoon.

The bomb had taken out one wall of the garage, blown a big hole in the roof, and shredded the bodies of two cars with thousands of tacks. What it had done to Hallie and Billy was unimaginable, but sometimes, against his will, Stromsoe did imagine it. Billy was eight. Stromsoe hadn't gone into the garage since that day. He was afraid he'd find something.

Stromsoe inwardly shivered at the sound of the nails going into the drywall. None of the reconstruction men had ever spoken to him or looked him directly in the eye. They were all Mexican, and familiar with the presence of the dead.

Use your words, he thought: tell the story and save your self.

"The marching band wasn't a very hip thing back then," he said. "It was us and them. But I liked us and them. That made it easy for me to become a cop. Anyway, the band members made friends pretty easy. One night some of the football players bombed our practice with rocks. We were under the lights, marching and playing, and these goofballs stood off behind the chain-link fence in the dark and let the rocks fly. A dumb thing to do. We didn't know what was going on at first—just a bunch of yelling and screaming about what fags we were. But then Kristy Waters sat down on the grass and covered her face and the blood was coming out from between her fingers. Kristy was first flute, a real sweetie, her dad ran a tire shop on First. I jumped the fence and caught up with a couple of those guys. I messed them up fairly well. I wasn't the type to get angry but I got very angry then. It seemed wrong that they'd thrown a rock into Kristy's face because she played the flute in the marching band.

Three of my musicians stuck with me—he was one of them."

"Mike Tavarez?"

Stromsoe nodded and touched the vase. He looked at his four-fingered hand then slid it casually beneath the bench.

"Yes. It surprised me because he was small and quiet. But he fought like a demon. It said something about him. Anyway, he was a good musician and nice kid, a real wiseass when you got to know him. So we became friends. That seems like a hundred years ago, you know? Part of another world, or someone else's past."

"I can only imagine what you're going through, Matt."

Stromsoe met her gaze and looked away. She had arrived today with the wildflowers in the vase, and a bag of fancy cheeses, salami, and crackers from an overpriced market nearby.

For relief he looked at his house. It was an older home on the Newport peninsula, on Fifty-second Street, two blocks in from the ocean. It was white. There was a fence around it and you could hear the waves. It was a nice little place, yet in the month that Stromsoe had been home from the hospital, he had come to hate it because it seemed complicit in what had happened.

But he loved it too—it had been their often-happy home—and the power of the two emotions made him feel paralyzed.

He thought about selling the place, fully furnished and as is, and moving away. He thought of selling the place but renting storage space for Hallie's and Billy's things, so he could visit them when he wanted to. He thought of just staying here and living in it as it was. He thought of burning it down and never coming back, and of burning it down with himself in it. The idea of never seeing his son's stuffed bears again broke his heart a little more, and the idea of seeing them every day broke it again in a different place.

He took off his sunglasses and noted again the odd sensation of breeze cooling his good eye while his prosthetic eye felt nothing at all.

"How long did your friendship with Mike last?" asked Susan.

"Four years. It was a good friendship. We disagreed about a lot of things and argued about everything. But always the big stuff—does God care or does God laugh at us? Is there heaven and hell, do we determine our lives or is there a divine or a satanic plan?"

"I had a friend like that too," said Susan. "Funny how we talk about those things when we're young, then stop talking about them when we get older."

Stromsoe thought back to the endless games of eight ball on the slouching table in Mike's garage. The talk, the competition. Two boys looking for a way to face the world.

"We both went nuts for Hallie Jaynes when she transferred in but we were good friends by then. We figured she was out of our reach. That was our sophomore year. She was pretty and smart. Stayed above things, had an edge. Unafraid. Unfazable. Always said what she thought—called Mike and me the marching gland. Sarcastic twinkle in her eyes. Nice face, curly blond hair, pretty legs. Our senior year, I finally got her to go steady. I knew her heart wasn't in it, but I was flattered that she'd do it for me. We didn't want to leave Mike out, so the three of us did a lot of things together. The summer after we graduated, Hallie took up with him."

Sometimes, as he remembered something good about his wife, terrible visions rushed in and destroyed his pleasant memories. How could he keep Hallie in his heart with these hideous pictures attached?

He cleared his throat and focused his attention on a hummingbird.

Talk on, he thought. Tell the story, shed the skin.

"That must have hurt," said Susan.

"Sure. But I was busy. I was getting ready to go to Cal State Fullerton. I was set to study prelaw because I wanted to be a cop. He was on his way to Harvard on scholarship because his grades were high and he was a great musician. He made the news—barrio kid bound for Harvard, all that."

"Did you see it coming, Hallie and Mike?"

Stromsoe nodded. "I wasn't totally surprised. Hallie always liked the hidden side of things and he had secrets. One of them was that at the same time he took up with Hallie, he was taking up with the Delhi F Troop. He hinted what he was doing. She dug it at first—the secrecy, the whiff of violence."

"Unafraid and unfazable."

"The minute that game started, she was out of her league."

Susan finished writing and looked at him. "You don't like to say his name, do you?"

"No, I don't."

"Does it bother you when I say it?"

"That's okay."

"I'll get you another beer if you'd like."

A minute later she was back with a cold bottle, then she set out the cheese, meat, and crackers on a plate that she had found in his kitchen. Stromsoe was annoyed that this reporter would commandeer a dish last touched by Hallie.

"When did Mike join Delhi F Troop?"

"They jumped him in that summer."

"Jumped him in?"

"They'd beat the shit out of you to see if you fight back. If you fight back, they give you a heavy job to do—an armed robbery, a retribution, maybe a killing. Once you do it, you're in. Usually, the kid is thirteen or fourteen. He was old. But they wanted him because he was smart. His parents tried to keep him away from the gangsters. They had him attend Santa Ana High instead of Valley, because Valley had the gangs. But Flora Street was Delhi turf, so he was surrounded by them anyway."

"What did he do to get in?"

"He held up three stores at gunpoint down in San Diego, where the Ten Logan 30s would get the blame. He did a good job, got some old plates for his car, cased the stores, waited until the end of the night. He hit the mom-and-pop places that didn't have fancy safes. He dressed preppie for the jobs, never banger, so it was a big surprise when the gun came out from under his sport coat. He got eleven hundred bucks, something like that. Turned half of it over to his homies, and he was in."

"They let him keep half?"

Stromsoe nodded. "He was supposed to give them all of it but he learned early to pay himself first."

Susan wrote quickly. "Did Hallie go east with him when school started?"

"No. But he came back to Santa Ana often while he was a Harvard student."

"To run with the Delhi F Troop and rob liquor stores," said Susan.

"And to be with Hallie."

Stromsoe sipped the beer. He allowed himself a memory, one that seemed useful: after Hallie had taken up with Tavarez, Stromsoe understood that she would come back to him someday. He didn't know when or why, only that she would.

Susan frowned, tapped her pen on her notepad. "How did Mike Tavarez go from being a clarinet player to an armed robber? And so quickly? Why?"

Stromsoe had given these questions more than a little thought over the last fourteen years, since he'd learned that Mike Tavarez had pulled off a string of nine armed robberies in Southern California while posting a 3.0 GPA as a Harvard undergrad.

"The robberies were a rush for him," said Stromsoe. "He told me that in jail. He said they were better than coke or meth or Hallie, or any combination thereof."

Susan nodded. "But he was giving up his future."

"He thought he was making his future. He hated Harvard. He felt dissed and out of place. He told me he just wanted to be a homie. Not a poster boy for Equal Opportunity. Not a newspaper feature about the poor kid in the Ivy League. He felt like a traitor to *la raza*, being singled out for all that praise and promise."

He didn't tell her that Hallie liked it when Mike came back from those robberies, jacked on adrenaline. She didn't know exactly what he was doing out there, but the mystery turned her on. Hallie told him so. And Mike had told him how much he enjoyed fooling her. A binding secret.

"What did he do with the money?"

"He told the court that he'd robbed to help his mother and father. But he didn't—he bought stocks and did well for himself. Most of that money he lost under asset forfeiture laws. His attorney got the rest. That was the last time he did anything traceable with cash. Anyway, the judge hit him pretty hard. Mike got ten, did a nickel, and walked in '93. By the time he left prison, Mike Tavarez wasn't a Delhi street hood anymore. He was La Eme."

"The Mexican Mafia. The most powerful prison gang in the country."

"They made the Delhi F Troop look like Campfire Girls."

"And by the time he got out, you were married to Hallie."

"Yes," Stromsoe heard himself say. "Billy was one and a half. It took us a long time to have him. Hallie had a hard time getting pregnant after what he did to her."

"Tell me about that," said Susan Doss.

"I can't," said Stromsoe. Exhaustion closed over him like a drawn blind. "I'm sorry. Maybe later."

"Tomorrow? Same time. I'll bring lunch, how's that?"

4

That evening, Dan Birch, Stromsoe's good friend and former narco partner, arrived unannounced. It was the third time he'd come to the house on Fifty-second Street since Stromsoe had been released from UCI Medical Center. Birch and his wife and children had been guests here for the better part of twelve years. Birch now stood in the kitchen and surveyed Stromsoe with his usual heavy-browed glower.

"You look bad," he said.

"I feel bad sometimes," said Stromsoe.

"What can I do?"

"There's nothing, Dan."

"I can put you to work when you're ready."

Stromsoe nodded and tried to smile. "A one-eyed security guard?"

Four years ago Birch had quit the Sheriff 's Department and started his own security company. Thanks to an engaging personality and some family connections to Irvine high-tech companies, his Birch Security Solutions had billed $1.15 million in its first year, and tripled that number since. They did some of everything: residential and industrial security, patent and copyright protection, patrol, installations, and private investigations.

Birch chuckled. "I can do better than that, Matt."

"Divorce work?"

"We've got some interesting industrial espionage going down in Irvine. And some jerk-off at the med school selling cadaver parts, but the university can't afford the scandal of busting him. We're going to…dissuade him from further business."

"No cadaver parts, Dan."

"I understand. I shouldn't have said that. What can I do to help? I'm trying here."

"Let me make you a drink. It's only the Von's brand. I'm trying to reduce my dependence on foreign vodka."

They drank late into the night, Stromsoe outpacing his friend roughly two to one. He laid off the painkiller as long as he could but by midnight the pins in his legs were killing him so he took more pills.

"One for the road?" he asked Birch.

"No."

Birch came over and knelt next to Stromsoe. "I didn't know it was this bad."

"It's temporary. Don't worry."

"I'm so fucking sorry, Matt."

"I'll get there," he said, wherever there was.

"Tavarez is an animal," said Birch. "And Ofelia's death wasn't our fault."

"No," said Stromsoe. "Not our fault at all."

A long silence lowered over them during which Stromsoe did not hear the waves breaking nearby. "Is there any way to get to him?" he asked.

Birch's eyes tracked behind his heavy brows. "Mike? In Orange County Jail? You might be able to bring some annoyance his way—get his privileges and exercise time cut back. You'd need to get a deputy or two on your side."

"I had something more substantial in mind."

"Such as what?"

"Five minutes alone with him."

Birch stood, shaking his head. "The visitation setup is all wrong for that. Besides, the only one who can grant you a visit is Tavarez."

Stromsoe thought about five minutes with El Jefe.

"Forget it, Matt. You kill him, you may as well just move right into his cell, put on his jumpsuit."

• • •

WHEN BIRCH HAD gone Stromsoe limped through the house with a big vodka in hand. He walked with his head down, focusing on the ice in his drink, and when he came into a room he lifted his head and looked around but then would have to close his eyes against the memories. Every cubic inch of space. Every object. Every molecule of every object, tied to Hallie and Billy. Their things. Their lives. Their life. It was impossible to endure.

He stood swaying in the courtyard for a moment, watching the sliver of moon slip down then rise back into place over and over.

His cell phone pulsed against his hip and Stromsoe slid it off, dropped it, and then knelt and picked it up.

"The bomb was for you," said Tavarez. "God put them there for reasons we don't understand."

"You blew up a woman and a little boy."

"But you made it possible."

"You'll burn in hell for what you did."

"Hell would be better than this," said Tavarez. "Now you understand how bad it is, don't you? Living without the ones you love?"

"If they ever let you out, I'll find and kill you," said Stromsoe.

"Life can be worse than death," said Tavarez. "So I'm going to let you *live.* Live first in the smell of their blood. Then live without them, month after month and year after year. Until you begin to forget them, until your memory is weak and uncertain. Because you know, Matt, wives and lovers and even children can be forgotten. They must be forgotten. But an enemy can live in your heart forever. The more spectacular his crime against you, the more durable your enemy becomes in your heart. Hate is stronger than love. I tried to kill you but I'm much happier that I didn't. Tell me, are you blinded by fury?"

"Inspired by it."

"Pray to your God for vengeance, to the one who ignores you. And welcome to prison. The bars here keep me from freedom. The bars around your heart will do the same to you."

With a dry little chuckle, Tavarez clicked off.

Stromsoe hurled his drink against the side of his house. He turned and lurched toward the garage. He pushed through the construction site tape, got tangled and kicked his way out as his legs burned with pain. He pulled open the garage door and flipped on the light.

Here it was, his personal ground zero, the heart of his loss.

He forced himself to stand where they had been standing. The concrete floor was thick with drywall dust and he swept aside some of it with his foot. The floor had been bleached. He looked at the wall in front of him— new drywall. And the wall to his left—new drywall too. He looked up at the new framing that was being roofed with new plywood and new paper and new mastic and new tiles. He didn't see a drop of what he was dreading to find. Not one tiny trace. New was good.

He walked slowly around the Ford to the far corner of the garage. Here were some cabinets he had built many years ago. The bottom cabinet was long and deep and fitted with duckboards. The slats were now stained from years of two-cycle oil spills and gas-can seepages, leaking weed eaters and blowers and chain saws.

Stromsoe bent over and rocked the red plastic gas can. It sloshed, heavy with fuel. He hefted it out, twisted open the cap, and pulled out the retractable spigot. The fumes found his nose.

The smell of escape, he thought.

He backed the Taurus into the driveway, set the brake, and killed the engine. Back in the garage he poured gasoline where Hallie and Billy had last breathed, then across the cement floor, out the door and across the bricks of the little courtyard to the back porch, then through the slider and into the dining room, kitchen, living room, the bedrooms.

He set the can down by the front door, got a plastic bag from under the sink, and slid most of Hallie's jewelry into it. He found a pack of matches in the coins-and-keys drawer of his dresser. Then, in Billy's room, he added three of his son's favorite stuffed bears to the bag.

He went back to the front door, opened it, and continued his gas trail outside to the porch. The door he left ajar. Dropping the gas can and the plastic bag to the porch boards, Stromsoe then fished the matches out of his pocket. The moths and mosquito hawks flapped against the porch lights and the waves swooshed to shore in the dark.

He sat down to think it over.

With his back to the door frame he brought up his knees and rested his face on his forearms. The nail wounds in his body flared like struck matches. His ears rang. He could feel his glass eye moving against the skin of his arm, but the eye itself felt nothing. The matchbook fell from his hand. He asked God what to do and got no answer. He asked Hallie and Billy what to do and they told him not this—it was dangerous and stupid and wouldn't help. Hallie's argument that he couldn't let his son be without a home made sense to him.

Stromsoe got up and went back inside and fell asleep on the living-room couch with the gas fumes strong around him and the waves breaking in the black middle distance.

He opened some windows before he crashed, a precaution that brought to him both cool night air and a sense of cowardice and shame.

THE NEXT MORNING he woke up with a tremendous hangover, for which he used hair of the dog and more Vicodin. After a shower and shave he dressed in pressed trousers and a crisp plaid shirt and called the neighborhood office of a national realty company.

Twenty minutes later a Realtor showed up, and by 11 A.M. Stromsoe had listed his home for sale. He offered the place furnished and as is. The Realtor's suggested asking price was so high he could hardly believe it. The Realtor smiled fearfully as they shook hands out by his car. He said he'd sell the place within the week, though an escrow period would follow.

"I'm sorry for what happened," he said. "Maybe a new home can be a new life."

5

By noon Stromsoe and Susan were back in his courtyard, sitting on the picnic benches again. She'd brought a new cassette for the tape recorder and a handful of fresh wildflowers for the vase.

"When I saw Hallie again it was '86," said Stromsoe. "We were twenty years old."

Mike's phone call the night before had convinced Stromsoe that he had to tell what Tavarez had done to Hallie, and how she had survived it. Tavarez could take her life but he couldn't take her story. Or Billy's. And El Jefe could not make Stromsoe kill himself, or diminish his memories, or make him burn down his house. Tavarez could not break his spirit.

"I was at Cal State Fullerton. I was taking extra units, and judo at night, and lifting weights—anything to not think about her. Them."

His words came fast now, Stromsoe feeling the momentum of doing the right thing.

"Every once in a while I'd read about Tavarez in the papers—they loved the barrio-kid-conquers-Harvard story—and I'd think about her more. Then one night I just ran into them in a Laguna nightclub, the old Star. She was wearing a gold lamé dress with white and black beads worked into the brocade. Tight, cut low and backless, slit up the side. It was very beautiful. And her hair was done up kind of wild, and dyed lighter than it used to be. She came running over and wrapped her arms around me. I remember that she was wearing Opium perfume. I looked past her at Mike, who was watching us from a booth. He looked pleased. She pulled me over there and he invited me to sit with them but I didn't."

Stromsoe remembered how the strobe lights had beveled Hallie Jaynes's lovely face into something exotic and unknowable.

It was so easy to see her now:

"You look good," she had told him.

"You do too."

"We miss you."

We.

"You're the one who left."

"Oh, Matty, you're much better off without us," she said with a bright smile. "Mike doesn't know how to apologize. He doesn't know what to say. I wish we could laugh again, you and me."

She looked both radiant and famished. It was an appearance he would see a lot of in his generation as the decade wore on. Looking at her for the first time in almost two years, he realized that she had moved past him in ways that until now he hadn't known existed.

"She was different," Stromsoe said to Susan Doss. "So was Mike."

He told Susan how Mike had gotten taller and filled out, grown his wavy black hair longer, wore a loose silk suit like the TV vice cops wore. His face had changed too, not just in breadth but in a new confidence. His sense of superiority was the first thing you saw—the quarter smile, the slow eyes, the lift of chin. He looked like an angel about to change sides.

"They were there with three other couples," said Stromsoe. "The dudes were older than us by a notch or two—early thirties, good-looking, Latino, dressed expensive. Versace and Rolex. The women were all twentysomething knockout gringas—extra blond. I was there with some friends from school and we ended up sitting across the dance floor from Hallie and them. I could hardly take my eyes off her. You know how it is, that first love."

"Sure," said Susan. "Richie Alexander. I wrote poetry about him. But I won't quote it for you, so don't ask."

Stromsoe smiled and nodded. Susan had freckles on her cheeks and a funny way of holding her pen, with her middle finger doing most of the work. Atop the garage, the crew commenced nailing the plywood to the roof frame and Stromsoe felt his nerves flicker.

He told Susan that on the drive home to his Fullerton apartment that night, he had lost his old faith that Hallie would come back to him someday. It was obvious to him that she and Tavarez were knocking on the door of a world in which Stromsoe had no interest. He had seen enough cocaine use at his high school and in his extended college circle to know the large sums of money attached. He had seen the white powder do ugly things to almost everyone he knew who used it. It made them pale and inward. Everything they did was for the high.

He didn't tell Susan that when he had imagined Hallie becoming like that—an inversion of everything about her that he loved and lusted for—his heart had hardened against her. But it had broken a little too.

Stromsoe believed back then that people soon got what they deserved.

Now he did not.

Now, sixteen years later, Stromsoe understood that Hallie had become everything he had feared, and that Mike Tavarez had gotten much more good fortune than he had ever deserved.

Tavarez had demonstrated that coke was venom to body and soul, and that anyone who ignores this fact can make many, many millions of good Yankee dollars.

Hallie had demonstrated how right Mike was. She was his first customer.

WHEN THEY FINISHED the lunch Susan pushed the paper plates away to make room for her notebook. She had brought the plates with her today, and Stromsoe wondered if she had sensed his anger yesterday over Hallie's dish.

"I didn't see her again until the night I graduated from college," said Stromsoe. "That was June of '88. After the ceremony a bunch of us went to the Charthouse here in Newport. We took up two long tables on the far side. Steak and lobster. Cocktails and wine. We blew enough money that night to live on for a semester. Hallie came in around midnight. I saw her spot me and I watched her come through the tables toward us."

Sitting in his courtyard now, Stromsoe could as good as see her. She was smiling at him but he could tell something was wrong. She walked carefully. She had lost weight. She wore a pink trench coat over a black-and-pink floral-print dress. Her hair was up and her earrings dangled and flashed.

Up close he saw that her face was clammy, with sweat beads at her hairline, that her pupils were big, and behind her pretty red lips her gums were pale.

"Congratulations," she had said, then hugged him. "I'm back at Mom's and Dad's after a little tiff with Mike. I saw your announcement in their mail pile. Not raining on your parade, am I, Matt?"

"Not at all," he'd said.

She touched his face. "I miss you."

Stromsoe got her seated and ordered her a soda water but Hallie told the waiter to make it a Bombay martini, rocks with a twist. She drank three of them in short order. He introduced her to his friends. The guys smiled and glanced knowingly at Stromsoe when they thought Hallie wasn't looking. The women were actively disinterested in her. She made several trips to the ladies' room.

Hallie ordered a double at last call, took one sip, then collapsed to the floor.

Stromsoe carried her back to the restaurant manager's office while one of his friends called paramedics. She was conscious but stupefied, trying to focus on

Stromsoe as he lowered her to a couch and wrapped a blanket around her. Her eyes were swimming and her teeth chattered.

"*Ohhh,*" she whispered, closing her eyes.

He smartly smacked her cheek. "Stay awake, Hallie. Look at me and stay awake."

She was half awake when the paramedics got there and took her away. Stromsoe followed them to Hoag Hospital in his old Mazda, called her parents from the waiting room. His hands were shaking with anger at Mike while he talked to Hallie's mom.

It took the doctors two hours to stabilize her. Inside Hallie boiled a witch's brew of Colombian cocaine, Mexican brown heroin, Riverside County methamphetamine, Pfizer synthetic morphine, and Bombay gin.

"She was okay," said Stromsoe. "Too much dope. Too much booze. It wasn't until later that I saw the really bad stuff."

Susan looked up from her notepad.

The day after Hallie had gone to the hospital Stromsoe had gotten a call from Sergeant Rich Neal of the Newport Beach police. Neal told Stromsoe to meet him outside Hallie's room at Hoag at 2 P.M. sharp.

Neal came from her room and shut the door behind him. He was stout and florid and asked Stromsoe what he knew about Hallie's drug problem. Stromsoe told him what had happened at the Charthouse. Neal asked about Mike Tavarez and Stromsoe confirmed that he knew him, and that Mike and Hallie were a couple.

"The parents think he supplied her with the drugs," said Neal. "They think he did that work on her body. She says no. What do you think?"

"He probably gave her the drugs. I don't know what bodywork you're talking about."

"Ask her about it," said Neal. "Where is he? Where's Tavarez right now?"

"I have no idea."

Neal asked Stromsoe about other friends of Hallie's, other boyfriends in particular. He asked if Stromsoe had met Mike Tavarez's parents and the answer was yes, Rolando and Reina, he'd spent some time in their home back in high school, eaten dinner with them on rehearsal nights, and sometimes he and Mike would just hang out there on weekends, shooting pool and drinking sodas, maybe ride their bikes or, when they got older, go for a drive. Stromsoe had always liked quiet Rolando and large, expansive Reina.

He asked if Stromsoe had given Hallie any of the drugs she had ingested last night and Stromsoe told him just the last few drinks.

Neal gave Stromsoe a card and an unhappy stare, then walked away.

"So I went into the hospital room," he told Susan. "Hallie was sitting up. She had some color back but her eyes were flat and her face was haggard. I held her hand for a minute and we didn't say much. Then I asked about her body and she told me to give her some privacy. I faced the door and heard her rustling around. When she said okay, try to control your excitement, I turned back and she had rolled the hospital smock just to her breasts, and pulled the sheet to just below her belly. Her torso was pretty much one big black-and-purple bruise, with a few little clouds of tan showing through."

Stromsoe now remembered the bend of Hallie's ribs under the livid skin. He remembered the pert Muzak version of "Penny Lane" that was playing while he stared at her. Susan Doss looked up from her notepad.

"She'd gotten an abortion a month earlier," said Stromsoe. "She told him it was her body, her decision, that she was a druggie and not ready to be a mother. There was no discussion. Hallie was that way. She said Mike went quiet, didn't talk for days, didn't even look at her. One night they went to a club and Hallie drank some, got talking to a guy. For the next couple of days, Mike drank and did blow, and the more loaded Mike got, the more he accused her of having a thing with this guy while he was away at school. She'd never seen him before in her life. Just when Mike seemed to be calming down a little, he and some of the guys drove her out to the middle of nowhere and the men held her while Mike hit her. And hit her some more. She passed out from the pain. They left her by the side of the Ortega Highway in the middle of the night. Mike flew back to Boston the next morning."

"My God."

Talk on, thought Stromsoe. Tell how Hallie handled that pain. Words, don't fail me now.

"She hitchhiked to the nearest house, called a friend to pick her up. Stayed in bed for three days at her Lido apartment, medicated herself with antibiotics, dope, and liquor. She forced herself to make an appearance back home for her parents' twenty-fifth anniversary, saw my graduation announcement, called my folks, and found out where the party was. By the time the doctors saw her, she was bleeding inside, infected, poisoned by the dope. Three of her ribs were broken and there were internal injuries to her spleen and ovaries. They took one ovary and said she'd probably never conceive. Three years later she had Billy."

"What did she tell the cops?"

"That she picked up the wrong guy one night. They knew she was protecting Mike but they couldn't crack her. Hallie was tough inside."

"Why cover for him?"

"The beating was five days old, so she knew it would be hard to make a case against four friends with their alibis lined up. And pride too—Hallie thought it was a victory not to go to the law. She also realized he might kill her. The cops busted him from a liquor-store video-tape a week after Hallie left the hospital. So, she thought Mike would get at least a partial punishment for what he did to her. Big news, when the Harvard boy was popped for a string of armed robberies in California."

"I remember."

He closed his eyes and could see Hallie as she was in high school, and again as she was on the day they were married, and then as she lay in the maternity ward with tiny William Jaynes Stromsoe in her arms.

But again, as had happened so many times in the last two months, his mind betrayed him with a vision of the nails and his wife and son.

He watched a neighbor's cat licking its rear foot in a patch of sunlight on the courtyard bricks.

His felt his heart laboring and he admitted to himself that telling this story was far more difficult than he had thought it would be. Where he had hoped to find some moments of fond memory, he found the awful truth instead. The truth he thought would set him free.

Then Stromsoe admitted another truth to himself—
he was feeling worse each day, feeling farther from
shore. It was like swimming against a tide. Wasn't he
supposed to get closer?

He was astonished again, almost to the point of disbelief, that he would never see Hallie or Billy as they
were, only as they had ended.

*God put them there for reasons we don't under-
stand.*

"Maybe we should take a walk on the beach while
we talk," said Susan.

6

They came to the ocean at Fifty-second Street and turned south. The sun was caught in the clouds above Catalina Island like an orange suspended in gauze. The stiff breeze dried Stromsoe's left eyelid and the pins in his legs felt creaky as old door hinges. The skin graft on his left breast tended to tighten in the cool evenings. He pulled up his coat collar and slipped on his sunglasses.

He told Susan about taking Hallie into his little college apartment in Fullerton and getting her off the drugs. And about how he had escorted her into court to testify in Mike's robbery trial, traded mad dog stares with Tavarez, how Mike's mother sobbed after the sentencing, and how Mike nodded to them—a courtly, emotionless nod—as he was led back to his cell.

"Do you mind?" Susan asked, taking a small digital camera from the pocket of her jacket.

"Okay."

She set her notebook in the sand with the pen clipped to the rings, and started snapping pictures. "I'd like some candids of you and Hallie and Billy too. From your home."

"Okay," he said.

Okay, because their story must be told and their pictures must be seen. Okay, because Tavarez can't take away their stories or their pictures. Or my memories. Ever.

"I know it hurts," said Susan, "but face the sun, will you? It lights your face beautifully."

He faced the sun, his right eye shuddering with the brightness and his left eye registering nothing at all. Susan circled him, clicking away. He turned to face her and he began talking about their wedding and their life while he went through the Sheriff's Academy, about their attempts to have a child and the doctors and tests and doctors and tests and the sudden presence of another life inside Hallie, detected by a drugstore pregnancy test on what was probably the happiest day of their life together until then.

Billy.

They walked on, then stopped to watch the sun dissolve into an ocean of dark metallic blue. To Stromsoe none of it looked like it used to. He wondered if this would be the last time he'd walk this beach. That would be okay. That's why he listed the house for sale. The world was large. A new home can be a new life.

"When Mike ordered the bomb, was it intended for Hallie and Billy, or just you?"

"Just me."

"Why does he hate you so much?"

"I loved Hallie and spent my life trying to put him in a cage."

There was Ofelia too, and what happened to her, but that was not something he could tell a reporter.

"You accomplished both," she said. "You won."

Stromsoe said nothing.

They started back across the sand toward the houses. Stromsoe looked at the beachfront windows, copper in the fading light.

"Thanks for everything," she said. "For telling me your story. I know it hurt."

"It helped too."

"If you need a friend, I'll be it," said Susan Doss.

"Oh?" He glanced at her and saw that she was looking down. "I appreciate that. I really do."

"What I mean is, this is me. This is what I look like and this is what I am. And I think you're wonderful and brave and loyal and I'd be proud to be your friend.

Maybe more. I'm sorry to be clumsy and insensitive. I think my moment is right now and if it passes I'll never see you again."

He looked at her, not knowing what to say.

"Plus, I get four weeks' paid vacation, great medical, and good retirement. I've got good teeth, strong legs, and an iron stomach. I'm relatively low maintenance."

He smiled.

"And I only look clean-cut."

"I can't."

They came to the street and headed toward Stromsoe's house.

"I talk too much at the wrong time," she said. "It's a problem."

"Hallie was the same way."

"You're a beautiful man."

"You're a beautiful woman but I can't."

"I understand, Matt."

Susan lightly held his arm until they came to the house. She waited in the living room while Stromsoe chose a framed picture from the spare bedroom wall: Hallie, Billy, and him on the beach, not far from where he had just watched the sun go down, smiling back at the stranger they'd asked to take the shot.

She looked at the picture then at Stromsoe. "You'll find all this again. Somewhere, someday."

He wanted to tell her it was impossible, but saw no reason to belittle her opinion.

One thing Stromsoe knew for certain about life was that things only happen once.

LATER THAT NIGHT he packed and loaded the car. It didn't hold much, but he got his bare necessities, the bag with Hallie's jewelry, and the one with Billy's things.

He cooked canned stew and drank and limped through the house again as the memories collided with one another and the waves roared then hissed against the beach.

He signed a power-of-attorney form downloaded from the Web and left it on the kitchen table with a check for five thousand dollars, made out to Dan Birch.

He'd call Dan from wherever he was tomorrow, explain the situation.

He slept in his bed for the last time.

EARLY THE NEXT morning he gassed up and headed east toward Arizona. By two that afternoon he was in Tucson, where he called Birch and talked about the selling of his house. Dan was unhappy about Stromsoe's plans but said he'd handle the sale and have the money deposited in the proper account.

"I want you to call me," said Birch. "I'm not going to let you vanish."

"I'll call, Dan. I don't want to vanish."

"What do you want?"

"Forward motion."

By midnight Stromsoe was outside of Abilene, Texas. He parked in a rest stop, unloaded boxes from the backseat, and slept. At sunrise he was on the road again.

He began drinking in Jackson, Mississippi, ten hours later. In the morning he took a city tour by bus for no reason he could fathom. He threw his cell phone into a trash can on Gallatin Street, then gassed up the Ford and stepped on it.

Mississippi became Alabama, then, troublingly, Indiana. He aimed south again, got a motel for the night, but by then it was morning. Georgia was humid and Florida was flat, then suddenly Miami was wavering before him like the Emerald City itself. He rented an upstairs apartment on Second Avenue, not far from the Miami-Dade College campus. Once he had the boxes upstairs he sold the Ford for five thousand and opened a checking account with fake ID from his undercover days with the Sheriff's Department. He got a new cell phone but never told Dan the number. The restaurant below his apartment was Cuban-Chilean and the food was extremely hot. Lucia the waitress called him Dead Eye. He ate and drank, drank and ate. Months later he flew back to California to testify against Tavarez. Other than that one week, he didn't get farther than walking distance from his Second Avenue apartment. Downtown Miami swirled around him, a heated closed-loop hallucination featuring Brickell Avenue, Biscayne Bay, and the ceiling fan of his small, box-choked room.

TWO YEARS LATER Stromsoe woke up to find Dan Birch hovering over him. A potful of cool water hit him in the face.

"It stinks in here," said Birch. He dropped the pot with a clang. "There's cockroaches all over your floor. Get up, Matt. No more of this."

"Of this?"

"Get the fuck up. Then we can talk about it."

PART II

The Heart of the X

7

S tromsoe sat in Dan Birch's Irvine office and looked out at the clear October morning.

It was thirty-two days since Miami and the pot of water in his face. He had come back to California with Birch, completed a monthlong detox program in Palm Springs, then taken a furnished rental in downtown Santa Ana, not far from where he had grown up. He'd started jogging and lifting weights during his detox, with arguable results. Everything hurt.

Today, Monday, he sat in his friend's office with a cup of coffee, like any other guy hoping for a job. He could hardly believe that over two years had passed since he last talked with Birch in his haunted, long-sold home in Newport.

"How are you feeling, Matt?"

"Good."

"Drinking?"

"Lightly."

"You idiot."

"It's under control."

Birch tapped his desktop with a pen. The office was on the twelfth floor and had great views southwest to Laguna.

"We got a call last week from a woman down in San Diego County," he said. "She's a weather lady for Fox down in San Diego—Frankie Hatfield is her name. Nice gal. Seen her on TV?"

"No."

"I hadn't either, until last night. She's good. A year ago I did some work for one of the producers there at her channel. Frankie—Frances Leigh is her full name— told him she had a problem. The producer recommended me. I recommended you."

Stromsoe nodded as Birch stared at him.

"Up for this?" asked Birch.

"Yes, I am."

"You would be an employee and representative of Birch Security Solutions," said Birch. "I use the best."

"I understand, Dan."

"The best control themselves."

"I can do that. I told you."

Birch continued to look at his friend. "So, Frankie Hatfield is being stalked. Doesn't know by whom. Never married, no children, no ugly boyfriends in the closet, no threats. The last time she saw the guy, she was doing one of her live weather broadcasts. They shoot live on location, various places around San Diego. He might be an infatuated fan—some guy who follows the Fox News van out of the yard and around the city. I've got some letters and e-mails she's received at work but I don't see anything to take seriously. She's caught glimpses of this guy—dark hair and dark complexion, medium height and weight—three times. Twice on her private property. She filed a complaint with SDPD but you know that drill."

"They can't help her until he assaults her."

"More or less."

Birch tapped his keyboard, adjusted the monitor his way, and leaned back. "Yeah, here. She's seen this guy outside her studio in downtown San Diego, on her residential property in Fallbrook, on her investment property in Bonsall, and possibly following her on I-5 in a gold four-door car. She hasn't gotten plate numbers because he stays too far back. He takes pictures of her.

He has not spoken to her. He has not called. He has not acknowledged her in any way except by running away from her."

"She's tried to confront him?"

"Confront him? Hell, she *photographed* him. Check these."

Birch flicked four snapshots across the desk to Stromsoe. Stromsoe noted that they were high-pixel digital images printed on good picture paper.

"Frances is not a fearful sort," said Birch.

Two of the pictures showed a sloping hillside of what appeared to be avocado trees. In a clearing stood a tapered wooden tower of some kind. It looked twenty feet tall, maybe more. In one picture a man stood beside the tower looking at the camera, and in the next three he was running away. He was dark-haired and dark-skinned, dressed in jeans, a light shirt, and athletic shoes. He looked small.

"That was taken on her Bonsall property," said Birch.

"How big is the parcel?" asked Stromsoe.

"A hundred acres. Says she goes there to be alone."

"Where's Bonsall?"

"Next door to Fallbrook."

Stromsoe pictured a woman sitting in the middle of a hundred-acre parcel to be alone. It seemed funny, but it also seemed like she had a right to her privacy on her own land.

"Frankie has a decent home security system," said Birch. "I set her up with a panic button that will ring the Sheriff 's substation in Fallbrook and you simultaneously. I set her up with one month of twice-a-day patrol. I sold her a bodyguard—that would be you—for trips to and from work and while she's on the job, for the next thirty days. Handle it?"

"I can handle it."

"This guy is pretty bold, Matt. She's seen him three times in twelve days, plus the maybe on the freeway. I don't think he's a weenie wagger—he'd have whipped it out already. Obsessed fan? Rapist? Find out. Arrest the creep if you can, let the cops chew his sorry ass. Give Frankie some peace of mind. I told her you were our best. She's expecting you at her home at noon today, to follow her into San Diego to the studio. She starts around one in the afternoon and heads home after the live shoot at eight o'clock. Keep track of your hours. If you shake this guy loose before thirty days are up, we'll all talk."

Birch handed Stromsoe the panic button, a concealed-carry sidearm permit for San Diego County, and a sheet of paper with Frances Hatfield's numbers on it.

. . .

FALLBROOK WAS A small town fifty miles north of San Diego, twelve miles inland, tucked behind Camp Pendleton. Stromsoe had never been there. The road in from Oceanside was winding and the traffic was light. He looked out at the avocado orchards and orange groves, the flowered undulating valleys of the big nurseries, the horses in their corrals, the houses on the hilltops or buried deep within the greenery. There was an antiques store, a feed and tack store, a drive-through cappuccino stand. He saw a tennis court hidden in the trees, and a very small golf course—obviously homemade—sloping down from a house with a red tile roof. He drove through a tunnel of huge oak trees then back into a blast of sunlight and thousands of orange butterflies. The sky was filled with them. A herd of llamas eyed him sternly from an emerald pasture. He rolled down the window of his new used pickup truck and smelled blossoms.

Frances Hatfield's voice on the gate phone was clear and crisp. She enunciated well. The gate rolled to the side without sound.

Her property was hilly and green, planted with avocado and citrus. The avocado trees were tall, shaggy and heavy with small fruit. Stromsoe had no idea how much of the land was hers because the orchards rambled on, a hilly, fenceless tableau in the clean October sunlight. A hawk shot across the treetops with a high-pitched keen.

Frances Hatfield was a tall woman, dark-haired and brown-eyed. She looked to be in her midtwenties. A straight, narrow nose and assertive bones gave her a patrician face, but it was softened by her smile. She was dressed in jeans, packer boots, and a white blouse tucked in.

"Hello, Mr. Stromsoe. I'm Frankie Hatfield."

She offered her hand. A golden retriever itemized the smells on Stromsoe's shoes and legs.

"My pleasure, Ms. Hatfield."

"This is Ace."

"Hey, Ace." He looked up. "Nice butterflies."

"Painted ladies," she said. "They migrate by the millions every few years. They'll be gone with the first rain."

"Are these your orchards?"

"I almost break even on the avocados," she said. "They take a lot of water and water is expensive here. Please come in. Want to just go with Frankie and Matt?"

"Good."

The house was cool and quiet. Through the mullioned windows the orchard rows convened in the middle distance. Ace produced a ball but gave no hint of giving it up. Stromsoe smelled blossoms again, then a recently used fireplace, then brewing coffee. A grizzled gray dog with a white face wandered up to Stromsoe on petite feet and slid her head under his hand.

"Hope you don't mind dogs," said Frankie.

"I love dogs."

"Do you have any?"

"Not right now."

"That's Sadie."

They sat in the living room. It was large, open-beamed, and paneled with cedar. With its many windows the room seemed to be a part of the patio beyond it and the avocado orchard beyond that. The patio fountain trickled faintly and Stromsoe could hear it through the screen doors.

A series of softened explosions seemed to roll across the sky to them, powerful blasts muted by distance.

"That's artillery exercise at Camp Pendleton," said Frankie. "The sound of freedom. You get used to it."

"I used to live near the beach and I got used to the waves. Didn't hear them unless I tried to."

"Kind of a shame, actually."

"I thought so."

Stromsoe felt the faraway artillery thundering in his bones.

"I have no idea who he is, or what he wants," said Frankie. "He does not seem threatening, although I take his presence on my property as a threat. I have no bad people in my past. I have skeletons but they're good skeletons."

Stromsoe brought her snapshots from his coat pocket and looked at them again. "Does he resemble anyone you know?"

She shook her head.

"Brave of you to whip out the camera and start shooting," he said.

"I lack good sense sometimes."

"I'm surprised it didn't scare him off. What's this wooden tower for?"

Stromsoe held out the picture and pointed.

"I have no idea. It's been on the Bonsall property forever."

"Is that where you go to be alone?"

"Yes. I escape from me."

Stromsoe noted that the tower didn't look old enough to have been somewhere forever.

He brought out the panic button and set it on the rough pine trunk between them.

"You flip the cover like an old pocket watch, push the button three times," he said. "If you hold the button down for five seconds or more, the call is officially canceled but I'll show up anyway. So will the sheriffs if you're out here in the county, or the San Diego PD if you're downtown."

"GPS?" She examined the gadget.

"Yes. It's always on."

"Can it differentiate between all the cities in the county?"

"Any city in the United States, actually."

"Impressive."

"Not if you don't have it with you."

She smiled. The smile disarmed the angles of her face and brightened her dark eyes. "I will."

Stromsoe told her he'd follow her to and from work, said not to get out until he'd parked and come to her vehicle, to leave the engine running until then, and if he didn't get there within two minutes to hit the panic button, drive to the exit, get on the nearest freeway, and call the police.

"Do you have a gun?" she asked.

"Yes."

"Are you good with it?"

"Yes. I used to be very good," he said.

"Do you adjust for the monovision?"

"Of course."

"Your prosthetic is a beautiful match, really," she said. "A friend of mine in school had one. She was a poet."

Stromsoe nodded. He reflexively balled his left fingers into a loose fist to obscure the missing one. "I suppose you've got a gun."

"It's a Smith and Wesson thirty-eight revolver, two-inch barrel. I've got a valid CCP and I've done ten hours of range training. To be honest I'm shaky outside of twelve feet. Fifty feet, I can't even hit the silhouette. It kicks like a mule."

"Those short barrels make it tough," he said.

"It makes lots of noise though. I feel better with it."

"You possibly are."

"It's a very unpleasant feeling, being watched."

"Tell me about it."

"No matter how ready I am, it always comes as a surprise when I see him. And I almost always *feel* watched before I realize I'm being watched. But then, I *feel* watched and a lot of the time I'm not. That's what it does to you. You begin to doubt your senses. And that makes a person feel weak and afraid."

Frankie's hands were large and slender and she used them generously while she talked. Since losing the finger, Stromsoe had paid special attention to people's hands. He considered the way that weather forecasters like to swirl theirs over the projection maps to show the path of coming fronts and storms.

"Don't feel weak and afraid," he said. "My job is to make your job easier. Forget about this guy. He can't hurt you. Leave him to me."

She looked at him straight on, no smile, the dark eyes in forthright evaluation.

"I can't tell you how good that sounds," she said. "I've lost more than a little sleep over this."

"No more."

Her intense scrutiny dissolved into a smile. "We should go. It takes an hour to get to San Diego this time of day. We're going to the Fox building off of Clairemont Mesa. I drive fast."

"Don't worry, I'll keep up. After you're past the parking-lot booth, don't drive to your space. Wait for me while I explain myself to the attendant."

"He's a tough old guy," said Frankie. "Suspicious and not friendly. You drive up for the five hundredth time and he looks at you like he's never seen you before. Then he takes an hour to check your number."

"He'll see the light," said Stromsoe. "Your job is to pretend I'm not there. Things will work best that way."

She half smiled, said nothing. Ace continued to hoard his ball and the artillery went off again in the west.

8

By 4 P.M. Frankie's video team had set up on a sidewalk overlooking Seal Rock Reserve in La Jolla. The big elephant seals lolled and roared in the cooling afternoon. The painted-lady butterflies filled the sky by the fluttering thousands. The ocean reminded Stromsoe of Newport, and Newport reminded him of Hallie and Billy, and for a moment Stromsoe was back in an earlier time when he and his wife and son could walk on a beach together. Now, two plus years after their deaths, his memories of them were less frequent but more distinct, and, somehow, more valuable.

Frankie—with a black windbreaker and her hair whipping in the breeze—held up her microphone and explained that the ridge of high pressure would continue through the week, gradually giving way to cooling and low clouds as the marine layer fought its way back onshore. However, a "substantial" trough of low pressure was waiting out over the Pacific. She smiled enthusiastically and said that rain was possible by Sunday, something in the one-inch range, if the current jetstream pattern held.

"Now I remember what the farmers used to say about the rain when I was just a girl," she told the cameras. "Early in, late out. So if we do pick up some serious rain this early in October, we could be in for a long, wet season. Okay with me—we need it! Just be sure to keep your umbrellas handy and your firewood dry. I'm Frankie Hatfield, reporting from Seal Rock Reserve in La Jolla."

Stromsoe watched almost everything except Frances Hatfield: the families and tourists out enjoying the fall day, the cars parked along Coast Boulevard, especially the single men who perked up when they spotted Frankie and the unmistakable Fox News van. A semicircle of onlookers formed as Frankie finished her report and Stromsoe spotted a dark-haired, dark-complected young man who stood and calmly stared at her. In that moment Stromsoe got a glimpse of what being a public figure was like, the way people assumed they had a right to stare at you. No wonder celebrities wore sunglasses. The young man backed away and continued his walk along the shore.

When Frankie was finished she took a few minutes to talk with the crowd and sign some autographs. She was half a head taller than most everyone. She knelt down to talk to a little girl. After the last fan walked off, she looked at Stromsoe, took a deep breath, then exhaled.

And that was when her secret admirer stepped out from behind the gnarled trunk of a big torrey pine, saw Stromsoe break toward him, then wheeled and sprinted for Coast Boulevard. Stromsoe saw that he looked a lot like his picture—young, dark-haired, and dark-skinned. He was square-shouldered and small, and he ran with rapid, short-legged strokes. He had what looked like a camera in his right hand.

Stromsoe was a big man and not fast. The pins in his legs caused a tightness that hadn't gone away. A month of jogging and weights and rehab didn't erase his poor condition after two years of boozing in Florida, and by the time he hit the sidewalk he saw, far down on Coast Boulevard, Frankie's stalker slam the door on a gold sedan and a moment later steer into the southbound flow of traffic. But the traffic was dense and his truck was parked way up by the Fox van, so Stromsoe powered down the sidewalk as fast as his pinned legs would carry him and almost took out a mom and a stroller but he detoured onto the grass as the gold car stopped behind a blue van about to pass through a stop sign. Stromsoe saw that it would be close. He cut back to the sidewalk then into the street. He ran through a cloud of orange butterflies. The blue van started across the intersection with the gold car glued to its bumper and honking. Stromsoe raised his knees and clenched his fists and charged up near the car just as it screeched around the van in a blast of white smoke that left him blinded and lumbering out of the way of a monstrous black SUV driven by a young man looking down on him assessingly. Stromsoe hailed the young man in hopes of following the stalker but the driver flipped him off and stomped on it right through the stop sign.

Stromsoe stood on the grass, hands on his knees, panting as he watched the gold sedan sweep around a corner. He'd gotten the first four of the seven plate symbols: 4NIZ or 4NTZ. It was hard to get a fix on that license plate with his feet jarring on the asphalt and his one good eye trying for a decent look at the driver.

So, 4NIZ or 4NTZ. Fuck, there were a thousand combinations to check. He kicked a trash can and looked back toward the Fox van. Thirty-nine years old, he thought, and I can barely run two hundred yards.

Furthering his humiliation, Frankie Hatfield was already halfway toward him, loping across the grass while her video man shot away.

He squared his shoulders and tried not to limp as he walked to meet her.

FRANKIE WAS RATTLED but went on to do live reports from downtown La Jolla, Torrey Pines State Park, and UCSD. Stromsoe didn't see the stalker or the gold sedan again.

Five lousy yards away, he thought. *That* close.

By nine that night he was following her brilliant red Mustang up the long driveway through the darkened avocado orchard in Fallbrook. Only a sliver of moonlight showed in the black sky.

She pulled into her garage, locked up her car, and came to his truck. He rolled down the window. He heard her dogs barking inside the house.

"Thank you," she said. "You gave our little friend something to think about."

"I'll get him next time. Are you sure you're all right?"

"I'd feel better if you lived a minute away instead of an hour," said Frankie.

"I'll park down at the gate for an hour or two, if you'd feel better," said Stromsoe.

"No. It's okay. That's not in the contract."

Stromsoe killed his engine. She took another step toward the truck and crossed her arms.

"Look," he said. "The sheriffs are tied to the panic button, and Birch got them to A-list you. The substation is only a couple of miles away."

Stromsoe had intended this to be comforting but he knew she was calculating response time the same as he was. By the time the alarm came through, dispatch made the call, and the nearest prowl car blundered through miles of unlit country roads and found a home lost on ten acres of grove and orchard?

Who knew.

Stromsoe heard a car engine idling back in the orchard. Then the engine died. He looked at Frankie but she apparently hadn't noticed it.

"Thank you," she said. "And good night."

"You're going to be just fine, Frankie."

It sounded lame and he wished he hadn't said it.

"I know I will."

When she opened the door he saw the dogs bouncing around her. She looked back at him and he started up the truck.

Stromsoe drove back through the orchards, looking for the car that had been idling. He saw nothing.

When he finally got down to where the orchard ended at the main avenue, he parked and turned off the engine and waited, just to see if someone might start up the slope toward Frances Hatfield's place.

Half an hour later he'd seen plenty of cars going up and down the avenue, and an opossum that barely made it in front of a tractor trailer with a gigantic bouquet of gladiolas painted on the rear doors, and three coyotes that trotted past the front of his truck with the harried concentration of young executives. The painted ladies billowed by.

But no cars on their way to Frankie's house.

Five minutes later her flashy red Mustang nosed out from the black orchards, then roared onto the avenue.

Stromsoe brought the truck to life, checked his clearance, and barreled off after her.

True to her word, she drove fast. But it was easy for Stromsoe to see her in the light traffic, so he kept back behind a tractor trailer for a half a mile, then behind a truck very much like his own, then behind a new yellow Corvette.

She took Old Highway 395 south then headed west on Gopher Canyon. She was going toward Bonsall, he thought—her investment property? He glanced at his watch: almost eleven-thirty. Kind of late to be going somewhere to escape from yourself, wasn't it?

She turned right and left and right again, longer and longer stretches of darkness between the turns, and Stromsoe followed as far back as he could with his headlights off.

The road turned to gravel, rising gently. Stromsoe eased his truck into the wake of Frankie's dust and crept along in the pale red glow of his parking lights.

When he came over the top he could see down now, to where the Mustang had stopped in a gateway. He killed his parking lights and engine. He watched the driver's-side door of the Mustang swing out and Frankie pull herself from the little cabin. Her two dogs spilled out behind her.

In the spray of her headlights Frankie lifted a thick chain off a post, then swung open a steel-pipe gate. After the Mustang was through, she got out, called the dogs, swung the gate closed, and lifted the chain back into place. She got the dogs back into the car and rolled off.

Stromsoe gave her a few minutes then drove slowly to the gate. He made a U-turn and left his truck parked on the far side of the dirt road, facing out.

He took a small but strong flashlight from his glove box and locked up the truck. A sign on the gate said NO TRESPASSING—VIOLATORS WILL BE PROSECUTED. He lifted the chain from the gatepost and let himself in.

He limped down the dirt road in the faint moonlight, climbed a rise, and stood now at the top of a hillock looking down on a wide, dark valley. He smelled water and grass and the butterscotch smell of willow trees.

A barn sat a hundred yards off the road. The red Mustang was parked beside it. Next to the Mustang was a white long-bed pickup truck. The barn door was closed but light inside came around the door to fall in faint slats on the ground. A window glowed faintly orange and Stromsoe thought he saw movement inside.

He stayed on the dark edge of the dirt road as he moved toward the barn. Above him the sky was pin-pricked by stars and again he smelled water and grass. A horse neighed in the distance. He could hear the ticks and pops of the Mustang's cooling engine as he approached the barn, crept slowly to the window, and looked in.

Frankie's side was to him. Ace and Sadie lay on a red braided rug not far from their master. Frankie was standing at a wooden workbench fitted with a band saw, a circular saw, a drill press, and half a dozen vises. She wore jeans and boots again, and a pair of oversize safety goggles. She squared a length of two-by-four on the bench, hooked the end of a yellow tape measure over one end, took a pencil from her mouth, and marked it. Then she pressed the board forward into the circular saw and a brief shriek followed. The motor died and Stromsoe heard the clink of the board on the concrete floor.

Beyond Frankie's workbench there was a similar bench, at which a white-whiskered old man drilled holes in lengths of two-by-four like the one Frankie had just sawn. He wore safety goggles too, but they were propped up on his head. A cigarette dangled from his mouth and a lazy plume of smoke rose toward the high rafters.

A tall wooden tower stood beside the old man's bench, the same type that Stromsoe had noted in Frankie's photograph of the stalker. It looked larger than the one in the picture. It was newly made. The redwood was still pink and Stromsoe could see the gleam of the new nuts and bolts and washers that held it together. The top was a plywood platform about the right size to hold a person, a fifty-five-gallon drum, or a couple of small trash cans. There was a one-foot-high railing around the edge of the platform, as if to keep something from tipping over or falling off. The tower rose up twenty feet high, at least. Beside it stood another tower that was only about one-third finished.

The old man carried two lengths of wood, joined at right angles, over to the tower in progress. He pulled a socket wrench from his back pocket and began bolting the boards to the tower.

The dogs looked up and the old man's gaze started his way and Stromsoe moved away from the window.

From this point he could see the west wall of the barn. There were four long benches along it, similar to the workbenches at which Frankie and the old man worked. These were covered not with tools but with books and notebooks, beakers and burners, tubes and vials, canisters and bottles, boxes and bags, all overhung with a series of metal lamps hung by chains from the rafters. There were two refrigerators and a freezer along the far wall. There was a small kitchen area with four burners, an oven, and a sink. A fire extinguisher was fastened to every fifth post of the exposed interior frame. In the far corner was what looked like an office, separated from the main barn by a door that stood open.

Stromsoe thought of the meth labs he'd seen out in the Southern California desert not far from here. Riverside County was ground zero for the labs, but there were plenty in Los Angeles and San Diego and San Bernardino counties, too. Interesting, he thought— except that he was pretty sure Frances Hatfield and the old man weren't cooking drugs.

He heard Frankie's saw start up and eased his face back to the window. She pressed the board into the blade, then another. She worked with assurance, and no hurry.

The old man wrestled another set of bolted boards off his bench, walked them across the floor, and fitted them into the growing tower. He took out his socket wrench and looked at the structure appraisingly.

"Nice, Ted," said Frankie. Stromsoe could just barely make out her words.

"When this one's finished I'm done for tonight," said Ted. "Been at it since four."

"We'll be ready for next week," said Frankie.

"I hope so."

"We need that jet stream to stay south. Just a little help from the stream is all we need."

The old man said something back but Stromsoe couldn't make it out.

He eased away from the barn, found the dark edge of the road, and walked back to his car. Ready for next week, he thought. Need the jet stream to stay south?

He wondered if the wooden towers were a decorative garden item that Frankie and her partner sold to local nurseries. He'd seen little windmills that looked a lot like them, though Frankie's were four times the height and had no blades to catch a breeze.

Then he thought of water wells and storage tanks and railroad structures and mining rigs and weather stations and airport towers and fire observation decks and oil derricks and guard towers and wind turbines for making electricity.

Ready for next week could mean for the distributor, or to complete an order, or …

Frankie, you have some explaining to do.

He smelled the river water again, then the sweet aroma of oranges and lemons carrying on the cool night air.

9

M ike Tavarez surveyed the exercise yard and listened to the inmates counting off their sit-ups:
thirty, thirty-one, thirty-two, thirty-three...

Their voices rose in crisp unison into the cold afternoon air of Pelican Bay State Prison. They sounded like
a small army, thought Tavarez, and in a sense they
were, because the Mexican gangs here in Pelican Bay
didn't stand around like the Nazi Lowriders or the
Aryan Brotherhood or the Black Guerillas.

No, La Eme and Nuestra Familia—though they
would kill one another if you put them together in the
same exercise yard at the same time—worked out here
in the general population yard for two hours every day.
Different hours, but they worked out hard. They heaved

and strained and yelled the cadence, in training to stay alive when it was time to fight.

Give people a beat to follow and they'll do anything you tell them to, thought Tavarez. Like a marching band.

Forty-nine, fifty, fifty-one...

"Why don't you work out with them?" asked Jason Post. Post was one of the correctional officers who had helped get Tavarez transferred from the Security Housing Unit to the general population. That was six months ago. The Prison Guards Union held substantial power at Pelican Bay, and Post was a union activist.

"I like watching," said Tavarez. "I like their discipline. I never got to see this in the X."

The Security Housing Unit was known as "the X" because it was shaped like one. Sometimes it was called the Shoe. Tavarez had spent his first year there. It was a living hell. The SHU was made up of pods—eight glass-faced cells per pod—arranged around an elevated guardhouse. It was always twilight in the X, never light and never dark. Tavarez was watched by guards 23/7 on television. When he used the toilet it was televised onto a guardhouse monitor. The toilets had no moving parts that could be made into weapons. For one hour a day he was allowed to exercise alone in "dog run"—a four-walled concrete tank half the size of a basketball court. A guard watched him do that too, from a catwalk above. In the X, time stopped. His great aloneness swallowed him. There had been days in the X when Tavarez had had to bite his tongue to keep from weeping, and swallow the blood.

It was solitary confinement, but in full view of the guards. The X was designed by an architect who specialized in sensory deprivation. Even the warden admitted that it was designed to make you insane. The feeling of hours stretching into years was indescribable for Tavarez,

unbearable. He never thought he would actually feel his mind leaving him. Finally, he found a way to get to Jason Post and Post had begun the process that saved his life.

The difference between the SHU and general population was the difference between hell and freedom. Or at least between hell and the possibility of freedom, for which Tavarez was now planning.

He saw that the count was slowing as his men approached eighty push-ups.

Seventy-six...seventy-seven...

"Besides," he said. "I like having the pile to myself."

"I'll bet you do," said Post. He was a thick young Oregonian with a downsloping head of yellow hair. "Nobody gets that except you."

Tavarez got an hour a day on the iron pile, where he could lift weights alone and let his mind wander. He had arranged this privilege through Post also, and paid for it by having money wired into various bank accounts. His iron-pile hour was generally between 11 P.M. and midnight but Tavarez was largely nocturnal anyway. He'd grown very strong.

And one night per week, usually Monday, Tavarez would skip his late-night workout and instead be escorted to the far corner of the southeast compound perimeter, where he would stand handcuffed while a prostitute serviced him through a chain-link fence.

"How's Tonya?" asked Tavarez.

"Chemo sucks, you know?"

Tavarez figured that Post would need some help.

"With her not feeling good, you know, the kid doesn't get decent meals and he doesn't ever get his homework done. I'm here in this shithole forty-eight hours a week 'cause we need the money, so I can't do everything at home, you know?"

"Sounds difficult," said Tavarez.

"That's because it is difficult."

"As soon as you get me the library, I can make a transfer for you."

Post was predictable and self-serving as a dog, which was why Tavarez valued him.

"It's done," said the young guard. "You have the library for one hour tonight. The laptop will be inside in the world atlas on the G shelf, down at the end, up on top, out of sight. Lunce will come to your cell at ten to take you in. Then he'll take you to the iron pile at eleven, then back to your cell at midnight."

Tavarez suppressed a smile. "Batteries charged?"

"Hell yes they're charged."

"I'll make the transfer."

"Ten K?"

"Ten."

Tavarez watched the men labor and count. The ten K infuriated him but he didn't let it show. Plus, he had the money.

...ninety-eight...ninety-nine...one hundred!

"Behave yourself, bandito," said Post.

"Always," said Tavarez.

"You don't want to go back to the X."

"God will spare me that, Jason."

"God don't care here. It's every man for himself."

"That's why I value our friendship," said Tavarez.

"Yeah, I bet. Make that transfer, dude."

• • •

PRISON INVESTIGATOR KEN McCann delivered a cloth sack full of mail to Tavarez in his cell later that afternoon. Mail was delivered to Tavarez only twice a week because he got so much of it. The Prison Investigation team—four overworked Corrections employees overseeing a prison population of almost 3,500—had to read, or attempt to read, every piece of Mike El Jefe Tavarez's incoming and outgoing correspondence.

"Strip out, Mikey," said McCann, making a twirling motion with his finger.

Tavarez faced the far wall and spread his arms and legs. "Looks like quite a haul."

Then the guard unlocked the cell and McCann tossed the sack onto the bed. The door clanged shut with a faint echo, and the lock rang home.

Tavarez backed again to the door slot—it was called the bean chute because meals sometimes came through it too—then went to his bed. The bed was just a mattress on a concrete shelf built into the wall. He dumped the mail onto the thin green blanket. He sat and fanned through the correspondence. True to form, McCann and his investigators had opened every envelope except the ones from law firms. Attorney-client privilege was a constitutional right even in a supermax prison, though

Tavarez suspected that McCann opened and read some of them anyway. Which was fair, since several of the law firms with very impressive letterheads were fictitious, and others were counterfeit. There were fifty or sixty letters in all.

"How many letters did you write this last week?" asked McCann.

"Seventy."

"Every week you write seventy."

"Ten a day," said Tavarez. "An achievable number."

Tavarez knew that most of the inmates got little or no mail at all. He'd seen printouts of the pen-pal ads on the prison Web site, which were full of pleas for letters from inmates who hadn't received a letter in years, or even decades.

But Tavarez was El Jefe, and he got hundreds of letters every month from friends and relatives—long, usually handwritten tales of life in the barrio, life in jail, life in other prisons, life in general.

"It's pure numbers, isn't it, Mikey?" asked McCann. "Enough mail comes and goes, and you know your messages will get through."

"No, Ken. I just have lots of family and friends."

"You have lots of business is what you have."

"You overestimate me."

"Well, the piss trick won't work anymore."

"No. You're too smart for that."

Tavarez had used his urine to write a coded message on the back of a letter to a cousin in Los Angeles. The message was about raising "taxes" on a heroin shipment coming north from Sinaloa to Tucson, then on to L.A., though McCann couldn't decipher it. It was an old prison trick—the urine dries invisible but the sugars activate under a hot lamp and the code can be read. McCann had had the good luck of picking this particular letter for his heat-lamp test.

But Tavarez had written the same message in a kite—a small, handwritten note—that a trustee had smuggled out for him through a friend in the prison kitchen, so the tax hike had gone into effect anyway.

Tavarez noted a letter from Ruben in San Quentin. Always pleasant to know what's going down on death row.

And one from the nonexistent law firm of Farrell & Berman of Worcester, Massachusetts, which would contain news of La Eme's East Coast business.

And one from his mother, still on Flora Street, still chipper and full of gossip, no doubt. Money was no longer a problem for his parents, though why they insisted on staying in the barrio Tavarez couldn't understand.

There was a letter from Jaime in Modesto—trouble with La Nuestra Familia, most likely.

One from a real lawyer—Mel Alpers—who was representing him on appeal. It looked like a bill.

One from Dallas, where the Mara Salvatrucha gang had butchered two local homies in a war for narcotics distribution in the south side. Blood was about to flow. We should exterminate the Salvadorans, thought Tavarez. Bloodthirsty animals with no sense of honor.

And another letter from Ernest in Arizona State Prison, a supermax prison like Pelican Bay. Ernest was doing a thirty-year bounce on three strikes. Tavarez knew that Ernest's boys in Arizona were busy these days. Since so much attention had been focused on California's border, Arizona was now the nexus for drugs, humans, and cash going in and out of the United States. In many ways Arizona was better, Tavarez believed— the deserts and mountains were filled with dirt roads and impossible to patrol. Much of the land was Indian, and the state and federal agents were not welcome there. Also, Arizona had one-tenth the population of California, and was closer to good markets like Chicago, Detroit, and New York. Business was good. Very good.

Tavarez sighed and picked through more mail, looking for the one letter that never came.

"What are you worth these days, Mike? Two million? Three?"

Tavarez shook his head, sorting through the mail. "Nowhere near the millions you dream of. My life is about honor."

"The honor of La Eme. That's funny."

"I don't think honor is funny," said Tavarez.

La Eme's code of silence forbade him from so much as saying those words—La Eme—let alone admitting membership.

McCann grunted. He had long accused Tavarez of secretly hoarding funds that should have gone into La Eme "regimental banks," though McCann had no evidence of it.

"Fine," he said. "Lie about your money. But if I do my job right, you won't have one dollar left to give your children when you die. Undeserving though they are."

Tavarez looked up from his mail. "Leave my family out of it."

McCann shrugged. He enjoyed chiding Tavarez about the fact that, despite getting hundreds of letters a month, Tavarez's letters to his own children always came back marked *Return to Sender*.

In the beginning McCann had opened these letters both going out and coming back, suspecting that the Tavarez children had marked them with coded messages before resealing the envelopes and having their mother write *return to sender* on the front. But all he'd ever found were heartfelt pleadings from the great Jefe, asking for understanding and a letter back. No urine messages, no pinprick "ghostwriting" that would come alive when a pencil was rubbed over them, no writing in Nahuatl—the language of the ancient Aztec—which was La Eme's most baffling code.

"Must be lousy, sitting in a stinkhole while your kids grow up without you."

"You've said that before."

"Better here than in the SHU though."

Tavarez looked at McCann and McCann smiled. "Those millions don't do you much good, do they?"

"They don't do me much good because I don't have them."

McCann stared at Tavarez for a long beat. He liked staring down the inmates. It was a way of saying he wasn't afraid of them. McCann was large and strong. Tavarez had heard the story about the Black Guerilla gangster who had jumped McCann and ended up knocked out and bleeding. McCann loved talking about the SHU. To anyone who had been incarcerated there, it was like having a knife waved in your face. Or worse.

"Honor?" asked McCann. "How do you stand yourself, Mike? Blowing up a woman and a little boy? A woman you knew, someone you lived with and slept with? The wife of an old friend?"

"I had nothing to do with that. I was framed by a U.S. government task force. The real killers were his own people, of course—the same task force. Because he was corrupt, on the payroll of La Nuestra Familia. Everyone knows what bunglers the government people are. All this was proven in court by my lawyers. The reason the government sent me here was so they could continue their fictional war on drugs against a fictional gang. It all comes down to dollars, jobs, and budgets. I am good for their business."

McCann whistled the tune of a *corrido*. Even the guards knew the *corridos*—the Mexican songs that romanticized the exploits of criminal heroes who fought against corrupt police torturers and bone breakers, usually Americans. This particular song was very popular a few years ago, and it told the story of El Jefe Tavarez and an American deputy who love the same woman.

Tavarez stared at the investigator.

"All three of you went to high school together," said McCann. "Later, the deputy took your girlfriend. So what do you do? You kill her, you fucking animal."

Tavarez said nothing. What was the point of defending himself to a fool?

"What did you and Post talk about today?" asked McCann.

"Family. He likes to talk."

"What's in it for you?"

"The X made me talkative. He's just a kid."

"Going to help him out?"

"My hands are cuffed."

"Don't get any big ideas, Mikey. Behave yourself and who knows? Maybe you'll actually get a visit from one of your own children someday."

Tavarez nodded and picked up a letter. Ears thrumming with anger, he could barely hear the sound of McCann's shoes on the cell-block floor as he walked away.

When he got out of this place, when the time was right, maybe he'd come back here to Crescent City and settle up with McCann.

But McCann was right. Tavarez yearned for letters from them—John, Peter, Jennifer, and Isabelle. John was the oldest at ten. He had gotten his mother's fretful character. Isabelle was eight and a half, and she had her father's ambition—she was acquisitive and calculating. Jennifer, only seven, had inherited her father's lithe build and her mother's lovely face and was excelling at tae kwon do, of all things. Little Peter had learned to run at nine months and walk at ten. He was three and a half when Tavarez had shuffled through the series of steel doors that took him into the heart of the X.

They still lived in the Laguna Beach mansion he had bought, along with his ex-wife, Miriam, and her parents from Mexico.

Miriam had cut off all communication with him after his conviction for the bombing. She had told him that she forgave and pitied him for what he had done and she would pray for his soul. But she would not allow him to poison their children. No visits. No phone calls. No letters. No communication of any kind. Her word was final. She was filing.

The Tavarez children all spoke English and Spanish, and attended expensive private schools. Their gated seaside haven was a place of privilege and indulgence.

Tavarez had removed his children as far as he could from the barrio near Delhi Park where he had grown up. He wanted them to be nothing like him.

He fanned through the last of the envelopes, his heart beating with the fierce helplessness of the caged.

10

That night at ten Brad Lunce called him out. Lunce was one of Post's buddies. There were three kinds of guards: the bribable, the sadistic, and the honest. Group One was small but valuable, and Post had introduced Tavarez to a few of his friends.

Lunce watched Tavarez strip naked, open his mouth wide, spread his toes and butt, then get dressed and back up to the bean chute so Lunce could handcuff him before opening the cell door. Lunce never seemed to pay close attention, Tavarez had noticed, something that he might be able to use someday.

When Tavarez was handcuffed, Lunce let him out.

Murmurs and grumbling followed them down the cell block. Any other inmate being led out at this time of night would have brought yelling and catcalls and demands for explanation. But all the Pelican Bay cell blocks were segregated by race and gang. And this block was populated by La Eme and the gangs with which La Eme had formed alliances—the Aryan Brotherhood, the Nazi Lowriders, and the Black Guerillas. So when the inmate was El Jefe, respect was offered.

Tavarez walked slowly, head up, eyes straight ahead. Something fluttered in his upper vision: a kite baggie on a string floating down from tier three to find its intended cell on tier one. Night was when the kites flew.

Lunce unlocked the library just after ten o'clock. It was a large, windowed room with low shelves to minimize privacy, pale green walls, and surveillance cameras in every corner.

Tavarez looked up at one. "Cartwright again?"

"What do you care?" said Lunce. Lunce was large and young, just like Post. He resented his manipulation more than the other guards and Tavarez was waiting for the day when Lunce would turn on him.

Cartwright was the night "situations" supervisor, which put him in control of the electric perimeter fence and video for the eastern one-quarter of the sprawling penal compound. This made Cartwright the most valuable of all the cooperative guards, and a kickback to him was included in almost every transaction that

Tavarez made with lower-ranking men such as Post and Lunce. There were kickbacks to mid-level COs also, to those lower than Cartwright but above Lunce and Post. That was why favors were expensive. The western, northern, and southern perimeter guard-tower sharpshooters and attack dogs were under the control of other supervisors but Mike had found no way to influence them.

"He can turn the cameras back on whenever he wants to," said Tavarez.

"Not with me in here he won't. You got less than one hour. I'll be watching you."

Tavarez nodded. Having an L-Wop—life without parole—meant that there weren't too many punishments they could give him if he was caught. They could move him back to the SHU, which was something he didn't even allow himself to think about. But he didn't pay all that bribe money for nothing, and after all, he was only in the library. No violence intended, no escape in mind, no drug abuse, no illicit sex.

"The cuffs," said Tavarez, backing over to Lunce. It made the hair on his neck stand up—giving his back to a hostile white man—but if prison taught you anything, it was to overcome fear. Outside, you might have power. Inside, all you had was the bribe and the threat.

He found the world atlas on top of the G shelf, which he now slid toward him with a puff of dust.

Both the table and the chairs were bolted to the floor, so Tavarez plopped the heavy book down on the metal table, then worked himself into a chair in front of it.

He lifted the big cover, then the first hundred or so pages. Sure enough, the laptop sat in an excavated cradle. Post had come through.

For the next fifty minutes Tavarez sat before the screen, practically unmoving except for his hands, tapping out orders and inquiries in an elaborate code that he had helped devise for La Eme starting way back in 1988, during his first prison fall, before he had become El Jefe.

The code was rooted in the Huazanguillo dialect of the Nahuatl language that he had learned from Ofelia—his frequent visitor at Corcoran State Prison. The dialect was only understandable by scholars, by a few Aztec descendants who clung to the old language, and a handful of upper-echelon La Eme leaders. Ofelia was both a budding scholar and a nearly full-blooded Aztec. Back then, Paul Zolorio, who ran La Eme from his cell just eight down from Tavarez, arranged to bring Ofelia up from Nayarit, Mexico, to tutor the handsome young Harvard pistolero.

Now Tavarez's text messages would soon be decoded by his most trusted generals, then passed on to the appropriate captains and lieutenants. Then down to the 'hoods and the homeboys, who actually moved product and collected cash. Almost instantly, the whole deadly organization—a thousand strong, with gangsters in every state of the republic and twelve foreign countries—would soon have its orders.

Tavarez worked fast:

Ernest's Arizona men need help—everyone had a finger in that pie now that California had been clamped down. Move Flaco's people from the East Bay down to Tucson.

The L.A. green-light gangs would have to be punished severely. Green-lights won't pay our taxes? They're proud to go against us? Then peel their caps. Cancel one homie from each green-light gang every week until they pay, see how long their pride holds up.

Albert's men in Dallas are up against the Mara Salvatrucha. MS 13 has the good military guns from the United States but they don't get our south-side action. Move ten of our San Antonio boys over to Dallas immediately. Shoot the Salvadorans on sight if they're on our corners. Not a grain of mercy.

At the end of his fifty minutes, Tavarez had passed on more information than he could send in a hundred handwritten, coded letters and kites. Which would take him a week and a half to write. And a week to get where they were going. And half would still be intercepted, diverted, destroyed—perhaps even passed on to La Nuestra Familia by people like Ken McCann.

But with the computer he could write things once, in just a matter of seconds, then send his commands to a handful of trusted people, who in turn would send them down the line. His code was wireless and traveled at the speed of sound. It was practically untraceable and virtually indecipherable. It was clear, concise, and inexpensive.

Pure, digital Nahuatl, thought Tavarez, beamed exactly where it was needed.

All it had really cost him was a few months of subtle persuasion, then ten unsubtle grand to help the Post family through Tonya's cancer.

Tavarez turned off the computer, closed the screen, and set it back into the hollowed pages of the atlas of the world.

Like an alert dog who hears his master stir, Lunce appeared from behind the G shelf, dangling the cuffs.

"Looking at porn?" he asked.

"Yes."

"Are they cute as your whores?"

"Not as cute."

"I don't believe you. I think you're running your business. La Eme business."

Tavarez just shrugged. He felt the cuffs close around his wrists.

TAVAREZ LIFTED WEIGHTS furiously that night, putting everything he had into the repetitions, increasing the weight until his muscles gave out, doing sit-ups and crunches between sets, panting and growling and sweating for nearly an hour. Lunce watched him work out and shower but Tavarez was hardly aware of him.

By the time he was back in his cell, it was well past midnight. His body trembled from the exertion. He lay on his back on the bed and listened to the snoring and the distant wails from the ding wing—psych ward—and the endless coughing of Smith two cells down.

He closed his eyes and thought back to when he was released from his first prison term and he'd moved into Ofelia's apartment for six blessed weeks. All of the pent-up desire they'd felt for each other during her visits came charging out like water from ruptured dams. She was only seventeen, hopeful and innocent, a virgin. He was twenty-seven, the adopted favorite of La Eme kingpin Paul Zolorio, and suddenly free. He had been tasked by Zolorio to exact tribute from the Santa Ana street gangs for all drug sales—starting with his own

Delhi F Troop. Zolorio had given him a mandate of one hundred percent compliance.

There was nothing better, Tavarez had realized back then—than to be free, employed, and in love.

His heart did what it always did when he thought of Ofelia—it soared, then hovered, then fell.

He pictured her slender young fingers as they traced the Nahuatl symbols across the page in the Corcoran visitation room. He could hear her voice as she translated their sounds and meanings into Spanish and English for him. There was innocence in her smile and trust in her eyes, and luster in her straight black hair.

He remembered the simple shock on her face when he told her, six weeks after moving into her cheerful little apartment, that he was going to marry Paul Zolorio's niece from Guadalajara. He really had to, he explained, really, it wasn't quite arranged in the old-fashioned way, but his marriage to Miriam would solidify the families and the business they did, it was practically his duty to Paul to...

He remembered how softly she shut and locked the door when he left her apartment that night, and the heaviness in his heart and the painful clench of his throat as he drove south into the night. It was nothing like walking away from Hallie Jaynes and her insatiable desires, her murderous *guerra* selfishness. No, Ofelia was uncorrupted, untouched except by him. She was drugless and guileless and had the purest heart of anyone he had ever known, and the wildest beauty to her smile.

ONE YEAR AFTER he had married Miriam, shortly after she had given birth to John, Tavarez secretly traveled to Nayarit to find Ofelia.

With doggedness and patience he was able to learn that she had joined a convent in Toluca, Mexico's highest city. It took him another day to fly to Mexico City, then rent a car for the drive up to Toluca.

Sister Anna of the Convento de San Juan Bautista scolded him for coming here unannounced with such a request. She said Ofelia never wanted to see him again, after what he had done to her. Yes, she was healthy and happy now in the love of our Lord Jesus Christ, which was not a love given and taken away according to lust, commerce, or advancement. She looked at him, trembling with disgust.

Tavarez set five one-hundred-dollar bills on the desk between them. "For the poor," he said in Spanish.

"They don't need your money," Sister Anna said back.

He counted out five more. "Let the poor decide."

"I have decided for them."

"Okay."

Tavarez rose, leaned across the desk, and grabbed the holy woman by her nose. He pulled up hard and she came up fast, chair clacking to the tile floor behind her. He told her to take him to Ofelia or he'd yank it off.

"You're the devil," she said, tears pouring from her eyes.

"Don't be silly," said Tavarez, letting go of Sister Anna's nose. "I'm trying to see an old friend, and help the poor."

She swept the cash into a drawer, then led Tavarez across a dusty courtyard. The other sisters stopped and stared but none of them dared get close. Sister Anna walked quickly with her fist up to her mouth, as if she'd just been given unbearable news.

The vesper bells were ringing when Sister Anna pushed open the door of Ofelia's tiny cell. It was very cold, and not much larger than the one he'd spent five years in, noted Tavarez. She had a crucifix on the wall. His cell had pictures of Mary Elizabeth Mastrantonio.

Ofelia rose from the floor beside her bed. She looked up at Tavarez with a stunned surprise. She was thinner and pale, but her eyes still held the innocent wonder that he had loved. She was not quite nineteen.

In that moment he saw that she loved him helplessly, in the way that only the very young can love, and that the greatest gift he could give her would be to turn around and walk away. It would mean denying himself. Denying his desires, his instincts, his own heart. It would mean giving her life.

He reached out and put his hands on her lovely face. Sister Anna flinched.

"Love your God all you want, but come with me," he said.

"We'll both go to hell," she said, her breath condensing in the freezing air.

"We've got three days and a lifetime before that."

"What about your wife?" asked Ofelia.

"I have a son too. Accommodate them. I love you."

Tavarez watched the struggle playing out in Ofelia's dark eyes but he never doubted the outcome.

"I don't have much to pack," she said.

Sister Anna gasped.

Tavarez looked at her and smiled.

EVEN NOW, TEN years later, Tavarez thought of that moment and smiled.

But finally—as always—he remembered what Matt Stromsoe had done to Ofelia. And with this memory Tavarez canceled her image as quickly and totally as someone changing channels on a TV.

11

The first For Rent sign he saw in Fallbrook was for a guest cottage. The main house was owned and occupied by the Mastersons and their young son and daughter. The Mastersons were early twenties, trim and polite. She was pregnant in a big way. They were willing to rent out the cottage then and there, so long as Stromsoe would sign a standard agreement and pay in advance a refundable damage deposit. The rent wasn't high and the guest cottage was tucked back on the acreage with nice views across the Santa Margarita River Valley. A grove of tangerine trees lined the little dirt road leading to it. Bright purple bougainvillea covered one wall of the cottage and continued up the roof. It had an air conditioner, satellite TV, even a garage.

Within forty minutes of driving up, Stromsoe had written a check for first and last month's rent and deposit, and collected a house key and an automatic garage-door opener.

Mrs. Masterson handed him a heavy bag full of avocados and said welcome to Fallbrook and God bless you. Included in the bag was last week's worship program for the United Methodist Church.

Frankie called him around noon and asked him over for lunch before their drive south to the studio.

"I just moved to Fallbrook," he said.

She laughed. "You're kidding."

"The butterflies sold me. And I'm minutes away if you need me."

She was silent for a beat. "Thank you."

"You're welcome."

"**WHAT ARE THE** wooden towers for?" he asked when the lunch was almost over.

"The one in the picture?"

"The ones in the Bonsall barn."

Frankie set her fork on her plate. Her expression went cool. "For meteorological instruments," she said. "I study weather. How do you know about them?"

Stromsoe explained waiting for the idling car and seeing nothing until Frankie came blasting out of the dark in her Mustang.

"So, Mr. Stromsoe—are you a bodyguard or a snoop, or a little of both?"

"You're being stalked. I hear a vehicle idling near your house. Half an hour later, you leave your home on a code red. What would you have done?"

"Followed me."

Stromsoe nodded. "Who's Ted?"

Stromsoe tracked the emotions as they marched across her face—embarrassment, then irritation, then confusion, then control.

"Came right up and listened in, did you?"

"Yep."

"I don't like your attitude right now."

"It comes from thirteen years of being a cop."

"But you're a private detective now. You have to act polite and charming." She smiled. It reversed the stern lines of her face and Stromsoe remembered a time when he actually had *been* polite and maybe even a little charming.

"Ted's my uncle," said Frankie. "He's a retired NOAA guy. That's National Oceanographic and

Atmospheric Administration. They study climate and report weather."

"I apologize for following you. I was slightly worried."

"I'm glad you were worried. That's why I pay you. You were curious too."

He nodded.

"The towers are made of redwood and finished with a weather seal," she said. "They're twenty-two feet high, and we anchor the legs in concrete on-site."

"Where do you put them?"

"Mostly around the Bonsall property."

"You sit on the platforms to escape from yourself?"

She smiled and colored. "No. I told your boss the property was a place I went to be alone, because I didn't want him asking the same questions you're asking now."

"Who cares if you study weather?" asked Stromsoe.

"I was a lot more relaxed about it until I saw that guy on my fenced, posted property, inspecting one of my towers."

Stromsoe wondered about that. "Are there commercial applications to what you're studying?"

"Possibly," said Frankie Hatfield.

"You think the stalker is a competitor?"

"I don't believe so."

Frankie explained the value of weather prediction. Its applications were endless—agriculture, water and energy allocation, public safety and security, transportation, development—you name it. When you studied climate you had long-term charts to go on, she said, and generalities became apparent. But predicting *weather* was a whole different thing from predicting climate. Within a general climate, the weather itself could be very unpredictable. That's where she came in. She was trying to find ways for extremely accurate thirty-day forecasts. Right now, the best they could do was five days. Seven tops, but even NOAA had dropped its seven-day radio forecasts because they were so often wrong, useless, and sometimes even dangerous.

"Global warming is interesting but it's not my thing," she said. "I'm interested in telling you what's going to happen—I mean *exactly* what's going to happen—*exactly* where you live, one month from now. The precise temperatures, wind, and humidity. The exact amount of precipitation, if any."

"I didn't think the conditions arose thirty days ahead."

"They do but they're not apparent. That's where I come in. I'm on the verge of nailing a way to see and measure them."

Stromsoe waited for that smile again but it didn't come. He watched Frankie Hatfield's face as she stared out the window of her dining room to the bright

Fallbrook afternoon. She didn't blink. A flat patina came over her eyes, and it looked as if she were seeing nothing, lost in a thought that overrode vision.

"Right on the verge," she said quietly, glancing at her watch. "I guess I should go to work."

FRANKIE AND HER crew shot the live spots around downtown that evening—outside the ballpark, in front of the old Horton Grand Hotel, up on the Cabrillo Bridge leading into Balboa Park. She wore a polka-dot sundress with a white cotton jacket, and a straw fedora. Her weather forecasts were almost identical to the ones of the day before, making Stromsoe wonder how challenging a San Diego meteorologist's job really was.

Frankie did say that it was looking more and more like the jet stream would carry the low-pressure system into San Diego County, and that Sunday night would very possibly be wet. Monday looked "promising" for rain too, with two more low-pressure troughs "stacked up" behind the first.

The little crowd that had gathered groaned at the thought of a wet weekend in mid-October.

"Rain is life," said Frankie, smiling. "Sorry."

The urban settings in which Frankie did her stories made Stromsoe hypervigilant and a little nervous, and he realized how limiting his monocular vision was when it came to surveillance. He wondered if he could accurately fire the Colt Mustang .380 he carried on a Clip-draw on his belt. He hadn't fired the thing since the bomb. This was one more reason to regret his two-year decomposition in Miami, though at the time it had seemed his only choice. A time for casting out stones.

By Frankie's last broadcast at 8 P.M. Stromsoe hadn't seen the stalker, much less entertained drawing his sidearm.

Just after nine o'clock he was once more following her through the dark orchards toward her home in the fragrant Fallbrook night. The butterflies lilted through the beams of his headlights.

Again she pulled into her garage and again Stromsoe stopped to make sure she got into the house safely. He heard the dogs start barking inside again too, and he wondered what it was like for this young woman to live alone in the middle of ten acres of avocado and citrus trees, with two dogs, a stalker, and a gun.

She came up to his window, pulling up the collar of her coat against the October chill. Her hat sat back at an end-of-the-workday angle.

"Come in for a cup?"

"I'd like that."

12

Frankie pushed open the French doors to let in the breeze and the smell of the orange blossoms into the living room. Ace sniffed systematically at Stromsoe's pants. White-faced Sadie lay down and looked up at him.

"I read those articles about you," she said. "And Dan Birch told me some things."

"So, are you a weather lady or a snoop or a little of both?"

"I haven't followed you anywhere yet."

"You might have a better chance of running down your secret admirer than I did."

"My money's still on you," said Frankie.

Stromsoe nodded.

"I want to say I'm sorry that all those things happened to you and your family," she said. Her voice was softer than Stromsoe was used to, more confidential. "I felt very strongly that you had endured more than your share. And your wife and son, well, there's nothing I can say that would do them any justice."

They were silent for a moment.

"They got the guy, so there's some of that kind of justice," said Stromsoe, trying to be helpful.

"There's no justice when the irreplaceable is taken away," she said. "Someone's vision, someone's life."

"No. After that you settle for what's left."

She looked down at aged Sadie. "Dogs have less problems with that."

Stromsoe smiled and nodded. For a moment they sat and said nothing. He listened to the frogs and crickets.

Frankie was gone for a while, then back with tea service and a basket of biscotti on a tray. She set it down on the coffee table between them.

"Dan told me you took some time off," she said.

"Yes, down in Florida mostly. I was here for part of the trial."

"Are you satisfied with the life sentences?"

"Yes."

"I would have wanted death," said Frankie.

"At first, I did too," said Stromsoe. "Then I realized that if you aren't alive you can't suffer."

"Brutal and true," she said.

"Exactly. I've seen Pelican Bay. He did a year in the Security Housing Unit, which is so bad it can drive men crazy. But he conned his way out. Still, the line is nobody's idea of fun."

"Line?"

"The general population."

Frankie swirled a tea bag through her cup. "I can't compare any tragedy of mine to yours," she said. "My parents are alive. I've never married and have no children. A good friend died of cancer when we were both twenty-one. That's the biggest loss I've had."

"I think we're measured by what we give, not what's taken," said Stromsoe. "That was awfully pompous. I mean, I just now made it up. I was talking about you, not me."

She looked at him with a frankly evaluative cock of head. Again they said nothing for a few moments.

"You seem like a good man, Matt. I'm done with my questions for now. I just like to know who I'm in business with."

"No apology needed. Questions bring up memories and memories can be good."

"I'm glad you feel that way."

"It took a while, but now I do."

"Will you tell me about them someday, your wife and son?"

"Okay."

More silence, during which Stromsoe drank his tea and looked out to the very distant lights beyond the avocados.

"Want to see my pickled rivers?"

"I thought you'd never ask."

"Come on back."

The first room off the hallway contained three rows of glass-topped exhibition tables as might be found in a museum. Each row was lit from above by strong recessed bulbs.

But instead of rocks or gems or spiked insects there were mason jars filled with varying shades of clear liquid.

"One hundred and eighty-two rivers, creeks, and streams," she said. "So far. They have to run year-round to qualify. Eight of them don't even have names, which I think is majorly cool. My furthest one is the Yangtze in China. My favorite is the Nirehuao in Southern Chile. Very sweet to the taste, very clear, and full of large trout. I boil and filter the water before I taste it. I'm not a complete fool."

"No, I can see that."

Stromsoe noted that each mason jar was approximately three-quarters full. Some had sediment on the bottom. In a small stand beside each jar was a color photograph of the body of water, with the name, location, date, and time of day handwritten in elaborate cursive script. On another stand was a map of the world with a tiny blue-, red-, or white-headed pin marking the location.

"Blue for river, red for stream, white for creek."

"What's the difference between a stream and a creek?" he asked.

"A stream is a small river. A creek is a small stream, often a tributary to a river. A creek can also be called a branch, brook, kill, run, according to where you go. The truth is there are creeks bigger than streams or rivers. The terminology isn't precise, which adds to the romance and fun of it."

Stromsoe nodded as he toured the tables. The woman had traveled to every continent to collect jars of river water.

"Why not lakes?" he asked.

"It has to be moving water. That's just a personal standard I have."

Stromsoe stopped at the Nile and looked at the pale, sandy-colored water.

"They didn't turn out quite like I'd hoped," she said. "I thought each jar would have a kind of spirit to it, something talismanic. After fifty rivers I realized a jar of water is pretty much a jar of water, though the argument has been made that we drink the same water that Jesus did or Hitler or Perry Como. But when I sign up for something, I'm in for the duration, you know? I go down with the ship. I don't quit on anything, ever."

"I'm impressed," said Stromsoe. "I don't think I've ever seen a passion displayed so literally and scientifically."

"I am a scientist."

"It clearly shows. Interesting that different rivers have different shades of water."

"Isn't it?" asked Frankie. "Really, a hundred and eighty-two shades of water in one room. And each one is from just one *fraction* of its river. Some people might consider this a useless collection of jars. But aren't they lovely? I had this idea of emptying them all into a clear, curvy, tube like they make for hamsters, and running the little river all over the house. *World River,* I was going to call it. But who wants a river in a tube? They actually have one—the Lower Owens comes out of a concrete tube into the Gorge Power Plant. Then it comes all the way to L.A., mostly in a tube. Weirdest thing to put a river inside something. Makes you want to let it go, like an animal in a cage."

Stromsoe saw that there were more tables around the perimeter of the room. These were glass-topped also, and contained rocks.

"Those are just river, stream, and creek rocks," she said quietly. "One from each."

Stromsoe moved slowly from table to table. Some of the rocks were beautifully shaped and colored; others were dull and common.

"The Blackfoot in Montana has the best rocks," she said.

"Very nice, almost red," said Stromsoe.

"If you get that one wet, it has owl eyes."

"Unusual."

"The Liffey River jar broke on my way home from Ireland," she said. "Customs at LAX took the Mures River from Romania, which broke my heart because Vlad the Impaler drank from it. They said it was illegal to import because I hadn't purchased it. Then Security at San Diego confiscated my Congo from Zaire right after 9/11, which you know darn well Conrad touched. So I've got some replacements to get."

Stromsoe turned to face her. "Is part of your interest which people have touched which river?"

"Part. A river is liquid history."

"I like your collection."

"Thank you. What do you think of me?"

"You're one of the least ordinary women I've ever met."

She blushed and shrugged. "When I hit five-ten in the eighth grade I figured, hey, I'm not ordinary. Collecting rivers was easy after that."

"Not ordinary is good."

She nodded. "Well, I'm great, then. Maybe we'll finish that tea."

AFTER HE LEFT Frankie's house, Stromsoe waited at the end of her road again but the red Mustang never materialized. He saw no stalkers or suspicious vehicles. The coyotes hustled by.

He retraced his way out to the Bonsall property, parked in a tight little turnout just past the gate, and walked up the rise. There was no pickup truck out front, no lights on inside. Stromsoe got his flashlight and walked down the dirt road in the waxing moonlight. It had been a while since he'd noticed the difference twenty-four hours can make in the amount of moonlight.

The sweet smell of water hit him—what little river was it that flowed through here, he thought, the San Luis Rey?—no wonder she bought a parcel. He heard owls hoo-hooing to one another from the trees but they stopped as he got closer.

The big sliding barn door was locked. So were both of the convenience doors, front and rear.

He stood on an empty plastic drum and jimmied a window with his pocketknife, climbing through with great slowness and pain. He hadn't twisted himself into such complex postures in years.

Inside, as he moved his flashlight right to left, he saw in installments the same basic scene as last night—the workbenches in the middle, the tables along the far wall cluttered with their beakers and bottles and drums, the office in the back.

But the second tower now stood complete beside the first. Stromsoe went over and touched it, smelling the clean odor of freshly cut redwood and waterproofing compound.

He went to the tables against the far wall and looked at the labels on some of the containers: sulfates and sulfides, chlorides and chlorates, hydrates and hydrides, iodides, aldehydes, alcohols, ketones.

This close to the chemical containers the barn smelled different—the air was sharp and aggressive.

Stromsoe walked over to the corner office, following his light beam. The door was open and Stromsoe went in. He flicked on the lights and the large, neat room came to life. There were bookshelves nearly covering two of the walls. There was a long table with a computer and peripherals, a phone/fax, and a copier. There were four weather-station monitors with current readouts for exterior and interior temperature, humidity, wind velocity and direction, barometric pressure, daily rain, monthly rain, yearly rain. There was a black leather chair on wheels. The top of the table was littered with notebooks, science journals, and loose papers held down by rocks. Stromsoe lifted a piece of gray-and-black granite. The sticker on the bottom said *San Juan River, 8/1/2002* in Frankie's ornate handwriting.

On the office walls were framed black-and-white photographs of a young man with a thin face and a cutting smile. In most of the pictures he wore a shirt with the sleeves rolled up, a necktie, and fedora. In some he was standing on towers that looked just like the ones out on the barn floor. In others, he was using gloves and longhandled tools to mix something in five-gallon drums. The smile was self-conscious and playful. It was hard to place the year. Stromsoe guessed the 1920s. He could have been Frankie Hatfield's great-great-grandfather. A moonshiner? A country still? That would explain the containers, the towers, maybe even the guy's smile.

Stromsoe went to one of the bookshelves and scanned titles. Most of the books dealt with the sciences—chemistry, astronomy, physics, biology, hydrology, meteorology. Some were state history. But most were about weather and weather forecasting. And most of the volumes appeared to be decades old.

Stromsoe picked one out: *Semi-Tropical California: Its Climate, Healthfulness, Productiveness and Scenery,* published in 1874. It was hardcover, with illustrations, charts, and maps. There was a 1907 edition of *The Conservation of Natural Resources* by Theodore Roosevelt. And an entire shelf devoted to *Weatherwise* magazines dating back to 1948.

But the shelves along the other wall held more recently published books and articles: *Deepest Valley: Guide to Owens Valley,* 1995; *Water and the California Dream,* published in 2000; *Weather Modification Schemes,* 2002; and *Cloud Seeding in Korea* from 2003.

There were booklets and stapled abstracts: *Daily Weather Maps, Weekly Series,* collected since 1990; *Making the Synoptic Weather Map,* 1998; and *Useful Symbolic Station Models,* published in 1999.

Stromsoe moved down the shelf and looked at titles. On one shelf he found a stack of national weather maps. He could hardly make sense of them for all the symbols and designs. On another, two boxes labeled *letters from g-g-g'pa.* He opened one. The first envelope he lifted out had a return address for Charles Hatfield of San Diego. He set it back in the nearly full box.

A handsome leather magazine holder caught his eye. The first magazine was *The Journal of San Diego History* from 1970. On the cover was an illustration of the same man pictured on the office walls—slender, wearing a suit and hat—apparently analyzing the contents of a test tube of some kind.

The title of the article was "When the Rainmaker Came to San Diego."

He scanned through the article. "Professional rainmaker" Charles Hatfield had contracted with the drought-stricken city of San Diego to bring forty to fifty inches of rain to the city's Morena Reservoir in 1916. He was to be paid ten thousand dollars, but only if he was successful. He set up his wooden towers near the reservoir and mixed his "secret chemicals" that he guaranteed would bring rain. A short time later it started raining and didn't stop. So much rain fell it overflowed the reservoir, flooded the city, broke a dam, and ruined thousands of acres of property. Hatfield was run out of town without being paid.

The last part of the article was interviews with experts who said that Hatfield's success was simple coincidence, that his secret chemicals were bogus, that Hatfield was a hustler who simply studied the weather patterns for San Diego and tried to defraud the city.

I'll be damned, thought Stromsoe. *Frankie's trying to make rain.*

He took the magazine over to the wall where the pictures hung, held it up, and made sure that he was looking at the same guy. No doubt, he thought. Same face. Same hat and clothes. Hatfield, the rainmaker.

He compared the pictures of the towers to the towers that Frankie and the old man had made.

Stromsoe shook his head. *Frankie Hatfield's trying to make rain like her great-great-granddaddy did.*

In an odd and admiring way, he wasn't surprised.

Stromsoe turned off the office lights, found his way to the leather chair, and sat. He aimed his flashlight beam on one of the photographs of Charles Hatfield. Stromsoe smiled slightly, then clicked off the light and set it on the desk. He locked his fingers behind his head and closed his eyes.

The weather lady who makes rain, he thought.

He wondered if she had met with any success in her rainmaking venture, if she'd told anyone about it, if she was sane.

It was possible that the answer to all three questions was no.

He sat for a few minutes, thinking about how easy it was for catastrophe and heartbreak to kill your hope and your wonder. The death of hope and wonder was the hidden cost charged by every criminal, torturer, and terrorist. Few wrote about that, how the facts of loss are not the truth of loss. Few seemed to realize how often and easily the beautiful things vanish, except those from whom they had vanished. And most of those people didn't have much left to say, did they, because without hope and wonder you can't even move your lips. A lot of them were in their own private Miami hotel rooms, as surely as he had been, ending things slowly, good citizens to the end.

So why not put a river in a bottle?

Make it rain.

Amen, sister.

A FEW MINUTES later Stromsoe turned off the lights in the office, followed his flashlight to the window, and climbed back out. He landed on the drum with a hollow thud, hopped off.

When he turned and looked up the dirt road he could see the guy fifty yards out ahead, looking over his shoulder and hauling ass for the gate.

13

Stromsoe broke into a run, swinging his arms and getting his knees up as best he could.

When he came over the rise he saw that he might actually catch up before the guy got to his car, or at least in time to throw himself onto the back of it like a PI in a movie.

Maybe.

Pins smarting and joints stiff, Stromsoe dug down for all the speed he could get. The guy hopped the gate. Same guy as in La Jolla, Stromsoe saw—same square shoulders and squat-legged sprint. Same gold sedan.

The man was at his car, struggling with his keys while he stared at Stromsoe in apparent fear. The car door swung open. Stromsoe timed his stride to launch himself over the gate like a pole-vaulter. It worked.

Midair he saw the car door open and the lights flash on but Stromsoe landed square, took three quick steps, and tackled the guy just as he hit the seat.

Stromsoe immediately felt his weight advantage, so he used it. Covering the struggling man with his big body, he found the guy's hands and pinned them back onto the passenger seat. It was harder than he thought with his little finger missing—an entire one-tenth of his hand tools gone. The guy yelled in pain and head-butted Stromsoe hard right between the eyes, so Stromsoe butted him hard back. He used his weight to slow the guy's breathing. When he felt him getting tired he let go and punched him in the jaw and wrestled him over. Then Stromsoe swiped out the plastic wrist restraint from his back pants pocket. He wrenched the guy's arms back, cinched the restraints with the flourish of a calf roper, dragged the now unstruggling man out of the car, lifted him by his belt and collar, and dumped him facedown across the hood of his own sedan. The guy's chest heaved and his breath made a patch of fog on the gold paint. Stromsoe patted him for weapons and tossed his wallet onto the front seat. Then he flipped the guy faceup and patted him for weapons again.

Stromsoe stepped back, panting. "Relax, hot rod. You're mine now."

"*Chinga tu madre!*"

"Yeah, sure, first chance I get."

"Gimme my lawyer."

"I'm not a cop, so you don't get a lawyer. You just get me. How come you're following Frankie around?"

"Frankie who, man? I don't follow no guys around."

"Damn," said Stromsoe. "I work that hard just to collar an idiot. Look, let me sketch this out for you— I'm calling Frankie Hatfield and the cops, she'll ID you, and you're going to jail for trespassing, stalking, and aggravated assault. They'll set bail sometime tomorrow and it will be high because she's a star and you're a dumb-ass. She's got pictures of you lurking around her property, for chrissakes. So you're meat. Right now we're going to my car to get my cell phone."

Stromsoe pulled on the guy's foot to slide him off the hood.

"No! Okay, okay, okay. I'm just doing what I do, man. Just…don't call any cops."

"So you're going to talk to me?"

"Yeah, man, yeah."

"Get started."

Stromsoe tied the guy's bootlaces together. They were workingman's boots, grease-stained suede and soles worn smooth. The laces were regulation brown, not *sureño* gangster blue or *norteño* gangster red. He wore jeans and a gang-neutral black T-shirt. The guy was younger than Stromsoe had figured—midtwenties at most. He was short—five foot six, maybe. He looked Hispanic, but could easily be something else. The only accent Stromsoe could detect was Southern Californian. Stromsoe ran his flashlight over the guy's arms for gang or prison tats but saw none.

"I saw her on TV, man. I'm her biggest fan. I went to her work and followed her to the different places where she does her show. I used the Assessor's office to get her parcel numbers and from there I figured out what she owned and where she lived."

Stromsoe picked up the wallet and sat in the driver's seat. He checked the glove box for a gun but came out with a handful of digital snapshots and a cell phone instead. He put the phone back and flipped through the pictures in the poor interior light: Frankie Hatfield outside her home, going into the Bonsall barn, doing a live report from what looked like Imperial Beach. The shots had probably been printed side by side on picture paper, then cut out in a hurry.

"Yeah, hot rod—Assessor's office. Keep talking."

"So I went and looked at her, man. I just looked. I didn't do nothin' wrong."

"You just like to look?" asked Stromsoe.

"You seen her. You know."

"Know what?"

"She's beautiful."

"There are lots of beautiful women you don't stalk."

The guy said nothing for a beat. "But she's totally giant, man. A perfect, giant lady."

"You're stalking her because she's tall?"

Again, the guy was quiet for a moment.

"Because she's tall *and* beautiful," he said. "That's what it is, all it can ever be, man."

Stromsoe used his flashlight and both sides of a business card from his wallet to take down the driver's-license information:

John Cedros
300 N. Walton Ave.
Azusa, CA 91702
Sex: M
Hair: BRN
Eyes: BRN
Ht: 5-6
Wt: 170
DOB: 12-14-80

"Yep, she's six inches taller than you, John."

"You see what I mean then, man. You her boyfriend? Or are you a bodyguard she hired?"

"You like to wag it while you look, John?"

"It ain't that! I don't do that never, ever."

Stromsoe counted the money in the wallet—sixty-four dollars, plus an ATM card, a video-store membership, and a car-wash card with three washes punched out and dated.

"Ever been in her room?" asked Stromsoe.

"No, man. I'm not a panty bandit. I ain't that kinda stalker. I can prove it."

"What do you do with these pictures?"

"They're for me and my own information. That's my private shit, man."

"Private. That's a good one, John. Where'd you do your time?"

"Six months L.A. County, that's all. They said I was a deadbeat dad but I wasn't. The post office fucked me up. I taught that boyfriend of hers some manners, though."

"Way to go, John. Why come all the way to San Diego to stalk a tall woman? Don't you have any closer to home?"

"Not like her I don't. You seen those hats she wears on TV?"

"What channel is she on up there in Azusa?"

"Uh, six, I think."

"You think."

"I got TiVo. I can watch whatever I want whenever I want to."

"You can watch Frankie Hatfield over and over."

"That's the truth. What's your name, man? Who am I talking to, sitting there in my own ride?"

"Call me Matt."

Cedros shook his head slowly. "I call you bullshit."

"You got a job, John?"

"Centinela Valley Hospital. Janitorial."

"You can keep up on the child support, then."

"Bitch married the punk and I still gotta pay," said Cedros.

"Your kid's worth it," said Stromsoe.

"She's the cutest little thing you ever saw in your life."

"Then hope nobody like you follows her around and takes her picture," said Stromsoe. "What's your cellphone number, John?"

Cedros gave it. He gave the same home address that appeared on his CDL. He knew his employee number by heart, which Stromsoe took down also. The name of his supervisor at Centinela Valley too—Ray Ordell. On still another business card Stromsoe wrote down the name of Cedros's ex-wife and her new husband and daughter—all residents of Glendora. He even got Cedros's parents' phone number. If the statements weren't true, Cedros was one of the best liars Stromsoe had ever seen.

Still, Cedros wasn't adding up for him.

"John," said Stromsoe. "I believe your details. But I think your main story—you stalking Frankie because she's tall and pretty—is a crock. What do you think?"

Stromsoe aimed his flashlight into Cedros's face while he waited for the answer. Cedros glared into the light, but Stromsoe saw calm and intelligence in the man's eyes.

"I think I'm telling you the truth and nothing but," he said. "When I saw her on TV, I just...*man.*"

Stromsoe let the crickets and frogs do the talking for a moment. There wasn't much left to do but the obvious.

"I need to use your phone," he said.

"What for? I get to meet Frankie?"

"You get to meet the sheriff."

"Homes, man, I been cooperating. You can't do this to me."

"Got to. But the sheriffs are close, so no roaming charge."

Cedros tried to wriggle off the car. His boot heels and head both pounded the hood and it looked like he might slip off. Stromsoe spun him back to the middle of it, where Cedros flopped like a fish on a rock.

"Oh, man, you cannot do this to me. Let me go. I'll give you anything."

"John," said Stromsoe. "When this is all over, if I catch you around Frankie again, you will be very unhappy."

Stromsoe dialed.

14

At ten-thirty the next morning Frankie Hatfield identified John Cedros in a Sheriff's lineup at the Vista Sheriff Station.

Stromsoe hustled her to her car and got her out of there before the crime reporters could figure out who she was and why she was there. He'd had her wear sunglasses and a ball cap.

At the nearby San Marcos Courthouse, Cedros was assigned a public defender who suggested that unlawful arrest by the county, and assault and battery by PI Stromsoe, might be more appropriate charges than the ones against his client. Stromsoe observed. The defender talked to a young bearded man afterward and the young man took notes.

Earlier that morning Stromsoe got a copy of Cedros's rap sheet from Dan Birch—assault, possession of stolen property, drunk in public. A total of six months in county. He'd never been convicted of failing to pay child support, as he'd said the night before. And no record of stalking, harassment, blackmail, exposure, or burglary.

Stromsoe was not surprised. After a night to think about him, Cedros still didn't add up.

For one thing, Cedros admitted right off to stalking Frankie because she was pretty and tall. He had pictures of her in his glove box—a sex rap right there, thought Stromsoe—exactly the kind of thing you try to cover up, not confess. Then Cedros didn't know what channel Frankie was on up in Los Angeles County because Frankie wasn't even on the air up there. L.A. County had its own Fox affiliate and its own weather people. Stromsoe had checked with the satellite and cable operators for Azusa, and neither offered San Diego's local stations.

There was also that cagey gleam in Cedros's eyes, even when Stromsoe had taken him down to the hood of the gold sedan. Like he was thinking, figuring, acting. The guy just didn't look right, in a way that Stromsoe could see but not explain.

So he sat in the courtroom and watched as tiny, muscular John Cedros was charged with stalking, loitering near a residence, trespassing on posted agricultural property, and unlawful interference with property. Cedros's lawyer entered a plea of not guilty. Bail was set at seventy-five thousand dollars. A temporary restraining order was issued.

Cedros posted a bond for seventy-five hundred through a bondsman and walked into the lobby of the courthouse at five o'clock.

Stromsoe was waiting for him.

"You're a nightmare, man," said Cedros.

"My head still hurts," said Stromsoe.

"What do you want from me?"

"I'll help you past the reporter outside if you'd like."

"Reporter? Where?"

"The short guy with the beard. I'm going to give you my coat in case he's got a cell-phone camera."

"You helping the weather lady or me?"

"The weather lady."

"Lead the way, man. Keep that reporter out of my face."

Stromsoe did exactly that, ushering Cedros to the parking lot and keeping himself between the accused and the young crime reporter. Cedros put the coat over his head even though the reporter never brandished a camera. Stromsoe got Cedros into his truck and started back to the Sheriff's substation.

Cedros threw the coat into the backseat and stared out the window.

"John, I'll tell you. I got to thinking and I talked to Frankie. I thought I could help you both out—you tell me why you've been watching her and I can get her to drop the charges."

Cedros looked at Stromsoe with a scowl, but his eyes were cool and analytical.

"I told you why I followed her, man."

"It was a good story but it wasn't the truth."

"It's my truth and I'm not changing it."

Stromsoe pulled into the substation and walked Cedros inside. He waited while Cedros submitted his bail papers to a large deputy, who handed them to an even larger deputy, who read them slowly and disappeared. A few minutes later he came back with Cedros's car keys.

Stromsoe followed Cedros out to the impound yard to get his car. Cedros plunked himself into the front seat, reached down for the lever, and slid the seat way up. He checked the glove box.

Stromsoe stayed back by the trunk.

"Oh, man," said Cedros. "They took my pictures."

"They took them for evidence, John. Pop this trunk and see what else they took."

When the trunk lock popped Stromsoe lifted the lid to shield himself, quickly reached down beneath the bumper, and felt the GPU locator jump from his fingers to the car frame. The locator was held in place by strong magnets and could broadcast to a receiver up to a hundred miles away. Birch had agreed that Cedros was worth a closer look, and the locator was one of Birch's favorite new toys.

Stromsoe was staring hopefully into the trunk.

"Just get away from me, man," said Cedros. "Let the whore hit me with trespassing—it's a fine is all it is. Let her hit me with harassment because I didn't harass her or nobody else, man. I never said one thing to her. I didn't stalk her either. I just … looked. I don't have any priors like that. The judge will throw it out. They got all my pictures, but that's okay with me because it's proof of what I did—I snapped some shots of a pretty lady I saw on TV. The *Enquirer* does it all the time and those guys get *paid* for it."

"Who paid you for it?"

"Man, you're stubborn as a goat. I told you and told you again."

For the first time since last night Stromsoe thought John Cedros might be on the level—a short, garden-variety stalker who got off spying on and taking pictures of a tall, celebrity woman.

USING THE LOCATOR receiver, Stromsoe tailed the gold sedan north toward Los Angeles in the dismal evening traffic. It was interesting to follow a blipping light on a map rather than an actual car.

Inching through Santa Ana, he saw a city that hadn't changed a lot in twenty years. His old home was just half a mile from this freeway. The high school wasn't far. Mike's house wasn't either. He passed a cemetery hidden behind towering cypress trees where as a twelve-year-old he had attended the funeral of Uncle Joseph, his mother's charming and humorous brother. At that service Stromsoe had had the revelation that people were constantly entering and exiting the world, so that the departing always left the gift of one more available space, and we should thank them.

Glancing into the rearview, he saw a man who had changed drastically. Where was the chubby-cheeked freshman with a passion for leading the marching band? He felt unrecognizable. He hadn't kept up with a single person from his high school, except for Hallie, who was dead, and Mike Tavarez, who had killed her. He couldn't think of one person from his past who would surely recognize him.

To his surprise, John Cedros didn't drive home to Azusa, but directly to the downtown headquarters of the Los Angeles Department of Water and Power.

Stromsoe had to pull over and watch as Cedros stopped at Gate 6, inserted a card, then drove in when the arm lifted.

Stromsoe looked up at the DWP headquarters. It rose fifteen stories high above Hope Street, a horizontally layered steel-and-stone fortress that looked down on the city it powered. One parking lot was shaded by solar panels. There were flowers in the planters of the walkway leading to the entrance.

Stromsoe swung his truck around and parked out front behind a LADWP van. He dialed Cedros's cell phone number and was surprised when he answered.

"John, this is Matt Stromsoe, Frankie's friend. Make it home okay?"

"Yeah, I made it home," said Cedros. "Gonna get a cold beer out of the fridge right now."

"Not coming back down to Fallbrook, are you?"

"It's a free country, *pendejo*. I'm not afraid of you."

"You working today? Going to tell Ordell about your adventure in jail?"

"Keep my boss out of it. And keep my work out of it. It's the only damned thing I got left."

. . .

AN HOUR LATER the gold sedan pulled out of the lot and headed toward the freeways. It was nine o'clock by now and Los Angeles was a sprawling jewel against the black October sky.

Stromsoe fell back and followed the locator again. Traffic was light now and Cedros got himself onto the 210 going east for Azusa. A few minutes later the GPU indicator stopped moving. Stromsoe pulled over and waited twenty minutes to make sure. Then he got within eyeshot of 300 North Walton and saw the gold sedan in the driveway.

He parked under a huge, drooping jacaranda tree that had soon littered the hood of his truck with pale purple-blue blossoms but made him feel invisible. Scrunched down in the seat, he could see through the upper arc of the steering wheel.

He could hear the traffic out on Azusa Avenue and the peppy rhythm of *corridos* coming from one of the houses across the street.

Stromsoe remembered a *corrido* written about Mike "El Jefe" Tavarez. In the song, Tavarez is a new Robin Hood, while his boyhood rival—who kidnaps and rapes Tavarez's young wife—is the "big swine" of the American DEA, a man called Matt Storm.

Stromsoe had first heard it back in 1995. It was based on a story by a Tijuana newspaper reporter who had come up with a few scant facts that inspired the *corrido* writer. Back then Stromsoe thought the song was deranged and amusing but now, almost ten years later, he was angered by the way it reversed the truth for entertainment.

Mike had been the subject of at least a half dozen *corridos*. In all but one of them he was a handsome leader forced by gringo racism into a life of armed robbery, but who also found time to play guitar, sing beautifully, and write stirring love songs. He killed without remorse but was loyal to the woman who was taken from him. In one *corrido*, which was commissioned by a leader of his rival La Nuestra Familia, Tavarez was portrayed as a musically gifted coward.

Stromsoe had been mentioned only in the one—Matt Storm, the big swine of the DEA. He remembered playing it for Hallie one evening. It made them smile uneasily, and speculate whether Stromsoe's interagency team of crimebusters would catch Tavarez before someone murdered him, and which would be preferable.

HE LISTENED TO the news, dozed fitfully, his legs threatening to cramp. He straightened them across the bench seat of the F-150, rubbing the backs of his thighs. He

hit the wipers and cut a cloudy swath through the jacaranda blossoms on his windshield.

Just after sunrise he saw John Cedros come from his
house and open a rear door of the gold sedan. A pretty,
pregnant young woman in a white robe and matching
slippers walked behind him. His hair was gelled back.
His shirt was short-sleeve, blue, and had an emblem on
the left breast. The collar of a white T-shirt showed at
the open neck. His trousers were blue too, his work
shoes were black and looked heavy.

Cedros kissed the woman, who hugged him once
before letting him go. She was taller than him by two
inches. He checked his watch as he got in and started
up the car.

The woman waved as the gold sedan pulled away,
then walked back into the house.

Stromsoe followed the car at a comfortable distance,
all the way back to the Department of Water and Power,
where it stopped again at Gate 6.

As he watched Cedros's car pull forward into the lot,
Stromsoe used the DWP phone directory to get his
number.

"This is the Department of Water and Power custodial ..." The recording gave an emergency number and
said to leave a message.

Stromsoe didn't.

Instead, he called Centinela Valley Hospital and was given the number of Empire Janitorial, which did not employ a John Cedros at Centinela Valley or any other of its contract sites. There was no Ray Ordell in their employ either.

Heading back down the freeway, Stromsoe called Frankie.

"We need to talk," he said.

"Sure, but about what?"

"Making rain," he said.

She was silent for a moment. "Sunday night we might really have something to talk about."

"Can you do it?"

"I don't know yet. But I think the answer is yes. Meet me at the barn at six Sunday evening."

PART III

Water and Power

15

John Cedros stood with his shoulders stooped and his head down, not quite looking at the director of resources.

Instead he glanced sideways through the blinds and saw Los Angeles below him, sprawling all the way to the ocean under a soft, white, cloudless sky.

Director Patrick Choat sat caged behind the bars of pale sunlight falling on his cherrywood desk and cabinetry. The light was low. He had a corner office at DWP headquarters, fourteenth floor—Water Operations.

"How long did he question you?"

"Half an hour."

"And the police?"

"An hour. They ask everything twice."

"What did you tell them?"

"What we agreed I would tell them," said Cedros. "It wasn't until I started talking that I saw how bad it sounded. Like I was some guy pulling my pud in the bushes. I wish you and I had worked out a better cover story."

"You weren't supposed to need the cover story."

"They took the pictures," said Cedros. "Just like we thought they would."

Director Choat nodded slightly, a barely perceptible disturbance within the slats of light and shadow.

"Were they convinced you were a common stalker?" he asked.

"The sheriffs were. The bodyguard thought I was lying."

"Then he'll come to us."

"I think that's possible, sir," said Cedros. "I think it's also possible that, if I stay away from her, he'll just leave us alone."

"You don't know who we're dealing with."

Overhead lights came on and Patrick Choat's great creased face emerged from the shadows.

Cedros looked at him—the trimmed gray hair, the oft-broken nose, the thick brush of a mustache, the pin-collared dress shirt snug against his thick neck, and the gray, seldom-blinking eyes.

Choat cupped the photographs in one big stubby hand, dropped them to the desk, then fanned them out in front of Cedros.

Cedros saw that they were from the batch he'd shot two days ago in La Jolla, just before the bodyguard had chased him.

"I ran your picture of the bodyguard through our risk assessment program in Security," said Choat. "His name is Matt Stromsoe. He's the cop who got blown up by the bomb a couple of years ago. A drug thing that got personal. His wife and son were killed."

"I don't know about any bomb, sir."

"You wouldn't. He's a PI now. She hired him because she'd caught you looking."

"I tried my best. I'm custodial, not a spy."

"Indeed. Though now you've been charged as such."

"I'm charged with worse than that. And my only way to protect you is to stick to my story and pretend I was stalking her for personal reasons. It's a sex crime, sir."

Choat looked at Cedros. "I can promise that this won't go to trial."

"I have a wife and we're expecting our second child."

"Everybody has a wife and kids. But you also have my word—this will not go to trial."

Cedros nodded and looked down at the polished marble floor. He could feel his briefly promising life caving in around him. It was the same feeling as a cell door clanging shut behind you. He had come so far in his twenty-four short years. Only to run smack into this.

"How can we guarantee that?" he asked. "Frankie Hatfield has pressed charges and I've been arraigned."

Choat leaned back. He lay his big leonine head against his chair. "Can you get me Ms. Hatfield's formula or can't you?"

"I don't even know if it's written down. I've been inside the barn, but it's stuffed with all kinds of things."

"Well, then, we're right back where we started."

"Which is where?"

"She can either accelerate moisture or she can't."

"It's going to be pretty hard to watch her any more, with this bodyguard around," said Cedros.

Choat nodded. "Prophylaxis."

"Sir?"

"I'm thinking."

"Think of a way to make those charges go away."

"I already have."

Choat stood. He was a very big man with a barrel chest made even more pronounced by the suit vests he wore.

"Sit," he said.

Cedros sat and felt the anger spike inside him.

Choat slowly circled the desk and stopped in front of the window facing west.

Cedros looked out at the whitening sky. The news had said that there were three storm fronts forming out over the Pacific and that one might hit L.A. this weekend. Today was much cooler than yesterday, down in cheerful San Diego County, where he'd made his bail, collected his car, and finally gotten away from the PI.

"Rain," said Choat.

"Only a small possibility, I heard."

Choat turned to look at him. Cedros was impressed by how much contempt the man could convey with just one expression.

"John," said Choat. "We need help. We need someone outside our immediate sphere here at DWP. Someone fair and impartial, with the power to help us, and a clear understanding of what a dollar means—and what a promotion can mean to a young family man. You're twenty-four."

"Yes."

"The wife, Marianna, is what, twenty-two?"

"Yes."

"Mexican-American, like you?"

"She's Italian-American."

"And Tony?"

Cedros swallowed and took a deep breath. Back in his badass days he would have been all over this pompous windbag. But you change in jail. You change when the world kicks your butt, seems to enjoy it, and leaves you with nothing. You change when you marry someone like Marianna Proetto and have a boy like Anthony and a daughter on the way.

"What about him?" asked Cedros. "He's an everyday, four-year-old American boy if that's all right with you. Sir."

Choat turned and looked at Cedros. "I can fire you faster than you can get out of that chair."

"I know. I saw you do it to Larsen and Kuyper."

"My point is that a lot is riding here."

"No kidding," said Cedros.

He watched Choat return to the window, where he adjusted the blinds infinitesimally. Cedros couldn't tell if it was to let in more light or less. He entertained the wild fantasy of simply telling the truth in a court of law. But it wasn't hard to predict what that would get him— fired for sure, convicted anyway, and a traitor's heart to carry around the rest of his life.

"How are we going to get those charges dropped, Director Choat?"

Choat lifted his hand with casual power, like a man shooing a fly. "I don't traffic in rumor. But I have been told by reliable people that you are related by blood to Mike 'El Jefe' Tavarez."

The name rang oddly in Cedros's ears. Tavarez and the DWP didn't belong in the same sentence.

"Very distant blood, sir. No. I won't consider going to him with this."

Choat glanced at him, then back to the window. "Would you consider a promotion to maintenance technician grade two, working the Owens Gorge Transmission Line, with a rent-free home? One of the Owens Gorge cabins could be yours, in fact—the two-bedroom, two-bath. And the base compensation is better than you're making now. Some maintenance techs make supervisor if they're diligent, and most maintenance supervisors *die* maintenance supervisors—and they're happy to. MS is the best career the DWP can offer a twenty-four-year-old with as much jail time as he has college. Hell, it's the best job we can offer anybody, if you ask me. They call themselves ditch riders and they're proud to. You work outside, in some of the most inspiring land in this state. You've got men under you. You've got responsibility and the power that comes with it. Sometimes, what happens on the Transmission Line is a matter of life and death. The job certainly beats custodial. You would retire at fifty-five with full salary and full benefits for your wife and yourself. That's a little better than most of us do here at DWP. But you're a friend and I will take care of you. As I've always said—it's not about the water, it's about the power. Christ in heaven, just talking about this promotion makes me jealous of you."

Cedros swallowed hard. His heartbeat actually sped up with mention of the Owens Gorge cabins up near the Sierra Nevadas, which is where some of the Transmission Line and Aqueduct One employees were billeted. DWP had built the homes decades ago, because DWP employees were often heckled, hassled, and harassed by the Owens Valley locals. The locals thought the DWP was pure evil for putting their river in a tube and sending it south 250 miles to build Los Angeles back in the early 1900s. When that happened, most of the Owens Valley went from being a verdant green paradise to a thirsty desert dust bowl, and it had never fully recovered.

But the cabins themselves were beautiful and serene, jostled together in the gorge near the DWP power plant, rough-hewn cabins with intersecting lawns of deep soft grass and the snowcapped peaks of the Sierra Nevada

Mountains shading them from the summer heat. The constant tumult of the Owens River in the background—briefly paroled from its tube to turn the power-plant turbines—was a hypnotic and powerful presence.

He had taken Marianna there once just to see the little community. They were cautiously welcomed onto the private compound by a guy who had helped get him on at DWP in the first place. They'd walked in the shade of the cottonwoods, going from cabin to cabin and house to house, meeting the people who lived there. And to Cedros's mind this private world, which looked so lovely and peaceful and beautiful from the outside, looked even *better* when you got inside: friendly people, kids playing on the grass, the moms barefoot and smiling, and the men talking water and drinking beer in the shade while the California sky smiled down the most unusual shade of blue that Cedros had ever seen.

It was no L.A.

No guns.

No dope.

No garbage flying and whores dying and junkies lying in their own vomit on the street.

No way.

"That," Marianna had said later as they walked to their car, "is heaven."

Cedros pulled himself from the memory to see Resources Director Choat looking down at him.

"Sounds good, doesn't it?" asked Choat.

"Sure."

"Joan and I lived there briefly. Some of the happiest days of our lives."

"I won't contact Tavarez," said Cedros. "I can't go to La Eme, ask for a favor, and come back a free man. You may not understand that."

"I certainly don't. And we're not asking any favors."

Cedros shook his head and looked away. "What would you expect him to do for us?"

"Neutralize the bodyguard. Discourage the woman from pressing her charges. Retrieve the formula for us to study."

Cedros just stared at Choat. "What exactly do you mean by neutralize and discourage?"

Choat shrugged. "Maybe El Jefe will have some ideas."

"What's in it for him, besides a promotion for a distant relative he's never even seen?"

"I can divert two hundred thousand dollars from the Resource Emergencies Fund, and replenish it at budget time," said Choat. "Some of the board of directors have spine. They are trusting and sympathetic. Mr. Tavarez can use the payment for his appeals. Or maybe just to provide for his family."

Spine was Choat's word for what it took to run the DWP. Members of the Board of Water and Power Commissioners—citizens elected to "guide" the gigantic utility—either had spine or did not. Spine meant the advancement of the DWP above all else. To Choat, DWP was larger than anything and anyone, even the individuals who ran it, including himself. It was exactly what its name said it was—*power.* Choat had once told Cedros that he was honored to be a pit bull for history.

Cedros thought now, for the thousandth time, that if they could just purchase Frankie's formula away from her, everything would be fine.

If they could manage that, then there would be no possibility of rain on demand. No "moisture acceleration," as old Charley Hatfield had called it. Los Angeles would stay as it was. DWP would remain the largest and most powerful water and power utility on Earth, right here in the middle of the desert that made it all possible. Choat could be what he'd always wanted to be—the modern relative of Mulholland and Eaton and Lippincott, the dreamers who first saw the Owens Valley and decided to bring its treasure to Los Angeles.

Guys with spine. Guys with their portraits in the lobby. The guys who brought water to the city, but not too much of it. Because, as Choat liked to say—*only abundance can ruin us.*

Of course Choat had already tried the straightforward approach—offered Frances Hatfield a substantial sum of money to do her work under the auspices of the Los Angeles Department of Water and Power. In fact, Choat had pretty much offered her the farm: a stupendously large salary; a support staff of meteorologists and hydrologists and chemists; virtually unlimited funding for R&D; and practically any DWP land in the state—hundreds of thousands of acres—on which to set up her rainmaking headquarters.

Naturally, if she made rain, DWP would own the know-how and the equipment.

Frankie Hatfield said no.

"I won't go to Tavarez, sir," said Cedros. "I know that world. If I step in I'll never get back out."

"The alternative," said Choat, "is to live your life as a known stalker of women. Marianna and little Tony deserve better than that. And the department, of course, would have to sever all ties with you."

Choat stared at Cedros then sat back down. "When you meet with Tavarez to explain our proposal," he said, "make sure he sees your pictures of the bodyguard—

the ones they didn't take away from you. It's essential that he knows who we're dealing with. He'll help us. I promise you. You have thirty seconds to decide what you're going to do, but don't even pretend to think about it."

16

Cedros signed in at the Pelican Bay visitors' room and emptied his pockets, watch, wallet, and shoes into a bin.

They scanned him for metal just as they had scanned him a few hours ago at drizzly LAX. He never thought he'd be an accused stalker, and a suspected terrorist and prison smuggler in the same day.

And he never thought he'd see Pelican Bay as anything but an inmate.

It was Sunday now, six days since he'd been chased by this Stromsoe *pendejo* down in La Jolla, four days since getting his butt out of jail, three days since getting his orders from Choat.

Now he was about to call on a distant relative he'd never met, one of the most powerful gangsters in the country, doing life for murdering a woman and a child, and ask him for a favor. A favor that would earn El Jefe lots of money, and would set Cedros and his young family free of Los Angeles forever, but a favor nonetheless.

Twenty minutes later Cedros was seated across a steel table from Mike Tavarez and one of Tavarez's lawyers. His heart pounded with fear of this hideous prison, but also with a deep thankfulness for not being confined to it—yet. He tried to picture the Owens Gorge cabin that he and Marianna and Tony and their daughter would share but he kept being pulled back by the calm, knowing eyes of Tavarez.

Tavarez was very pale, Cedros noted, but there was a sinewy hardness to his neck and arms. He was slender. His face was open and innocent-looking, and his hair was full and curly, which gave him the look of a soccer star. He was handcuffed in the front and his legs were in irons.

The lawyer was a young man with dark glasses and a sly smile. His presence here gave them privacy from the guards and recording equipment, explained Tavarez—attorney-client privilege, constitutionally guaranteed.

Cedros and Tavarez talked for a few minutes about relatives. There was actually only one that both of them had met—a third cousin of Tavarez's who had married the half sister of one of Cedros's incorrigible nephews from Azusa.

"Azusa?" asked Tavarez. "Who'd you click up with?"

"No one," said Cedros. "I stayed out. Some school. A job."

"Azusa 13?"

"I said, no one."

"You know Marcus Ampostela?"

"No."

"Tito Guzman? Ricky Dogs?"

"No. Sorry."

Tavarez smiled and nodded.

"You want to talk to Marcus Ampostela."

"I'll remember that name."

"You don't have to. He'll find you."

"Good," said Cedros.

"You look afraid right now," said Tavarez.

"Not my kinda place, man."

"The animals treat us like animals," said Tavarez. "But I'll hit the bricks soon. My appeal, you know. Now state your business."

Cedros glanced nervously at the lawyer, who was staring at him, then up at the cameras in each corner of the visits room. He wasn't sure how to solicit felonies from a convicted murderer without getting caught, but he had given it more than a little thought.

In fact he had spent almost the entire weekend in a break room at DWP, staring at the wall because there was no window, picturing this moment and what he would say. Marianna had given him wide berth the last few days. She knew that he had been trespassing and photographing the news lady down in San Diego at the behest of Director Choat—because the woman was trying to make rain. Now that her husband had been caught, Marianna would have to endure a trial and she was angry about it.

But she had soon sensed a crisis even deeper than the arrest, though she didn't ask what it might be. Not asking had little to do with fear, something to do with trust, and much to do with the peace and well-being of the baby girl inside her.

"I'd like you to speak to a woman who has stolen something that belongs to my company," said Cedros. He breathed deeply and continued. "She took information developed by scientists where I work. She hired a private detective for intimidation and to keep us from getting the information back. I tried to get the information from her and she has accused me of stalking her. My employers want the information returned, the bodyguard discouraged, and the charges against me dropped. Promptly. And they want it made clear that none of this will happen again."

Tavarez frowned and nodded, prying into Cedros's eyes with his own. "Information about what?"

Cedros shook his head. "No."

"The name of your company?"

"No," said Cedros.

Tavarez sat back, looked over at his attorney, then again at Cedros. "Why should your stalking problem become mine, little man?"

"I'll also be given a very good promotion."

There was a moment of faintly echoing, metallic silence, then Cedros laughed. Then Tavarez and the lawyer laughed too. For a moment Cedros felt a soaring joy and an unreasonable confidence that everything would be okay. He saw a guard's inquisitive face appear behind a window to his left.

When the guard moved away, Cedros reached into his pocket and flashed Tavarez the back of a business card on which he had written *$200K*. Tavarez widened his eyes theatrically, grunted like an ape, and started laughing again.

Cedros brought out the picture of Frankie Hatfield and the PI down by Seal Rock in La Jolla. He set them on the table before El Jefe.

Tavarez stopped laughing and looked at Cedros. Cedros had seen the look before, *ojos de piedros*—the eyes of stone—and he thought for a moment that Tavarez was about to kill him.

"Do you know who this is?" Tavarez asked.

"He's the PI working for the woman, Stromsoe," said Cedros.

"And the woman?"

"Frankie Hatfield, a TV weather chick in San Diego."

"She has your valuable company information?"

"Yes, she does."

"And he's protecting her and the information?"

"He is."

Then Tavarez laughed again. "Holy Mother. Holy whore of a Mother."

For a moment Tavarez just looked at the pictures and shook his head in apparent disbelief. Cedros wasn't sure what Tavarez couldn't believe—his promotion, the two hundred grand, how tall Frankie was?

"Any more pictures of them?" asked Tavarez.

"None with me," said Cedros. "Why?"

"Where do you live?" asked Tavarez.

Cedros had dreaded this question but he knew this was how Tavarez would move forward if he chose to move forward at all—through one of his trusted people, not over a steel visitation table in Pelican Bay State Prison. Which presented a problem, because Cedros couldn't exactly entertain La Eme personnel in a break room at the DWP. If you make a deal with the devil, he thought, you'll have to shake his hand. He told Tavarez his address on North Walton.

"Marcus Ampostela," said Tavarez.

"We want things taken care of quickly," said Cedros.

"No worries, Homes. None at all. That thing on the business card? Have half of it ready for my man."

Cedros nodded.

"And, John," said Tavarez. "If anybody wants to know what we talked about in here, let's say it was personal. We're relatives, see, but we never met till now. We talked about family. Family. That's all."

CEDROS DROVE AWAY from the prison under a pouring Northern California sky. It was still only afternoon but the day was almost black. The rain roared down on his rental car and jumped up from the asphalt like it was boiling.

He squinted through the flashing wipers and felt as if the small, neat box of his life had been pried open and would never fit back together right. La Eme would soon be standing in his living room, breathing the same air as his wife and son. God only knew what they'd do to the weather lady and her bodyguard.

Cedros told himself that he had done the right thing, acted with spine. With storms like this up here, it was obviously possible to get too much rain instead of not enough. Not enough is what had made the DWP. So, two hundred thousand bones to keep extra rain from falling? To keep the DWP in control of every faucet and light switch in Los Angeles, every kilowatt hour, every drop of moisture used by 3.9 million people every second of every day? What a deal. Two hundred grand was like one drop hitting the road out there, one tiny part of the vast cascade of water and money that fell from heaven and surged through the state each second, north to south, the aqueducts mainlining the great thirsty arteries of L.A.

Yes, Cedros thought—money well spent. Choat would be silently rewarded by his masters on the board. They could give their pit bull a shiny new collar. Maybe he'd even get his portrait in the lobby someday.

And practically nobody would know, thought Cedros, that the guy who'd really kept the DWP in charge was a twenty-four-year-old custodial grunt with almost four mouths to feed. Which was fine with him. He didn't want glory and he never wanted riches. To him, the DWP was not a God. All he wanted was a decent job and a cabin in the Owens Gorge, a place away from L.A. where he would love his wife and raise his children and not go through life as a guy who was tried for stalking a pretty TV personality because he was short. Even if he beat the charge, the stink would follow him forever. He could play golf with O.J. Drink with Baretta. Party down at Neverland.

Cedros wondered if the weather lady could really make rain. Maybe she really was as dangerous as Choat believed. Wouldn't that be something?

Only abundance can ruin us.

17

Frankie's uncle Ted drove the white long-bed pickup truck through the failing light of the breezeless, humid evening. The sky above Bonsall was soft and gray as the belly of a rabbit, and the fretful clouds in the northwest looked almost close enough to touch.

Frankie sat beside Ted, and Stromsoe rode shotgun. Stromsoe looked back into the bed of the truck, at the eight five-gallon containers with vented lids that gave off the aroma of copper and chlorine. The containers were steel and rode on pallets that were roped to cleats on the bed sides. There were eight small gas canisters of the kind used to fuel camp stoves, and eight circular steel stands that looked roughly a foot in diameter. An aluminum extension ladder clattered against the pallets.

There was an electric lantern and two large metal toolboxes, one red and one black. Three folding beach chairs were tied up snug to the bed and what looked like plastic rain ponchos were stuffed down between them. Ace and Sadie lay on blankets, panting contentedly as the truck bounced down the dirt road.

Stromsoe couldn't tell exactly where they were, just that they were south of Fallbrook, west of Interstate 15. They'd come here by a series of turns, gates, bridges, and other unmarked dirt roads. The Bonsall hills were dry now in the fall and Stromsoe smelled the clear, quiet sweetness of sage and chaparral coming through the open window at him.

Ted drove fast, a cigarette in his mouth. He had given Stromsoe a firm handshake and a dubious once-over when Frankie had introduced him as Uncle Ted Reed—Frankie's mother's oldest brother.

Frankie wore a brown fedora into which she had stuffed most of her hair. The pocket of her dress shirt held a folded handkerchief and three pens. The sleeves were rolled up. She held a jumping laptop to her thigh with one hand and tapped away with the other. Stromsoe spied a Southern California weather map with more contour lines, front indicators, and numbers on it than he could even focus on.

She zoomed in on northern San Diego County, her face bouncing in unison with the computer. Then she turned, looked straight into his eyes, and smiled. Up this close, it was an unexpected and personal thing to Stromsoe.

"It's moisture acceleration, not rainmaking," she said. "Great-great-grandpa Charley Hatfield made that distinction. You can't make rain out of a sky with no moisture in it. It would be ridiculous to try."

"Acceleration," said Stromsoe.

"One hundred percent is what we're after," said Frankie. "We want to get double the rainfall per event."

Stromsoe thought. "How do you know what number to double?"

"Because we've got four towers spaced three miles apart in the northwest-to-southeast storm line, that's how," said Ted. "We bait the two outside towers and compare the rainfall with the two inside towers. We're plugged into the Santa Margarita Preserve, which is right over the hill. So we get data over their five thousand acres, and real-time video if we want it. And the city, county, state, and federal weather stations are all online now. That's how we know what number to double."

Stromsoe thought.

"With a storm of any size, you won't get a one-hundred-percent fluctuation in that short a distance," said Frankie. "If we get double the local yield over towers one and four, that's our system at work. And it's not really baiting, like Ted says. It's not really seeding either."

"Tell him about the particles," said Ted.

Frankie shut down the computer, folded the screen, and looked at Stromsoe. In spite of the cool evening there were pinpricks of moisture just under her hairline.

"Every raindrop contains a very small particle of solid matter," she said. "Once an oxygen and two hydrogen atoms bond, you have water. But you don't have a raindrop. It won't form, and it won't fall. We're not sure why the inert grain is necessary. Maybe it's the same principle as a grain of sand helping to form a pearl. Way back in the seventeen and eighteen hundreds, soldiers noticed that big rainstorms often followed big battles in which cannon and black powder firearms were used. People also liked to say that rain 'followed the plow,' because the rainfall records distinctly showed a rise in precipitation over cultivated land. For years scientists thought these beliefs were just superstition about battle and the wishful thinking of land speculators. Now we know that the particulate matter caused by detonation and the dust rising from cultivation accelerated the rainfall."

Stromsoe nodded and looked out the window to the clouds advancing from the northwest.

"We're doing something similar," said Frankie. "But we've got something a lot better than heavy carbon molecules or plow dust, and we've got a way to put it right where it belongs. The basic formula comes down from Great-Great-Grandfather Hatfield. It's based on an easily made silver iodide isotope—everybody suspected that's what it was—but that's all I can tell you about it. His other ingredients were a secret and people thought they died with him until I found his old lab out in Bonsall. That's his stuff out there you saw—most of it was his, anyway. He was a genius. Then Ted and I went to work. It's taken us eleven years but we came up with a lighter, more versatile particle and a much more effective way of dispersing it. Our formula is secret too, so don't even ask. Charley would have absolutely *dug* it. We built the towers out of wood just like he did, but that's because I'm nostalgic and because they look inspiring. If you ever went large scale with this, you'd use cast aluminum if you needed them lighter."

When she looked over at Stromsoe again he saw the sheen of sweat on her forehead, the tiny droplets of moisture above her lips.

As if seeing what Stromsoe saw, she wiped her face with the hankie. "Man oh man, this might time out just right, Ted."

"I think it's going to, Frankie," said Ted. "Soon as that jet stream started coming south again we were looking good."

"And you, Matt," she said. "Maybe you'll see some history made."

"We won't know until after it stops raining," said Ted. "When we compare the rainfall numbers."

"But if it pours cats and dogs over towers one and two, I'm going to be one happy girl."

IN THE NEW darkness they parked by tower one and Frankie climbed back, turned on the lantern, then pushed two canisters to the edge of the lowered tailgate.

Stromsoe carried one from the truck to the ladder, handing it up to Ted, who muscled it with a grunt onto the tower platform. The containers were heavy and hard to handle with his modified left hand. The smells of copper and chlorine hung in the dense air.

Before handing up the second canister, Stromsoe tried to peer inside but the vent holes were tiny and the lantern cast only a faint light.

"Don't," said Ted. "It's not yours to know."

"It's mine to smell," said Stromsoe.

"We've done this fine a long time without you."

"Come on, kids," said Frankie.

Stromsoe heaved the heavy container up to Ted, who jerked it onto the tower platform then shoved it into the corner opposite the first. Frankie handed up two of the gas canisters and two of the circular steel stands.

Stromsoe saw the cluster of meteorological instruments affixed to one corner of the platform. The cups of the anemometer scarcely shifted in the still night.

"That's going to change," said Frankie, again seeming to see through Stromsoe's eyes.

Frankie reached into the truck again and slid out the red toolbox. By the dip of her right shoulder Stromsoe could see how heavy it was.

"Matt, I'm going to ask you to face due south right now and give me some privacy."

Stromsoe glanced up to find the North Star but the clouds were too low to locate anything at all. He faced what he thought was south and listened to Frankie's boot steps across the earth, then on the ladder, then the huff of her breath as she hoisted the toolbox to the platform, then the clank of the heavy thing on the redwood.

He heard the lid open, and the sounds of objects being laid out on the platform. The fumes found their way down to him, not a foul smell really, but one that seemed potent.

Ted came over and stood in front of him and offered Stromsoe a smoke, which he accepted. The old man lit it for him and stepped back where he could keep an eye on Stromsoe and still see Frankie up on the tower. "I'm really not doing an antler dance up here," Frankie called down from the platform. "This is science. Mostly."

"Mostly science," said Ted.

Stromsoe heard the sounds of various lids being pried off, then liquid being poured into liquid. The cigarette smoke tickled his memory as he listened to the scrape of something on the inside of one of the big canisters, the sound of Reina Tavarez stirring the pot of chile verde she made on Sundays while the boys watched sports on TV or shot pool on the ancient balding blue-felt table in the Tavarez garage or hung with the other adolescents down at the corner of Flora across from Delhi Park but never actually in the park because Mike's father, Rolando, threatened to punish his son if he ever set foot in Delhi Park or ran with the bangers in Delhi F Troop, which was why Mr. and Mrs. Tavarez had had Mike transferred across town to Santa Ana High School, because they didn't want Mike in with the bad boys at Valley High, which was F Troop's corner. Stromsoe imagined Mike then unimagined him and wished that he could edit that face from his memory forever but knew he never would.

An enemy can live in your heart forever.

"Good job bagging the stalker," said Ted.

"Thanks."

"Think he'll come back?"

"Maybe," said Stromsoe.

"John Cedros, right?"

"That's right."

"What do you make for a day's work?"

"Three-fifty."

Ted was quiet a moment. Then, "I thought of police work when I was young. Turned out I was better suited for meteorology. I could do the math but I couldn't toss people around."

"I liked tossing around some people," said Stromsoe. "I never thought of anything but law enforcement. My father told me I lacked imagination."

"Imagination, well, fine," said Ted.

"I liked the work okay," said Stromsoe. "It paid the bills."

"She's a sweet girl," said Ted.

"I know."

Stromsoe heard Frankie climbing down the ladder. The copper-chlorine smell had changed to a lighter, more ethereal aroma that came and went quickly.

He peeked up at the tower, where the tops of the containers glowed a pleasant shade of light blue, and pale vapors rose into the air. Each container sat atop one of the circular stands, and each had a propane canister attached to its bottom.

When they were finished at tower one, they drove off to tower two, a mile to the southeast. Here, Ted again climbed the ladder and checked the cables and contacts on the meteorological instruments bristling atop the platform.

"The bugs get up in the housings," said Frankie. "One time we had a bat in the rain collector and another time a bunch of wasps got into the module case."

"Looking right," Ted called out from the platform. "Load 'em up here, PI."

Stromsoe slid the first canister from the truck bed and lugged it over to the ladder.

AN HOUR AFTER Frankie climbed down from tower four it started raining.

18

The three of them sat in the beach chairs in the bed of the pickup truck, the plastic ponchos efficiently shedding the raindrops. The dogs were outfitted in the same gear, with the hoods bunched behind their necks and the tails of the ponchos trimmed for their shorter bodies. They squinted into the rain with the air of veterans. Ted came up with a pint of Scoresby that slowly made the rounds.

Stromsoe looked up at the tower in doubtful wonder. Frankie's secret brew had been percolating for an hour now. The tops of the five-gallon canisters were still glowing a light blue color as the last of the gases sputtered and hissed and climbed into the air, then wriggled into the sky like smoky embers. Before the rain had started, he'd been able to watch the vapors rise up a hundred feet into the air, but now Stromsoe could follow them only a few yards before they vanished into the wet dark.

A few minutes later the containers rocked and shuddered and the blue light dwindled out. They sat smokeless and silent, no more interesting than empty paint cans.

"What's your forecast?" Ted asked. "Unaccelerated."

Frankie was already nodding. "I came up with half an inch. NOAA says half an inch. UCSD says half an inch too."

"I'm liking this," said Ted.

"I want double at towers one and four," said Frankie. "Maybe even triple."

"Don't get your hopes too far up."

"What are hopes for?"

Stromsoe sat with Sadie's gray muzzle on his leg, feeling the rain hit his poncho. His shoes and socks were soaked. For the first few minutes the rain was light, then it almost imperceptibly gathered force until the drops were springing off the bed and roof. Stromsoe listened to the growing volume of it against the metal and the ground.

Frankie sat next to him with her feet up on the bed side and the rain streaming off the brim of her fedora. Her work boots were heavily oiled and shed the rain.

Ted was on the other side of her, cupping a smoke in one hand and wobbling the Scotch bottle on his knee with the other.

"That's the most beautiful sound on earth," said Frankie. "Don't you think?"

"Chet Atkins," said Ted.

"And you, Matt?"

"I like how it roars on the truck."

"I like how much time it took to get here," said Frankie. "It's a closed system, you know—and it's hundreds of millions of years old. We could get hit by a water molecule right now that evaporated up from the Atlantic a few million years ago, rained down in Egypt thousands of years later, ran with the Blue Nile south to Ethiopia, then perked down into the ground. Later it came up in a village well and somebody used it to water a barley plant, so it evaporated again and got swept up by a front that dumped on Bangkok, then it ran off into the South China Sea. Then it wobbled along the Tropic of Cancer over to the North Pacific, where it became part of the ocean for a few million years before the northeast trade winds led the currents all the way to this front off California. Where our little molecule rose up, found a particle, and became a raindrop that hit a dog lying in the back of a truck."

Silence then, except for the rain.

"Which dog?" asked Ted.

Frankie backhanded his leg.

"Wow," said Stromsoe. "That's a mouthful, Frankie."

"Or not," she said. "Every drop has a different story."

She pulled the bottle from Ted, took a small sip, and handed it off to Stromsoe.

"God *damn* I'm happy right now," she said.

"You're a cheap date, Frankie," said Ted.

"That's me. Two sips of Scotch and I'm good to go. And I know I'm verbose. It's bad. I just love this stuff. *This.*"

She stood up and jumped off the side of the truck bed to the ground. Ace and Sadie took the smart way, off the tailgate.

Stromsoe watched her walk out into the chaparral, raise her face and arms to the sky.

"She got straight A's at UCLA," said Ted.

Stromsoe dropped out of the truck, his landing padded by his rain-swollen shoes and socks. He walked over to Frankie and the dogs, stopping not right next to them but nearby.

"What?" asked Frankie.

Stromsoe couldn't remember being at a simple loss for words in many years.

"Looks like rain," he said.

• • •

BACK IN THE barn office Frankie and Ted pulled the rainfall data off the tower sensors while the dogs sprawled on the red braided rug in front of an electric heater. Stromsoe made instant coffee, took cups to the scientists, then pulled up a chair with the dogs.

He listened to the rain hitting the tin barn roof overhead, an amplified clatter that sounded much wetter than the lessening slant of drops visible against the yard light outside the window.

He thought of a trip he'd taken with Hallie and Billy down to Costa Rica one year to see a live volcano and collect seashells. They got caught in a thunderstorm on the Arenal volcano and Stromsoe had found an old sheet of corrugated tin that he held up as shelter. They sat for a while and watched the big boulders and molten lava heave forth from the cauldron in the distance while the rain thundered down on their roof. Stromsoe had felt particularly strong at that moment, captaining his little family on the journey of life, protecting them, showing them a good time.

Now, a lifetime later, he shuddered.

"It's going to be a while," said Frankie. "Don't feel like you have to wait around in wet shoes. I'll call you first thing in the morning if you want."

"I'll just sit here if you don't mind."

"There's sandwich stuff in the fridge."

"That'd be good."

BY MIDNIGHT THE rain had stopped, though Frankie said there was probably another cell out there swirling in.

"Come on in here, Matt," she called to him from the office. "I'll walk you through this part."

Stromsoe stood next to Ted and looked over Frankie's shoulder as she went online and collected the NOAA rainfall data. Then she linked on to the Santa Margarita Ecological Preserve Web site for real-time downloads from their weather stations. She paused on a camera feed from the Santa Margarita river gorge. In the scant moonlight the runoff pounded over the smooth rocks of the old riverbed. Frankie quietly murmured. Then she clicked off, printed some pages, and highlighted certain numbers with a yellow marker. She said the state and county figures wouldn't be available until morning.

Then she collected the data from the four towers. Stromsoe and Ted stood and watched over her shoulder as the information was relayed to her computer.

What looked to Stromsoe like several tables of diffi-cult-to-understand statistical information took her just seconds to read and digest.

"Gentlemen," she said quietly. *"We just tripled what a rainstorm gave everyone else!"*

She stood up, knocked over her chair, and flew into Ted's open arms. The dogs hustled over to participate. She slapped her uncle's back, then released him and turned to Stromsoe.

She offered her hand and he shook it.

"This is more than excellent," she said.

"Nice to be here for it," said Stromsoe.

"You brought the luck," she said.

"That doesn't sound very scientific," said Stromsoe.

"What science says is that we have to repeat our results time and time again," she said. "This could be some of your good luck. This could be an aberration. It's a beginning. We have to make it work predictably, reliably."

"Not right now we don't," said Ted. "It's pushing one in the morning."

"Celebration at my house," said Frankie.

She righted her chair and sat down in front of her computer again. She leafed through the pages she'd printed, checking the numbers, shaking her head.

Then she looked up at Stromsoe with one of the nicest smiles he'd ever seen.

THE CELEBRATION DIDN'T last long. Frankie brought out thick dry socks for the men, traded her work boots for enormous sheepskin lounging boots, and got a fire going in the living room. They pulled the sofa closer to the flame and sat three across, close like children. Ted poured three Scotches, a light one with water for Frankie. The dogs were there too, asleep and stinking of wet hair.

Frankie told Stromsoe about finding her great-great-grandfather's laboratory in the old Bonsall barn, how the first time she walked into it she knew it would be hers someday, the smells and the books and the chemicals still in their containers and his mountains of notes and formulas and experimental data. It had been very difficult to find—most of the Hatfield relatives assumed it was long gone. They'd never laid eyes on it. And the published lore that she had unearthed over the years stated—unconvincingly, to Frankie—that Charley had set fire to the lab before he was run out of San Diego for creating too much rain. She was sixteen when she'd found his old laboratory. She said that opening the barn door was opening the rest of her life. She would study weather and accelerate moisture. She was surprised that the other descendants of Charles Hatfield were not particularly interested in the barn or the formulas. To her it was like losing interest in finding the Holy Grail or Noah's Ark. She told Stromsoe that she'd seen the dumb Burt Lancaster movie *The Rainmaker* and wished they'd have shown some of Great-great-grandpa's scientific side rather than his dreamy hustler's side.

"He sold sewing machines most of the time he was rainmaking," she said, yawning. "He never made any real money at it. But he always wore nice clothes, a tie, and a good hat. The movie should have been more ... I don't know, more something..."

A moment of quiet, then, as the fire burned and popped and Ace's legs twitched in a dream of pursuit.

Then Frankie Hatfield's head lolled onto Stromsoe's shoulder and she was out.

Stromsoe looked over at Ted, who sipped his Scotch and looked into the fire. "Par for the course," he said. "Frances can't drink more than a thimbleful and stay upright."

Stromsoe sat awhile. Ted made another drink and sat on a chair not so close to the fire.

"I checked you out through the Web and your boss," said Ted.

"Good."

"Learn to shoot with one eye yet?"

"I'll find out soon," said Stromsoe.

"I wondered about the two years in Florida."

"Lost."

"I figured," said Ted. "I might have done the same."

"It's nice to be back."

Ace whimpered and his legs kept twitching.

"A guy named Choat at the L.A. Department of Water and Power tried to buy her out of the rainmaking formula," said Ted. "My theory is, if you follow up on this Cedros fellow, he'll lead you back to DWP."

"I have and he did," said Stromsoe. He told Ted about tracking Cedros to the DWP. "Did Choat threaten you?"

"Oh, no, not at all. Very civil, in a hard-ass kind of way. He offered Frankie seven-fifty a year and all the support staff she wanted, so long as her procedures and formulas belonged to DWP. Said she could set up shop on any DWP land in the state, and they own thousands of square miles and rivers and lakes and mountains. Three-quarters of a million bucks a year! She turned him down. It drove Choat bugshit that we might have our hands on a moisture accelerator that worked."

"How did Choat know about this?" asked Stromsoe.

"He'd been agitating her and other Hatfield descendants for years, off and on. Always poking around, looking for the barn, the formula, his papers, whatever. Just staying in touch. When he got wind that she'd found the barn, he was all over her."

Stromsoe thought. "Cedros was his threat," he said.

"Sure," said Ted. "Shake Frankie up. Take her picture. But I also think he broke into the barn one night.

There were footprints, and some of the files were laying out. Like somebody was looking for something."

"The formula."

"Yup. You're signed on for a month, right?"

Stromsoe nodded.

"If Choat sent Cedros, Choat's ass is in the wind," said Ted.

"Not if Cedros keeps his mouth shut. He didn't say anything about Choat. He says he stalked Frankie because he likes the way she looks."

"A jury could believe that," said Ted.

"I almost did," said Stromsoe.

They watched the fire burn. Outside the breeze came up and a shower of raindrops hit the roof then stopped.

"I don't think this DWP stuff is over," said Ted. "Choat made my scalp crawl, a quality few men have. Maybe you need to apply some pressure. If Cedros is protecting Choat, there might be a way to pry them apart. Cedros can't be happy about the charges."

"You think like a cop," said Stromsoe.

"I'm just a weatherman. Though I did shoot down some planes over Korea in '51."

"I might be able to make Cedros see the light," said Stromsoe. "If he rolls on his boss, we've got what we need."

"I like the sound of that."

"Frankie might have to call Birch Security, make it clear to Dan that she still wants me on the job. When a stalker goes to jail and gets charged, that usually means the PI is done."

"She already did that," said Ted. "Actually, I made the call myself. She thought it would look better coming from a man. Frankie tends to worry. Sometimes she worries too much, and she begins to see herself as hysterical. Which of course makes her hysterical. Gets even more worried."

Unworried, Frankie started snoring.

"There's been a reporter calling her," said Ted. "From a local paper. Frankie asked me to put him off, so I've been giving him the runaround."

"Good," said Stromsoe. "Let him find another story."

Stromsoe got up without waking her and arranged her on the sofa with her head on one of the pillows. He found a throw blanket by the fireplace and covered her.

"Something I don't understand," he said. "If the Department of Water and Power had a way to triple the rainfall, would that help them or hurt them?"

"Help them, I guess," said Ted. "Help everybody."

"Then why didn't Frankie let them finance the research, get rich, and make rain for the world?"

"Because Frankie liked Choat even less than I did. 'Creeped me out' is what she said. She thinks Choat would lock up the formula and toss the key."

Stromsoe thought about that. Hard to imagine.

Or was it? With triple the supply falling from the sky, wouldn't people need you for two-thirds less of it? Triple the supply of Chevys and you have to sell them for a third the price. And what court in the country would hand a utility company the sole right to increase rainfall and reap the rewards? If you couldn't monopolize the formula—or destroy it—someday you'd be a lot less needed.

"How come Frankie didn't tell me about Choat?" asked Stromsoe.

"She didn't think he'd stoop so far as to intimidate her. She thought Cedros was just a stalker. She's naive in a lot of ways, really. And stubborn."

Stromsoe nodded. "I like it that she loves the rain and collects rivers."

"She's not like anybody else."

He looked at her sleeping under the blanket, fire shadows playing off her face. "Well, 'night, Ted."

"Good night," said Ted. "Be good to her."

"You too."

Stromsoe drove home with the windows down and the smell of rain and soil and citrus in the cool air. The clouds had blown out and the sky was now black and pricked by stars. He thought of Frankie Hatfield and his heart rose and hovered like he was in an elevator coming to a stop or on a roller coaster when he was young.

19

Mike Tavarez lay on his bunk and listened to the steely hum of night-locked Pelican Bay State Prison, the tap of the guard's boots approaching on the concrete floor, the distant wails of men driven insane in the Security Housing Unit, the X.

Lunce arrived at El Jefe's cell with his usual Monday-night pout. This was Tavarez's "family"—conjugal—visit night, though it would not take place in the Pelican Bay apartments available for such visits, commonly known as the Peter Palace. Lunce was extra sullen on Mondays and Tavarez knew he was envious.

It was ten o'clock. Tavarez stripped, bowed, opened himself for Lunce's cursory visual inspection, then redressed and turned his back and put his hands to the bean chute for cuffing.

They walked wordlessly from the wing, inmates stirring, inmates watching. In the library Lunce released the cuffs and took his seat at the end of the long aisle. Tavarez pulled the world atlas down from the G shelf and went to work on the neat little laptop.

Much to do.

El Jefe's most recent batch of mail had contained a plea from La Eme captains in Los Angeles who wanted to deal with the south-side green lighters more forcefully. Tavarez tapped away in the code he had helped devise, the code based on Ofelia's impenetrable Huazanguillo dialect, then sent his instructions to five different addresses at once: permission granted.

He looked over at thick Lunce. The Web was the best thing that had happened to La Eme since the Nahuatl code had been invented. Now, using the two together, it was almost as easy as picking up a phone— and his orders were practically impossible to trace, divert, or crack.

Thinking about the code brought up memories of Ofelia. And with them came memories of what Stromsoe had done to her. He would deal with Stromsoe soon.

There was good news from Dallas and the problems with Mara Salvatrucha—La Eme gangsters had canceled two of the Salvadorans in broad daylight the day before—no arrests, no problems.

Tavarez quickly approved La Eme memberships for a Venice Beach gangster doing time in Corcoran and another who had just hit the bricks back in Ontario after two years in Vacaville. They had proven their loyalty and were willing to swear an allegiance to La Eme that would override their street loyalties once and forever.

This changing of loyalty, Tavarez knew, was what had turned La Eme from a simple prison gang into an empire of soldiers in every city in Southern California, and in many other states besides. La Eme's rules for membership were simple and had seemed right to Tavarez from the first time he'd heard them. You cannot be a snitch, a homosexual, or a coward. You cannot disrespect another member. Death is the automatic consequence for violation of any of the first three rules. Only a member can carry out the murder of another. Such murders must be approved by three members.

He coded his congratulations to the new members, to be passed on by higher associates in Corcoran and on the streets of Ontario, along with the usual warnings to keep close eyes on these new men. Loyalty had a price, just like everything else.

Tavarez ordered a payment of fifty thousand dollar to the widow of a La Eme OG—original gangster—who had been shot down by La Nuestra Familia gunmen in the "border" city of Bakersfield. He asked that the Bakersfield associates produce the name of the shooter within forty-eight hours. It would be a bloody season up there on the border between La Eme of the south and La Nuestra Familia of the north.

He approved a one-month extension on an eighty-thousand-dollar payment due from the Little Rascals' cocaine sales but ordered one of the gang's members killed each week if the deadline wasn't met.

He ordered a five-thousand-dollar withdrawal from a La Eme "regional account" and given to the daughter of a La Eme soldier on her wedding day next month.

He sent condolences to a new widow in Los Angeles; congratulations to a new father in Riverside.

Tavarez enjoyed the feeling of his fingers flying over the keys. It was something like playing a clarinet, but instead of musical notes his fingers produced action. It was like fingering a melody that didn't hover in the air and vanish but rather pushed itself across time and space into the lives of real people and forced them to act the way that Tavarez wanted them to act.

When his gang business was finished he visited his personal accounts online—three in Grand Cayman and two in Switzerland—and found them to be earning nicely at the usual three percent. He was worth almost $2 million now. Every original penny of it had come

from what he collected for La Eme through drug traf-
ficking, tributes from cowed 'hood gangsters twelve
and thirteen years old, extortion and protection money,
blackmail money, blood money—anytime Tavarez took
in a dollar for La Eme he chipped off a few cents for
himself. Never enough to show. Never enough to raise
an eyebrow. And he quickly delivered the cash to Iris, a
Harvard acquaintance who had become an investment
banker in Newport Beach and could electronically
credit the money to accounts thousands of miles away
that only Tavarez had the numbers to access. A few
hundred dollars here, a few hundred dollars there. He'd
started investing with her secretly right after being
released from Corcoran and having seen all of his armed
robbery loot taken by lawyers and the cops. He was
hugely proud of the fact that, though he was a convicted
murderer doing life in Pelican Bay, nobody had been
able to locate his money. Amazing, what twelve years of
compound interest and steady contributions could do,
he thought. He could still remember the rippling of his
nerves when he stole his first hundred dollars from La
Eme kingpin, mentor, friend, and uncle-in-law Paul
Zolorio. It was only a hundred dollars, but it was almost
as exciting as knocking off the liquor stores when he
was at Harvard, and much more dangerous. He and
Ofelia had celebrated that moment with a night of wild

lovemaking and huge happiness. Two days later he'd married Miriam.

Which brought him to Matt Stromsoe.

Tavarez shook his head again, still not quite able to believe that fate—a distant relative named John Cedros—had delivered Stromsoe back into his hands.

Tavarez had always been lucky. He was born with a high IQ, musical talent, and a gift for understanding people. He was handsome and women fell for him. He had courage and unusual physical strength. He had 20/10 uncorrected vision. He had met Paul Zolorio and found a direction for his life simply by being in the same prison.

Then there were other good fortunes too. He'd been shot through the side of his neck once with a .25-caliber handgun and the bullet hit nothing vital. He survived without seeing a doctor, just two painful black-and-red rips at either end of a tunnel that Ofelia had cleaned out by running a piece of alcohol-drenched T-shirt through it with a pencil. And there was the time his warrants had failed to show during a traffic stop and he'd come *that* close to grabbing the handgun from the console of his Suburban and killing a CHP officer. He had foreseen in a dream an attempt on his life and saved himself by taking a different road to Culiacán one day while meeting with cartel heavies in Sinaloa. He won at craps in Las Vegas and poker in Gardena. He rarely played the California Lottery games but had won more often than anyone he knew, and for good money—five hundred here, three-fifty there, a thousand once on tickets that had cost him three bucks apiece.

But this felt like something more than just luck, something heavier and less clever. This was having your life changed by a force intimately familiar with your desires. This was an act of God, *his* God—the God of Jesus and Mary and Aztlán.

The question was what to do. There was the obvious: he could have Stromsoe beaten and the weather lady tortured—that would almost certainly get Cedros's information returned. He would have his two hundred thousand in cash couriered to Newport Beach and Iris would credit his accounts, minus payments wired to his most trusted men. Cedros would move higher into the DWP bureaucracy. Cedros didn't know it, but he was already the property of La Eme, because the lawyer had tape-recorded the meeting and Cedros's solicitations were clearly of criminal intent.

Or he could kill them both, and Cedros too, and be done with it, leaving no trail back to Pelican Bay.

All of this was obvious.

But, what if?

What if he had been correct in sensing that Stromsoe looked at this weather lady in a special way?

What if that attentive angle of Stromsoe's head in the picture taken of them outside her house had betrayed a more than casual interest from the newly hired private detective?

If that was true, then Tavarez had a chance to send Stromsoe through the flames of hell on Earth not just once—but *twice*. By killing his new hopes. His new dreams. By killing his future.

I would do it right in front of him, Tavarez thought. Let him see and live and remember what it means to lose everything—*again!*

It would finally be fair revenge for Ofelia, who left the Aztec gods for Jesus and left Jesus for me and died for it. Fair revenge, because the deaths of insatiable, ignorant, arrogant Hallie and her offspring were almost valueless compared to the life of Ofelia.

It would be the stuff of a hundred *corridos* that I could listen to in the shade of my home on the beach in Sayulitos, Nayarit, where I will retire when I'm out of this prison.

When I'm out.

He looked over at Lunce. Lunce was reading a car magazine with a bright red roadster on the cover.

Look at him, thought Tavarez. If he's the best the *norteamericanos* have to offer, I can do it. Not long now. Not long. I have what I need.

Tavarez shook his head and pictured the calm, humorless face of Ariel Lejas, the most capable man he knew. Then his hands began to fly across the keys.

In a confounding amalgam of Nahuatl, Spanish, and English, Tavarez ordered Lejas to dispatch Marcus Ampostela to the home of John Cedros, 300 North Walton, Azusa. Ampostela would pick up one hundred K and Cedros would handwrite all needed details regarding his request. Ampostela would deliver the money and the information to Lejas and Lejas would FedEx seventy-five-thousand to Newport Beach, keep twenty thousand for himself, and lay off five to Ampostela.

Tavarez paused and looked down at the screen. The strange Nahuatl words jumped out and reminded him of Ofelia as they always did. *Ichpochtli* (young woman)...*Momatequia*(washyourhands)...*Tlazocamati* (thank you)...*Icniuhtli* (friend)...

Interspersed with the Nahuatl was some English: *My Dear Friend...PI Stromsoe...possibly armed... barn...Weather Lady...your account...*

Tavarez painstakingly went through the message and rewrote every third sentence backward—both words and the letters of the words. He randomly added three sentences beginning with the Nahuatl word for "to marry"—*Monamictia*—that contained nothing but Nahuatl-like nonsense that Lejas would know to ignore.

When Tavarez was finished he looked down on what would be just dizzying blather to anyone but a patient Mexican-American gangster with a knowledge of Nahuatl and Sinaloan slang.

He took a deep breath and organized his thoughts before he ended the message:

Ignore Cedros. Kill the woman. Make the PI watch and let him live.

TAVAREZ WALKED TOWARD the eastern perimeter of the Pelican Bay Prison grounds. He was handcuffed from behind again. The October night was cold and clear and the moon was loitering into its first quarter.

It was neither dark nor light, but a twilit truce between the blackness of the Northern California forest around them and the muted light straining out from the prison buildings three hundred yards to the west.

Out here away from the compound, the grass was sprayed with poison once a month so it would not provide cover for even the ground squirrels but the lavish rains dulled the herbicide enough for new shoots to grow and these stunted storm-drenched blades now soaked through Tavarez's prison sneakers and sent a chill up his shins.

He saw the North Star shimmering off the lip of the Big Dipper and smelled the wet green density of the Northern California forest that pressed right up to the prison fence line in front of him.

Lunce followed, tapping the rolled car magazine against his leg.

Tavarez approached the fence. It was twenty-feet-high, electrified chain link that carried 650 milliamperes and 5,000 volts—nine times the lethal limit for human beings. It was topped with two rolls of razor ribbon in case the electricity failed.

Seventy-five yards to his left a guard tower stood outlined against the autumn sky. Seventy-five yards to his right was another. The towers were staffed at this hour by one of Cartwright's loyal men, who included Post and Lunce and a few others. The interior lights brought a quiet green glow to their insides and Tavarez could see in the northern tower the black motion of the guard as he moved within. The floodlights were aimed away from them and they wouldn't begin their criss-crossing searches for the half hour that Tavarez had bargained for. The video cameras running along the fence were off now, activated when needed only by

Cartwright and his "situations" brethren who controlled the three other sides of the perimeter.

The flashlight flicked twice from the forest. It belonged to Jimmy, who belonged to La Eme. It came from a slightly different place each week, but there was a creek that wandered close to the fence between two stands of cedar trees and in the dark Tavarez could tell from the smell of the trees and the gurgling of the creek where Jimmy and his people would be waiting.

He came to the fence and stopped. A moment later Lunce stood to one side of him, removing the spare cuffs from the pouch on his duty belt.

Tavarez watched as Lunce took a step back and tossed the stainless-steel handcuffs against the chain-link fence.

They clinked lightly then fell to the ground.

Tavarez had always been curious what the 5,000 volts would have done, had Cartwright or one of his gang messed up, or had left the fence electrified on purpose.

Lunce collected the cuffs without taking his eyes off of Tavarez.

Tavarez took a step toward him and Lunce's hand went straight to his club.

"I want you to know I appreciate this," said Tavarez.

"Live it up," said Lunce.

"Thank you," said Tavarez.

"I won't be far away."

With this, Lunce took two small steps backward—he always took two small steps backward—then turned from Tavarez and lumbered into the near dark twenty yards away.

Tavarez turned to the fence. "Jimmy, my friend, is that you?"

"Your friend it is, Jefe. I brought you something sweet."

"Let's see."

A rustling in the cedars produced a figure that came toward Tavarez from the other side of the fence. He smelled her perfume before seeing her clearly. Her shoes glinted in the quarter moonlight and the spike heels sank into the damp earth and she had to lift them up as if from gum to get them free again.

"Hi."

"Hello."

"I'm Shavalia."

"Great."

She was light-haired and slender, nice face. She had costume diamond earrings and her jeans had similar jewels down the legs to where they ended midcalf. She wore a dark camisole under a loose red mesh shawl under a short black leather jacket. There was orange mud on her heels and the sides of her shoes but the rhinestone-studded straps looked bright and clean.

She smiled prettily. "Hope they don't turn the fence on. Blow my jewels all the way to Lake Shasta."

"Mine too."

She smiled. "Here, honey, come a little closer."

20

Early the next day Stromsoe bought rich food and good wine in Fallbrook. The people in the stores and deli were friendly and helpful. He learned that Fallbrook called itself the Friendly Village. Drivers in the parking lots stopped so he could get to and from his car, without the terse hand signals he was used to. He felt as if he should wave and smile to them, so he did. Girl Scouts sold cookies outside the market and he bought some Thin Mints.

He straightened up his tiny home.

Then he drove up to Orange County and met with Dan Birch, who agreed that Cedros was probably lying and wanted to know why.

"Think he's a danger to her?" Birch asked.

"I've got no reason to trust him."

Birch nodded, tapped something onto his keyboard. "Frankie says she's okay now, to and from work. She's not worried anymore."

"Okay."

Birch studied Stromsoe. "Look in on her at work anyway. Drop in. I know that's a lot of hours. Just keep track of them."

"Gladly."

"I talked to the publisher of the *North County Times*—boss of the reporter who's been calling Frankie. I got the publisher to keep a lid on this for now. I told her about copycat possibilities if the whole world knows there's a sicko watching a TV celebrity. Fox News double-teamed them with me. They love Frankie. Don't want to lose her."

"That's good planning, Dan."

"Security *Solutions*, Matt. What do you think of her?"

"I like her."

"I can't believe this shit about DWP. You'd think she'd have mentioned all that."

"Funny what she offers up and holds back," said Stromsoe.

"Making rain," said Birch. "Christ."

After that, Stromsoe spent the rest of the morning at the indoor range in Oceanside. It felt good to have a gun in his hand again and to feel the percussive pops through the muffs and smell the gun oil and the solvent and the burned powder. He was surprised how well he shot with only one eye.

He had been a distinguished expert on the OCSD pistol team for three years running, until workload and fatherhood had squeezed out his recreational time. He had learned to use his eyes and to trust his hands and fingers to do the right things at the right time. Practice, and more practice—range hours, competitions, dry-firing his sidearms whenever he could to build trust and familiarity, helping the new deputies—it was enjoyable.

Stromsoe had been surprised to see that most law enforcement officers did no more shooting than was absolutely necessary to qualify each year. They took poor care of their sidearms and their skills. They seemed to ignore their guns. Some actually disliked or feared them. He had been surprised too at his own interest in shooting, but he enjoyed using a precisely made tool, liked the hand-eye coordination, the concentration and rhythm.

Firing a revolver in PPC competition, Stromsoe could get off six rounds, shuck the empties, smack home the speed loader, squeeze off six more, and hit nothing but black at fifty feet without ever looking at anything but his target. The PPC events were almost leisurely because speed wasn't really important. But shooting an IPSC with an autoloader was about speed and accuracy and it was more exciting because you were moving and shooting at the same time. The magazines were faster than speed loaders, and you got more rounds besides. The secret for either competition was to keep the gun up at eye level during the reload, so if you needed to adjust the speed loader or get the magazine started, your eyes were still near the target. He felt connected to his target by his eyes, tethered almost, and it had been a simple visual skill to discharge the bullet that would follow the invisible connective thread to its mark. His target could be a guy hopping fences at night but Stromsoe had taught himself to truly see with a gun in his hands and to put his rounds where his eyes were looking. He was proud to have placed ninth overall in the Southern California Regional Sheriff 's Association competition of 1994.

Now it was different, but not all bad. Two years had given his body time to adjust. His depth perception was not as precise as before and his field of view was smaller. It was like looking down a tunnel. Through his one eye the world looked slightly flat and compressed, as if telescoped back toward him by an invisible hand. But the picture was clear.

At fifty feet he shot a decent group with his Colt .380. The shots hit right and high of the five-ring but almost all in the black.

At ten feet his right-side pull was one inch but the group was very tight.

He practiced his motion with the Clipdraw, first with a sport coat on, then with it off. Smooth was the ticket here, especially with the coat on—no jerks, nothing showy, no mistakes. The Clipdraw rode too high to quick-fire over like a western gunslinger, so it was left hand on the coat then the right arm drawing out the gun and extending while you bent your legs and let your left hand find your right while your eyes—eye— ate the target for lunch.

Boom. Boom boom boom.

Still got it, Stromsoe thought. He also thought it was oddly fitting that of all the skills diminished by the bomb, his ability to shoot a gun was pretty much unchanged.

He shot another six magazines with the Mustang, then fifty rounds from a Smith AirLite .22 that was small and light enough to slip into a pocket and had once saved his life.

BY FOUR THAT afternoon he was waiting across the street from John Cedros's house in Azusa. He parked under the same generous acacia tree and noted the fallen flowers collecting again on the windshield wipers and hood of his truck.

At quarter till five the pregnant young woman he'd seen last week parked an embattled white coupé in the driveway and slowly climbed out. She was dressed in what looked like a waitress's uniform for a Mexican restaurant—a brightly colored ruffled skirt, a white blouse with puffed sleeves off the shoulders, a comb with a red fan in her dark hair. She flipped the driver's seat forward, squeezed awkwardly behind it, then emerged with a little boy hiked over one shoulder. She pulled a purse off the front seat and slammed the door with her foot while the boy reached up and fingered the red fan.

A few minutes later she was back. She had changed to jeans and a flannel shirt rolled to her elbows. She opened the trunk and carried in plastic bags of groceries four at a time, two trips, then shut the trunk and locked it.

At five-thirty Cedros rolled up beside the coupé in his gold sedan and killed the engine. Stromsoe slid down again and watched through the crescent between the dash top and steering wheel. Cedros popped out of the car and hustled into the house. Stromsoe waited five minutes.

The security screen door of the Cedros house was closed but the wooden door behind it was open to the cool evening as Stromsoe knocked.

"Go away," Cedros said from somewhere inside.

"I think Frankie will see the light," said Stromsoe.

Cedros stood behind the screen door. Bare feet and a beer, a singlet and his blue DWP custodial chinos. Small as ever. "Make sense, *pendejo*," he said.

Stromsoe looked past Cedros to the kitchen, where the woman stood before the seated boy, lowering a bowl to the table.

Cedros looked at his wife then back at Stromsoe. "She's my wife, man. That's my son."

"Let's take a drive."

"Let's."

They headed up Azusa Avenue through town. The streetlamps and benches and planters were painted a flagrant purple blue that Stromsoe liked. The little city seemed caught in a time warp, with tenacious mom-and-pop stores downtown instead of the chain every-things he'd become so used to in Southern California. But the stores looked to be struggling. Some were boarded up, right along the main drag. There were lots of liquor stores with their faded cigarette posters and sale signs and Lotto ads fixed to the windows. CAMEL TURKISH BLENDS—CARTON OF 20—$39.99!!!

A half mile farther and they hit the residential area. The homes were small, some neat and some not. Front yards sat behind iron fences and gates and there were steel safety doors instead of the regular screen doors. The wrought-iron patterns over the windows looked more defensive than decorative. Flat-footed women slowly carried bags of groceries home from the *mercado* and pretty girls with flashy clothes and smiles crossed the streets away from the homies manning their corners or slinking up and down the avenue in older cars with thumping woofers and bright paint and the windows blacked out.

Stromsoe saw the contempt and impatience on Cedros's face as he looked out at the town.

"Didn't use to be like this," said Cedros. "The bangers."

"My hometown changed a lot too."

"Just the last five years, man."

"It doesn't look so bad."

"What do you know? And what do you want? The weather lady is ready to drop the charges?"

"She might," said Stromsoe. "But I need some information first."

"And if I don't have it, the charges stick."

"Yep. You go on trial."

"Name it, man."

"You work for DWP, not the hospital. It took me half a day to figure that out."

Cedros shrugged.

"I think Choat put you up to harassing Frankie."

"Choat? I barely know Choat. He's water operations, fourteenth floor. I'm custodial."

"You didn't answer the question."

"He didn't put me up to anything. The fuck is wrong with you?"

Stromsoe looked over at Cedros, who had slipped on a pair of shades.

"Here's the deal on Choat," said Stromsoe. "He wanted Frankie's rainmaking formula. Offered to pay her a lot of money for it. When she said no, he sent you to frighten her, maybe even steal that formula yourself. I think you got as far as the barn—inside the barn—but you couldn't find the formula because she's never written it down."

"I didn't break and enter. Never."

"Let's go back to Choat, then. What did he want you to do with Frankie?"

"Nothing, man. How many times I gotta tell you that?"

"You stalked her because you're obsessed with her?"

"I didn't say that either. I didn't stalk her. I'm not guilty of that."

"They got a stack of pictures you took of her. They got pictures *she* took of *you* on her property. I caught you trespassing on her private property and handed you over to the cops. John, let me help you out here— you're toast."

Cedros stared out the window.

Stromsoe said nothing for a minute or two. He pulled over where the San Gabriel River passed under the road, a narrow white-water ribbon racing down from the mountains. They got out and walked to the edge of the drop and watched the river below.

"You did good," Stromsoe said. "You pestered Frankie to the point where she hired a PI. You took the pictures of her, had the stalking story ready if you got caught. You even took the rap in court. Good for you. I hope you're in for a big promotion."

Cedros stared down at the water. "I'm waiting for you to say something that makes sense."

"Try this," said Stromsoe. "You have a nice wife back there at home, and a nice little boy, and another baby on the way. This isn't going to be easy on them, especially your wife. You get tried as a stalker, there's no winning it. Even if you're acquitted, people wonder. They talk. You get passed over. You're a stand-up guy, John. You can't live like that. I know you."

"Bullshit."

"You're a lousy liar," said Stromsoe. "I don't believe you'd leave that pretty woman back there at home, then drive all the way to San Diego to spy on a weather lady who isn't even on your channels up here. *That's* bullshit, John. You're covering for Choat and you're going to take the fall. I'm trying to help you here. Can't you see that?"

Cedros reached down, picked up a rock, and snapped it out over the river. His motion was compact and angry and the rock jetted far out over the water then vanished into the canyon shadows.

"And you also lied about being a deadbeat dad," said Stromsoe. "Just the idea disgusts you. You lied about being a janitor in a hospital because you're DWP and you're proud of that. You wear your uniform and you polish your shoes and you hope you're moving up the ladder. And you lied about stalking a woman because you're still so crazy in love with your wife it's the last thing you'd ever do. So, why? Choat? You know I'm going to talk to him. How can I help you if you don't tell me the deal?"

"There's no deal," Cedros said with soft-spoken hostility. "There's just me and something dumb I did. You saw my wife. She's tall. I like the tall ones."

"Okay, fine. Get back in."

Stromsoe punched a U-turn and headed back toward Azusa.

Cedros stared out the window almost the whole way back to his house. He seemed deflated, even smaller.

"I Googled you," he finally said. "I know all about you."

"Everybody knows all about me."

"You got my respect."

Stromsoe looked at Cedros but couldn't think of what to say. He just shook his head and opened his hands in frustration.

"You go get another job," said Cedros. "Get Frankie Hatfield to hand over her formula and promise not to use it to make rain. Everybody will be better off."

Stromsoe jerked the wheel to the right and his truck careened to the curb and when he slammed on the brakes John Cedros's head was pressed to the side window. Stromsoe leaned across and felt his pistol press his ribs as he jammed his face right into that of Cedros.

"But that's *not going to happen*. Choat doesn't own the rain. You can't scare that woman off of her work. You don't tell me who to work for. Get it? Can I make it any more clear to you?"

"That's all I'm going to say."

"No, you're saying good-bye to your future too, friend. You're dumber than I thought you were. You want to drag your wife and kids down with you just to kiss somebody's ass at work, that's your business. Fuck it, kid, I give up."

Stromsoe floored the truck from a dead stop and skidded to a halt in Cedros's driveway a minute later.

Cedros jumped out and slammed the door. He turned back to look at Stromsoe without breaking stride. His wife opened the safety screen door and Cedros blew past her and was gone.

Stromsoe backed out and saw the new Magnum parked under his acacia tree down the street, the pink blossoms littering the black hood, a face behind the wheel scarcely visible through the windshield and the darkly smoked side window.

Everywhere you look, thought Stromsoe.

He drove out to Azusa Avenue, cruised the street with the lowriders and the pretty girls for a few minutes, then circled back and came up on Cedros's house again. The Magnum was now in the Cedros driveway. Stromsoe parked well away and not under his acacia tree, then got his binoculars from the glove box and wrote down the Magnum's plates. He waited about twenty minutes until a guy came from the Cedros house with plastic grocery store bags swinging in each hand.

The man was big, his skin the color of heavily creamed coffee. His hair was buzzed. Wraparound shades and a chain with one end latched to his belt loop and the other disappearing into his front pocket. He wore black work boots and chinos and a sleeveless under-shirt and his arm tats included an elaborate Celtic rendition of "13," the letter *S*, and something Stromsoe couldn't quite make out involving an Aztec warrior and a bloody heart.

The "13" was for the thirteenth letter of the alphabet, thought Stromsoe—the letter *M*. *M* was for Mexican Mafia. And *S* for *sureño*, the gangs of the south that made up the thousands of foot soldiers of La Eme.

The guy swung the bags into the passenger seat of the Magnum and drove off. Stromsoe stayed in his truck, struck by the circularity of what he was doing, by the deadly comedy of it all.

Fourteen years of chasing these guys and I'm still at it, he thought. A wife and a son murdered, an eye lost and a body blown half to bits, no Sheriff's team around anymore to help keep me alive, but I'm still here, just like I had good sense. For what? Three-fifty a day before taxes, five vacation days your first year, a lousy

HMO medical plan, no dental, per diem enough for fast food and a few gallons of gas.

The upside?

It was a short list: doing the right thing, fighting the war that had taken the ones he loved, and Frankie Hatfield.

21

It was almost eight by the time Stromsoe got down to the San Diego waterfront for Frankie's last story of the night. She stood on the Embarcadero walkway with the yachts bobbing behind her in the marina and a firm breeze ringing the halyard swivels against their naked masts.

She smiled at Stromsoe as he came down the boardwalk, and waved the microphone at him. In the felt fedora and brown overcoat she looked like a gumshoe with big hair.

He stood behind the little audience that had formed, listening to tomorrow's forecast: clear and breezy throughout the county, with temperatures in the low seventies at the coast and midseventies inland, with the deserts at eighty and the mountains in the midsixties.

"And we've got some more rain to go along with that half inch from Sunday, coming along, well…I'm going to say Friday, maybe Saturday. Right now it looks like another substantial storm, and two storms this early in the season is good for our depleted lakes and reservoirs. Rain is life! I'm Frankie Hatfield, reporting live from the Embarcadero."

"Get 'em, Frankie!"

"Right on, Frankie!"

She signed a few autographs and Stromsoe walked her across the street to the county building parking lot.

"You look nice tonight," he said.

"Thanks. This was one of Great-great-grandpa Charley's hats. I'm trying to keep up with Loren Nancarrow on Channel Ten. He's got the coolest clothes."

She opened the door of the Mustang.

"I got food and wine for us," he said. "Even though my whole house is about the size of your living room."

"You really did?"

"The whole truth."

"For *me*?"

He looked at her.

"The shower work?" she asked.

"Perfectly."

She tossed her fedora into the air, caught it, and set it on Stromsoe's head. It was warm and smelled of her.

STROMSOE TURNED THE radio on low and got the omelets started while Frankie used the shower. With the windows open the breeze brought in the smell of tangerines from his drive and the distant hiss of the cars on Mission. The cannons boomed out at Pendleton, muffled thuds, the sound of freedom. The landlord's cat sat on the couch and licked a front paw. The Mastersons had left a red colander filled with homegrown avocados, tomatoes, basil, and cilantro on his doorstep sometime during the day.

He was wiping two wineglasses when Frankie came out in jeans and a silk tank top the same deep brown color of her eyes. She was barefoot and her hair was up and she made the little house seem even smaller. Stromsoe's heart rocketed.

"Can I go barefoot around here? It makes me shorter."

"I've got you by two inches either way," he said.

"Mom and Dad used to tape my shoulder blades together so I wouldn't stoop."

"Ouch."

"Not really. It was kind of a joke. But it worked. It reminded me to keep my back straight. If you don't slouch, the tape doesn't bother you."

She turned her side to him and stood ramrod straight.

He looked at her, wishing that she knew him better, that she was aware of the less-than-good things he'd done in his life. Maybe there would be time for that, he thought.

"Can you dance?" she asked.

"Oddly enough, I can. It came easy to me."

"Me too. Hey, cool place. I love the big windows and the little fireplace and all the bougainvillea. And, God, the smell of tangerine blossoms is like heaven on earth. There's a million little nooks and crannies like this in Fallbrook. I've lived here five years and I keep finding them. My friends all want to move here. Wouldn't that be great, or maybe not."

She smiled anxiously at her own nervous chatter.

"I'll get you a small glass of wine."

Stromsoe served the omelets, dimmed the lights, and lit two candles. They sat across from each other at a small table in the dining room. The red colander filled with treasures was the centerpiece. Stromsoe had used some of everything for the meal. He thought of Hallie's lobster extravaganzas and of Susan Doss bringing him the good deli lunch that day when he almost set his life on fire.

He poured Frankie some cool white wine and some for himself.

"I think Choat dispatched Cedros to scare you," he said.

"Then I was wrong. Ted thought the stalker was DWP all along."

"It doesn't matter who was right or wrong. What matters is we blocked someone with power. We busted his man and wrecked his program, and now he's free to find a new way to deal with you."

"Can't you stop him from dealing with me at all?" she asked.

"I think I can."

"I don't want people watching me. I don't want that man to turn my work into his business."

Stromsoe took a bite of omelet and had a sip of wine. "Frankie, some people don't discourage. Some people will take things all the way."

She looked at him and nodded.

"I'll talk to Choat," said Stromsoe.

"He'll just deny Cedros and say he made a generous offer for my work," she said.

"He did."

"Please."

"I understand. It's your work and your formula and your rain and you aren't going to sell it to someone who wants to profit by it—whether by using it or destroying it."

"Right on."

"You're not going to budge, Frankie? Not for a million dollars? Ten? Or all the staff and land you need to do your experiments? I have to know if you've got a price, and if so, what it is."

Frankie shook her head. "No price to Choat or the DWP. Ever."

"Okay," he said. "You don't discourage either."

This brought a smile to her face, then it left and she looked down at the tabletop. "Do you think I'm an idiot?"

"I think if you can make rain, you've got bigger problems than Choat. You've got half the power of the Lord Himself, just for starters."

"I'm getting close, Matt," she said, looking up at him. "You saw it. We got triple what the rest of the valley did."

"I saw it."

"*Triple.* And I'll have a chance again by Friday or Saturday."

They ate for a while in the near silence while the radio played something peppy and light.

"Cedros worries me," said Stromsoe. "He's got big things at stake and he's smart. He's covering for Choat and he has connections with La Eme."

She looked at him. "La Eme—I remember them from the stories about you. Your enemy, the guy who played in the marching band—"

"Right," said Stromsoe. "Cedros knows a guy named Marcus Ampostela. Birch ran him for me while I was driving up from Azusa just now—grand theft auto, extortion, armed robbery, assault with a deadly weapon—and plenty of minor charges. He's spent eight of his twenty-five years behind bars. Not bad, compared to some guys."

Stromsoe had been surprised at Birch's speed with the records check. Back in Stromsoe's day with the sheriffs, nobody but law enforcement could come up with a jacket that fast. But Birch was plugged into networks that barely existed two years ago and some that hadn't existed at all back then. The private was becoming public faster than he could imagine.

Frankie let out a small exhale. "Maybe Cedros was just buying drugs from him. Or a stolen car or something. Nothing to do with the DWP or me."

"True. But if Choat could get to the right people, he could hire it."

"Oh," she said quietly. "Through Cedros?"

Stromsoe nodded and took another drink of wine. "That would be one way. Cedros thinks you'll drop the charges."

"Who told him that?"

"Someone he believes," said Stromsoe. "Look, when I lay out the cause and effect for him, he hears it. He *gets* it. He knows he's risking his future, his marriage, his family. But he sticks to his original story—he was stalking you because he's obsessed with you. That's not the kind of story you walk into court with."

Frankie sat back and looked at him. In the candlelight the hollows of her face were both deepened and softened and her eyes shone the brown of polished walnut.

"What do you want me to do?" she asked.

"Wait. If Choat has a new idea, we'll know soon enough."

"He could just let the brake fluid out of my Mustang the way I drive. Or have me run over some night walking to my car."

"He wants the formula. Is it written down?"

"No. Charley never wrote it down either."

"Keep it that way."

"That I can do." She set down her fork, sighed very quietly, and shook her head.

"I won't let anything happen to you, Frankie."

She looked at him and Stromsoe had no idea what she was thinking. His own mind was a swirl of hope, fear, and contradiction. How many times had he told Hallie and Billy that, in his heart if not with words?

"Dance?" he asked.

"By all means."

The song was an old Dire Straits piece, "So Far Away," and Stromsoe led Frankie in a happy little fox-trot that dismissed the melancholy of the lyrics. At first he was self-conscious about his three-fingered lead, trying to use mostly palm, to keep his touch light but informative. He felt her little finger resting comfortably where his had been. He wished again that she saw him for what he was and was not and wondered if this was a sign that she would be able to. They danced around the table and into the living room, where the floor was cut small by the boxes he'd yet to unpack.

"I think I just bumped into your past," she whispered.

"I believe you did."

"Can I see some pictures?"

"Sure. When?"

"Now. After the song, I mean."

• • •

THEY SAT ON the couch and he showed her his Santa Ana High School yearbook for his senior year, replete with pictures of himself and Hallie and Mike.

He hadn't looked at these things in years and to see himself posed before the marching band, mace held high and shako hat worn low, was to see a child living his desires free of self-consciousness and history.

"I recognize you," said Frankie. "Look what chubby cheeks you had. And so serious!"

"Hey, drum majoring was an important job."

He showed her the pictures of Hallie—her senior shot, her picture as "Most Sarcastic Senior," and a candid image of her standing at a pep rally with a doubtful look on her pretty face.

"She was an outsider," said Frankie.

When Stromsoe turned to the first of the *T* seniors, he just tapped the page on Mike. Tavarez looked up at them, his expression wholly remote but the half smile in place like a casual piece of armor.

Frankie looked down at the picture and said nothing.

Caught between his desire to reveal and his need to protect, Stromsoe took out a favorite picture—Billy at age four standing on a dock with a yellow child's fishing rod in his hand.

Stromsoe's whole world immediately tilted and the questions of what could have been slid down on him with all their awesome weight.

"Billy," he said. "Four years old."

"He's beautiful," Frankie said quietly.

"He was very beautiful."

She bowed her head.

Stromsoe continued to look at the picture—it hadn't been all that long because he had visited these images in their boxes regularly over the last two years—but now, exposed to someone else, Billy seemed to flourish like a plant exposed to fresh air and sunlight and for the first time since Billy's death Stromsoe was able to see his son's particular traits instead of his tremendous absence. He saw Billy's intelligence and shyness. He saw his grave respect for the tiny perch he'd brought out of the pond and now dangled from the rod—the same gravity that his father had brought to drum majoring, of all things, and later to his work. Stromsoe saw too, in the firm set of Billy's jaw, a conviction that the moment and the fish were important. An attribute, thought Stromsoe, that might have later become valuable to Billy in this world of distraction and diluted faith.

Might have.

Might have later.

Might have later become.

"Not fair," said Frankie.

Stromsoe saw a tear hit the back of one of her big hands, which were folded on her lap.

"Oops," she whispered. "Sorry."

"I don't mind."

He selected another picture, Billy dressed in a pirate's costume for Halloween, brandishing a rubber sword. He was trying his best to look menacing but it was easy to see the self-mockery in him. There was also something seductive in his expression, as if he was inviting you and only you to team up and play along.

"That was the Hallie in him," said Stromsoe. "The part of him that couldn't take things too seriously. The part of him that smiled and laughed and played. The part that loved a secret. That Halloween night he finally went out to trick-or-treat with the pirate costume and sword and a pumpkin mask."

He rewrapped the picture in the crinkled newspaper, slid it back into the box, and took out another.

"Tell me a memory of him," she said. "The first one that comes to your mind."

"We used to love going through car washes together. You know, the ones where you stay in your car and pull in and the big brushes wash the car. Billy loved it when the brushes come toward you and it feels like the car's

moving forward. He'd *swear* the car was moving forward. We started going to different ones. He kept a log.
This one in Costa Mesa turned out to be the best all
around, based on the amount of soap and how thorough
the brushes were and how good the rinse was and how
long the dryer would go. Car washes. I miss that."

Frankie smiled and nodded. "Nice."

"Here's Hallie on her thirtieth birthday. I threw her
a surprise party in a restaurant. One of our friends is a
professional photographer, so this came out real well."

"She was beautiful too. I see her in Billy."

The photograph was just face, taken from across the
room with a big lens and without her knowing. It captured the obvious—Hallie's offhand loveliness, her blue
eyes and her freckles and easy smile, her sun-lightened
hair. It captured her delight in the moment. She didn't
look like she was trying too hard, which was just how
she was in life. Pure Hallie. Stromsoe felt for a moment
like he could scoop her up out of that frame and set her
on the couch next to him, pour her a glass of wine. The
image also hinted at another truth about her, which was
that Hallie was never content for very long. She was
always looking, reaching, tasting, taking. She was
always a step ahead, slightly to the side, sometimes
miles out of sight. She was a traveler. She went. And if
the journey took her to a bad place, then that's where

she went with all of her energy and charm and sometimes reckless gusto. Stromsoe had often thought that if
people could sprout wings, Hallie's would be the first to
grow, and the largest.

"She looks hard to catch," said Frankie.

"She let me when she was ready."

Stromsoe set the picture back in the box. His heart
was beating hard and for just a moment he doubted his
location in time and space. For the first time in his life he
saw no clear distinction between the past and the present and no meaningful difference between memories
and what he could see right now with his one good eye.
He felt as if he could stand up and walk into the next
room and his wife and son would be there, sitting cross-
legged on the bed over a game of Go Fish or reading a
bedtime story. Over two years had passed since their
deaths and somehow that terrible day seemed both closer
than before and further away than it had ever been.

In looking at these pictures with Frankie, Stromsoe
understood that he had crossed the great black barrier
that he had tried to cross by talking to Susan Doss but
couldn't. He saw that the dead are free only when we
remember them without death. Then the living are
finally free too.

"Thank you," said Frankie.

"Thank you. It's a good thing."

"Want to be alone?"

"No," said Stromsoe. "Take a walk with me?"

"Sure."

"I found a good spot the other day."

"I got some shoes in my car."

"I'll get the wine and something to sit on."

THEY SET OUT down the slope of the tangerine grove. The night was cool. A dog barked then lost interest. The moon was small but bright and it lit their way between the rows and along a dirt road and through the lemon trees. Then past an irrigation station and up a hill of chaparral and wild buckwheat from the top of which Stromsoe looked down on the sprawl of nursery flowers stretching all the way to the dark horizon. The colors were luminous in the moonlight and in the lights on the security fence. There were wide avenues of white and yellow and pink on the left, then a central highway of orange and red, then on the right a great boulevard of mysterious blue and purple receding into the distance.

"I'll have to do a report from here," Frankie said. "It's wonderful. Right in my own backyard."

Stromsoe doubled the blanket twice and they sat and drank the wine side by side with their arms touching, which sent Stromsoe into incommensurate distraction despite the Colt nudging him for attention on the opposite flank.

He told her about learning to drum major—the many hours of solitary marching to a boom box playing marches in his small backyard in Santa Ana, his many hours being drilled by grouchy old Arnie Schiller, who had led the Santa Ana Saints marching band from 1928 to 1930—and his happy dismay at being the only contestant at the band tryouts the summer before his freshman year. He touched on the basics of cadence and beating time, on downbeats, rebounds, and patterns, as well as the more advanced mace techniques which included tosses, spins, ground jabs, and salutes. He demonstrated a few moves with his wineglass.

Frankie told him about finding Charley Hatfield's secret lab in the Bonsall barn after following a map attached to an old trust deed she'd found in a Hatfield-family file cabinet. The barn itself was lost in a swale of bamboo and choked over by wild cucumber vines. She used a machete to find a door. When she first swung that door and stepped inside, all of Charley's stuff was there under decomposing sheets, covered in cobwebs and dust like a horror movie and she understood that she had been born with a purpose—to find this place and continue this work.

"They all thought I was crazy," she said. "I was fifteen and I believed them for the longest time. Now? I figure what's so crazy about making rain? It's a good thing. It's possible. Somebody's got to take the job and it may as well be me."

Later they walked hand in hand back to Stromsoe's guesthouse. They leaned against the Mustang and looked up at the stars. Frankie, as a meteorologist, knew the night sky well.

Stromsoe followed the line of her finger as she pointed skyward, listened to her voice, smelled her breath as she spoke: *Lacerta, Pegasus, Delphinus. Capricornus, Fomalhaut, Lyra.*

He wanted to tell her lesser, personal truths, but he didn't want to damage the moment, then the moment was gone.

She drove away with one bare arm waving back at him out the window.

22

People of your ilk usually have to deal with Security first," said Choat. He sat recessed in the near dark of his office, big hands folded on his desktop in dim slants of morning sunlight. The hands were practically all that Stromsoe could see of him. "But I agreed to give you a few minutes because you're a friend of Frankie's."

"Thanks," said Stromsoe. "I'm an employee of Frankie's."

"How is she?"

"Worried. She's been stalked at work, stalked at home. I had the guy arrested and he's going to stand trial but his story doesn't wash."

"Stalked?"

Stromsoe leaned toward Choat, still trying for a good look at the man. "Intimidated. Photographed. Trespassed upon. Watched." He sat back. "You know what stalking is, Mr. Choat. It's section sixty-forty-six point nine of the California Penal Code."

Choat rolled forward from the shadows, giving Stromsoe his first good look at the pugnacious, broken-nosed, battle-scarred face. He was one of those men with a neck as thick as his head. "If he's been arrested, then her troubles are over, right?"

Stromsoe paused a beat. "There's a temporary restraining order against him too. But there are plenty of other people besides him who could intimidate a young woman."

"I don't understand why you're here."

"Look, Mr. Choat," Stromsoe said calmly. "You don't fool me. You don't impress me. Frankie said no to DWP money, so you sent John Cedros to frighten her. You know Cedros—he's in custodial here. But Frankie hired me and I caught your man. He said he was stalking her because she was tall and pretty. He said that to cover your butt. It's a lousy story. He's a family guy. He doesn't even get Frankie Hatfield on his home TV."

Choat nodded, leaned back, and crossed his thick arms across his chest. Stromsoe noted the suit vest, the cuff links, the tie pin, the round-collared shirt, and the blunt barbershop haircut.

"I confess," said Choat. "We offered Frances Hatfield money for research and development of a moisture acceleration system. We are skeptical fans of the work her great-great-grandfather did back in the early 1900s. We are aware that he contracted to make rain for the city of San Diego and it rained so hard the reservoirs flooded, the Morena Dam burst, and people were rowing boats on the streets downtown. That interests DWP. And it was not his only success story—there were several. People have spent R-and-D money on climate manipulation schemes much more outlandish than his, I can tell you—defrocking hurricanes, melting ice caps—schemes that never worked half as well as Hatfield's secret formula. So when we heard what Ms. Hatfield was doing, well, we were damned curious. She had some promising numbers. But in the end she refused our best and final offer and that was that. Mr. Stromsoe, I've got no reason in the world to intimidate that lovely young woman. On the contrary, I'm pulling for her."

"That's good of you," said Stromsoe. He stood and went to the blinds and let some light in. "How come you keep it so dark in here?"

"I have very strong eyes."

"You're a lucky man."

"I was born with them."

"That's what luck is."

"I grew up with the son of a multimillionaire. The boy put a gun to his head when he was thirteen years old."

Stromsoe left the blinds open and sat back down again. "Maybe I had this wrong. Maybe the fact that Frankie turned you down and a guy who works for you was arrested for stalking her aren't connected."

Choat nodded. "It's a free country. I believe this Cedros fellow if that's what he told you. You can think what you want."

"I think Frankie scares the hell out of you and your bosses. Who are probably the people I should be talking to right now anyway."

"You're threatening me?"

"With what? You're Water and Power. I'm a one-eyed, by-theday PI."

"Then what do you want from me?"

"I want you to know that my bosses and I know who you are and what you did. And we want your guarantee that Frankie Hatfield won't be bothered anymore. We don't want another Cedros—or somebody worse—down in San Diego, pestering her. That's all."

"That's not within my power to grant or deny."

"Then maybe I should talk to somebody who gets things done around here."

Choat tapped some numbers on his telephone console. "I just called Security. They get things done."

Stromsoe stood and buttoned his coat. "Thank you for your time. We'll be watching."

Choat stood and came around the desk in a kind of swagger. He had an odd smile on his face, something bemused and occult. He was bigger than Stromsoe had thought, and his gray eyes were hard and calm.

"You can do whatever you want, Mr. Stromsoe," Choat said. "My only regret is that we had to have this conversation here in my office."

Stromsoe saw the movement on the low left edge of his vision but understood it not quite fast enough.

Choat's heavy fist clubbed the side of his jaw up high, by the ear, and Stromsoe spun away. Choat caught him by his lapels and drove Stromsoe back against the wall. Stromsoe had just found his vision and balance when Choat dragged him forward and pushed his battering ram of a face into Stromsoe's.

"Just a little something between men."

"Don't touch Frankie."

"Seize him."

Choat shoved him back hard and let go and Stromsoe felt the arms clamp around him from behind.

"Son of a bitch threw a punch at me," said Choat. "Get him out of my sight."

"Yes, sir."

"Happy to, sir. Come on, dirtbag. Back outside where dirt belongs."

TWENTY MINUTES LATER John Cedros was sitting where Stromsoe had sat. Choat held him with an unhappy stare.

"We need to accelerate the timetable," said Choat.

"I told them we wanted action fast."

"The PI knows. A million things can go wrong. You might be called to trial if we don't get moving here."

"I told you he knew," said Cedros.

"Do what you need to do. Tell them we need results quickly. Tell them we can add fifty thousand dollars to the budget, for results on or before Sunday. If they can't get the formula, they can burn down the barn instead. And I want the PI off the case and the woman *fully discouraged*."

Cedros's heart fell. One week ago he was a DWP custodial-staff flunky trying to raise a family, doing some low-life harassment on the side to please the Director of Resources. Now he was an accused sexual predator contracting for violence and intimidation with the most feared prison gang on Earth.

He thought of big Marcus Ampostela lumbering into his home the day before, leering at Marianna, kneeling to tickle little Tony under the chin, looking over at Cedros as if he owned his family and his life. And Ampostela was just the go-between, not the fearsome ambassador that Tavarez would dispatch for the job on the PI and the weather lady and the barn. Ampostela had actually smelled the cash, pushing his snout into the sacks to sniff the stacks of bills that Marianna had conscientiously double-bagged as if they had been her own. Ampostela had sat staring at her while Cedros painstakingly wrote out everything he knew about Frankie Hatfield and Matt Stromsoe—her address, her work numbers, the plates on her Mustang, the location of her barn in Bonsall, her hours of work and play, even the name of the gym she went to in Fallbrook on Saturdays and Sundays...

A cabin in Owens Gorge, he thought.

Two hundred and fifty miles from here. Marianna and him in the big bed with the curtains moving in the crisp mountain breeze and never once would they have to roll under that bed when the bullets flew, or hear the stupid *corridos* pounding all night or the scream of sirens or the deafening thunder of the police choppers rattling the walls and blasting their searchlights through the windows.

But just when his heart began to fall, Cedros picked it back up and put it in place again. There were times when a man could not afford to be hesitant or self-pitying. There were times when he had to take care of the ones he loved.

"Yes, sir. We need to move things along. I'll get the job done."

"You're a tough little man. I appreciate that."

"Does it bother you that Tavarez killed this PI's wife and son, and now we're making this happen?"

"Heaven puts people where they need to be."

"Man, I hope so."

"We're just hustling the little PI off to his next case," said Choat. "It's not like we're out to shoot his dog."

CEDROS MET MARCUS Ampostela at El Matador Mexican restaurant, where the big man had centered himself in a corner booth of the back room. The room was partitioned off with a light chain and a sign that said CERRADO/CLOSED. Ampostela's table was filled with plates of food.

A skinny gangster in a gray flannel shirt sat at the adjacent booth with two weary-looking women and a heavily muscled pit bull with a blue bandanna around its neck. The dog sat beside the man, snorting down the last scraps off a plate. The women looked bored but the man and the dog stared at Cedros as he walked toward Ampostela.

Ampostela, mouth full, waved him over like an old buddy, made a small show of sitting up a little straighter. He was wearing sunglasses. There was an empty beer pitcher on the table and a half-full one.

Ampostela flicked the empty pitcher with a big finger and said, "And a glass for Mr. Cedros." One of the women climbed out of the booth.

Cedros sat on the edge of the booth bench but he still felt too close. The big man's head was shaved but the hairline was a shadow on the prison-paled skin. Being this close to La Eme made Cedros feel even smaller than he was, but even worse, doomed.

Cabin. Owens Gorge.

The woman came back with a pitcher and a glass, set them in front of Ampostela. He slid the glass to Cedros and set the pitcher in front of him.

Cedros immediately got down to business. He explained the hurry in vague terms and quickly offered the fifty-thousand bonus to have everything taken care of by Sunday. There would be a change for the better, however. Instead of obtaining the information that he had talked about with Tavarez, now they would like the barn—it was described in the notes he'd written for Ampostela to pass along—to be simply burned to the ground. Ampostela offered no discernible reaction to the money or change of plan, just a shaved-head glower that could have meant anything.

Cedros thought some actual cash might make the deal. He moved to get an envelope from his breast pocket and the skinny gangster leveled a big automatic at Cedros's face and the pit bull growled and knocked a plate to the floor.

Cedros slowly pulled out the envelope with just his fingertips and dropped it between himself and Ampostela.

"You people make me nervous," he said.

"That's good," said the gangster. He looked like one of the Olmec heads in the Mexico Anthropology Museum that Cedros had once seen in *National Geographic*. Except for the shades, thought Cedros.

"This is half," said Cedros. He removed the other envelope and set it by the first. "This is the other half."

"Okay, Sunday," said Ampostela. "I'm taking all of this now. If it doesn't happen, we'll make it right. It's not an easy thing, you know?"

"I've got no assurance?"

Ampostela smiled. His teeth were white and straight. "That's right. No insurance."

Cedros tried to puff himself up a little but it felt pointless. Still, his respect was in question now and he knew he was expected to secure it.

He reached out and claimed one of the envelopes, slid it back into his coat pocket. His fingertips brushed the acetate lining of his jacket, which was soaked through with sweat.

"Half now," he said.

The Olmec head traced the movement of his hand, then aimed its sunglasses at Cedros's face.

"This comes back to you the second I know it's done," said Cedros. He was surprised at the relaxed strength of his own voice because every muscle in his body felt tight. "And done right."

Ampostela drummed his blunt fingers on the envelope. He brought it to his nose and drew in the scent of the money. His tattooed arm rippled and swayed, half muscle and half blubber. The Aztec warrior prepared to bite into the human heart he held in one hand like a peach.

"Ricky," said Ampostela. "You trust this guy?"

The man with the dog shrugged.

Ampostela reached over and poured Cedros some beer. "Good," he said. "Drink."

AMPOSTELA WAITED FOR Cedros's gold sedan to roll down Azusa Avenue then he called Jimmy up in Crescent City. He told Jimmy to get a pen and paper and copy down a message word for word.

Jimmy took the very brief dictation and said El Jefe would have it by eight the next morning.

Then Jimmy called Shawnelle down in Redding and she took the message word for word too, along with a warning from Jimmy about getting it to El Jefe with speed and accuracy.

Shawnelle called her sister, Tonya Post, back up in Crescent City even though it was past dinnertime and the chemo made her very tired, but Tonya was actually happy to hear from her big sister and they yapped awhile before Tonya took down the message for her husband, Jason. It was a hassle for him, sure, and it could cost him his job, but it was easy money.

A message to El Jefe? Two hundred bucks from Shawnelle after Shawnelle took her fifty, and it always came one week later, right on time.

Tonya wrote slowly and asked Shawnelle to repeat herself several times to make sure it was right.

Ced wants all done by Sun night. Fifty extra, half here now, smells good. MA.

A few minutes later she walked in on Jason in the garage, where he was playing "Halo," blasting alien soldiers into pools of blood hour after hour while the half gallons of supermarket vodka and the cream sodas he mixed them with disappeared at a breakneck rate.

She held her robe up snug at the chin but she felt the Northern California cold come instantly through her socks and into her feet then up her legs and into her feminine parts, where the remains of the tumor lay hopefully dead forever.

Jason wore an old down jacket and a blaze-orange hunter's cap against the chill. He didn't take his eyes off the screen. He hadn't looked at her with much of anything but hostility for a year before her diagnosis, and now all he could muster was a glazed resentment so thorough it sometimes frightened her but most often just made her wish he'd move out, send child support, and leave her and Damian alone.

"Money, honey," she said, waving the paper.

"Put it on the couch. I'm beating this level."

"It's right here."

"How you feeling, hon?" he asked, eyes on the screen.

"Kinda ragged. Damian's down. I'm thinking I'll do the same."

"I'll be a while."

"It's for El Jefe. Important stuff."

"You don't know what's important and what isn't."

"Two hundred is important to me."

"I said leave it."

"I heard you."

"You want us to fight or you want to just go get some sleep?" he asked. He still didn't take his eyes off the TV. A silver figure of some kind exploded in a storm of blood.

She turned back into the house without answering, heard another explosion.

"Ah *fuck,* I just died."

You died a long time ago, Tonya thought, but I'm not going to.

POST WENT THROUGH Thursday morning with a belligerent hangover. The aspirin bounced off his headache like it was armored but there wasn't a lot to do after the breakfast mess. There had been rumors of La Eme versus La Nuestra Familia, and he could feel the tension in the yard and the mess hall, an almost audible buzz that the officers learned to listen to like a broadcast from a distant radio. The numbers of officers had been doubled in the mess and yard for a week now and it made you feel better to look through that jungle of orange-clad felons and see the stalwart blue of your fellow bulls lined up along all four walls with bats and hats—helmets, actually—ready to put the wood to somebody if they got the chance.

He gave Tavarez the message as they walked back to the cells in near privacy, El Jefe given his usual wide berth by the other inmates. Post always memorized the messages rather than writing down something that could be intercepted or traced back to him. Through the headache he conjured the words and relayed them to Mike Tavarez not once but twice. El Jefe walked slowly and stared down at the floor while he listened, then nodded, then picked up his pace again.

"Can you get me into the library tonight?" asked Tavarez.

"Five hundred."

"I'll need the laptop charged and ready."

"I can handle it."

"Then my message back is, *yes.*"

"Okay," said Post.

"One simple yes."

"I can handle that too, El Heffie. Hey, how was your babe last night?"

"Very nice."

TWELVE HOURS LATER Ariel Lejas was rousted from a Spanish-language soap opera by his niece, who rushed into the darkened room to give her *tío* another message from El Jefe.

He took the printed sheet and thanked her and waited for her to leave the room. He looked out the windows at the blue-black Riverside sky and the great palm trees of Victoria Avenue drooping in the cricket-loud night.

The message was four words, all in English:

Do it by Sunday.

Lejas looked at his watch. It would be an honor to deal sooner than later with the Big Swine who had brought Mike Tavarez such misfortune.

23

Stromsoe trailed Frankie that evening and night on her rounds to report the San Diego weather. His ear rang and his jaw throbbed as regularly as a metronome, which he used as a reminder to be alert, careful, and ready. Choat's punch had left him spoiling for a fight.

Earlier Stromsoe told the X-ray tech the jaw ache was a karate-class sparring accident. After pronouncing the jawbone unbroken, he told Stromsoe he might want to try yoga.

Frankie's last dispatch was from the Cabrillo Lighthouse on Point Loma, behind which the city sparkled in the October night. Stromsoe stood away from her and the crew and audience, keeping tight to the shadows to watch and see. He felt proud to know Frankie and slightly disbelieving that she had danced with him the night before. He thought of her skin touching his arm. He thought she was interesting, unpredictable, and extraordinarily lovely. He liked being near her, something he could say about only a handful of people on the planet.

Now let's get to the rain that's developing for the weekend...

Stromsoe wished again that he could tell her a few more things about himself, just to give a balanced picture. It was hard to stand on half of a foundation. The last thing he was was a liar.

He knew that his affection for her was supposed to make him weak because that's what manly stories always told you, but he wondered why those feelings couldn't just as easily help him stay sharp and capable. He felt strong right now as he looked at her and he silently promised her again that nothing bad would happen.

As he sat across from Frankie at the Top of the Hyatt later that night, his jaw still throbbed and his ear still rang. He had co-opted the pain and noise and made watchdogs of them. Compared to the bomb two years ago, this was nothing.

"I'll bet you want a rematch," she said.

"Yes, I do."

"Something tells me you'll get it."

They had a light dinner and coffee. Stromsoe looked down forty stories to the shrunken city, at the bay busy with its ferry and yachts and lights that glittered across to Coronado and Point Loma, beyond which the water became the boatless black Pacific stretching all the way to the sky.

He quickly noted all of this, then his attention went back to Frankie Hatfield. Again he felt the gap between her innocence and his experience and it made him want to speak.

THEY WALKED THROUGH the Gaslamp Quarter, had a drink at Croce's, and listened to the singer.

She caught the look on his face. "Talk to me."

"There's something I want to tell you," said Stromsoe.

"I love secrets and I'm good at keeping them."

"I have one to tell you."

"Maybe we should go outside," she said. "Get some quiet and some fresh air."

They headed up the avenue past the bars and restaurants. The Gaslamp Quarter was busy with traffic and pedestrians and they could hear scraps of music floating out from the clubs.

"You don't have to hear this," he said. "No happy ending."

"You've got my curiosity up. Play fair now."

"It's a story that explains some things."

They walked on in silence while Stromsoe tried to find the right words.

"We'd been after Mike Tavarez for eight years," he said. "From just about the second he got out of Corcoran in '93. He was rising to the top of La Eme. He was number five in the organization, then number three. By 2001 he was El Jefe, number one boss, undisputed. He got there by being smart and by making people rich. Know what he liked at Harvard? Business and history. Way back in the eighties, in Corcoran, Mike saw that La Eme needed personnel if it was going to reach far beyond the prison walls. And he saw that the barrio street gangs needed direction, motivation, and a business plan. The old gangs, like F Troop that Mike clicked up with? Gangs that fought over turf and honor and girls? Mike came to believe that they were ridiculous. That was a radical thought at the time, for a gangster. He thought they were stupid, counterproductive, and a thing of the past. Reagan was deregulating the country, trying to make healthy competition. Mike, he wanted to do the opposite—get the gangs under one color, get a monopoly. Back then, La Eme was run by Paul Zolorio. He was doing time in the same Corcoran cell block as Mike. Zolorio had the power to make things happen, and believe me, they were happening. Coke was flooding the country big-time by then, and when Zolorio put La Eme's clout together with the barrio gangbangers, it made the biggest distribution network in the country. La Eme conscripted those gangs, those armies of potential drug salesmen. They killed the resisters, charged their taxes, and watched the money flood in. It was an ingenious move, because Mike and Zolorio were able to get all these factions working more or less together, making money. It was perfect timing, and in a perfect location—Southern California—right on the border and one of the biggest blow markets in the world. The money was phenomenal. And of course Mike learned to put away his share, plus some. Sure, he was La Eme but he was taking care of himself pretty damned well. By '95 they were bringing in millions of dollars a year in drug distribution taxes alone, and Mike had his finger in most of it. Some ugly things went down—nature of the business. Here I was, tracking my old friend, the guy who played clarinet in my band. The guy who had beaten Hallie half to death. I'd stay up late at night sometimes, thinking of ways to get to him. Sometimes I'd dream about him, what he'd done to Hallie all those years ago. It infuriated me that I was the good guy, a cop, and we had resources and manpower and we couldn't catch up with him. Hallie told me to take myself off the Narcotics Division, to try Homicide or Traffic or Fraud. I was too stubborn. It was personal and moral. The way I saw it, it was good against bad. Us and them. That was my simpleminded take. I've always been uncomplicated about the law, and breaking the law, and what's right and wrong. It's a flaw of mine."

He felt the great wave of the past towering over him just like the night before, when he'd shown her the pictures. But this wave was even darker and bigger because he was the perpetrator in this story, not the victim.

"So every time we caught a glimpse of Mike he was farther away, at a different level," Stromsoe said. "We couldn't touch him in Mexico—the corruption was too thick. We couldn't touch him in Colombia—it was another universe down there. And we had a helluva time putting our fingers on him here in the U.S., too. He'd sneak up to Laguna from Tijuana in an old car or in a cigarette boat called *Reina,* stay with his family for a few weeks. By the time we realized he was under our noses he would be gone again. You have to understand how many people were looking out for him. He had six men living on the Laguna compound alone. They were chauffeurs and gardeners and assistants to his wife and children, but they were pistoleros first and foremost. Mike was El Jefe. If you helped El Jefe you made a powerful friend. Hell, they were writing songs about him. He was a hero. Nobody was going to help us. He was safe in any barrio in the world, unless La Nuestra Familia was in charge."

"La Nuestra Familia? Rivals?"

"Sworn and deadly. LNF is mostly in the northern part of the state."

They stopped and looked in the window of a store devoted to lamps made from plaster seashells. The pure white whelks and conchs and abalone shells looked stark and peaceful glowing around their colored bulbs.

They crossed Island and headed up Fourth.

"Then, we caught a break," he said. "Mike had a longtime lover, a woman named Ofelia. She'd visited him a lot at Corcoran when she was just a girl—and coached him in the Nahuatl language. She was a nearly full-blooded Aztec, fluent in a dialect that Tavarez was using to build a language code for La Eme. After he got out of Corcoran in '93, Mike shacked up with Ofelia for a couple of months. She was seventeen. But Mike had plans—he dumped her and married Miriam Acosta, Zolorio's niece. Ofelia fled back to Mexico and entered a convent. A year later Mike went down there and talked her out of it. He never stopped seeing Ofelia, even married, even as a father. Which meant we never stopped watching her."

"Did she go and come back to the United States?"

"Not quite that far. Mike set her up in a nice apartment in Tijuana's Colonia district. You think TJ is all filth and poverty but it's not. I saw the place and it was nice—up in the hills and gated, always two gunmen outside. Always two. When Mike got more money and power he bought another apartment in Tijuana and one in La Jolla. Ofelia would rotate according to where Mike was going to be. Sometimes she'd rotate according to where Mike *wasn't*. They had handfuls of cell phones. They'd use them for a day or two and toss them. So, no way for us to set up good intercepts. It came down to physical surveillance of three known places, plus whatever safe houses we hadn't discovered yet. Between us, the TJ cops, and the La Jolla PD, it was just about impossible to get every place staked out at the same time to see who was where. Plus some of the TJ cops were on Mike's payroll. So you'd finally get a couple of TJ detectives to check one of the Colonia apartments and they'd run into two on-duty TJ uniforms who were Mike's. We'd find out a month later that he wasn't there anyway—he'd been way up in Laguna with his family. It was crazy."

"Cops on the drug payrolls," said Frankie. "Now that scares me."

"Me too. We felt completely handcuffed. Then I got an idea. We picked up Ofelia in La Jolla and flew her up to Santa Ana in a DEA helicopter. This was August 2001, just before 9/11, and we were a multiagency task force—we had a fat budget, toys galore, and latitude. They sat her down in a women's-jail interview room. I walked in and she recognized me immediately, called me Señor Matt. She was dark and pretty. Wild-seeming. Expensive everything. She had a temper but she was intelligent too. I told her she and Mike had a large problem. She thought that was funny. I told her that she and Mike were being shadowed by soldiers of La Nuestra Familia. She said that was impossible—LNF had no idea where she and Mike would be. I told her that in the course of our surveillance we had identified four of them. We had them in our sights, just like we had Mike and her in our sights. I rattled off their names. By then she was listening, sizing up my tale. Yes, I told her, we wanted to arrest Tavarez more than anything, but if we couldn't get a clean arrest on him, we didn't want La Nuestra Familia to get him. I was acting as a former friend, I told her, a man who respected Mike. I showed her some of our surveillance pictures of LNF gangsters on a stakeout of their own. We cropped them so you couldn't tell exactly where they were taken.

Ofelia was starting to believe me. She was easy to read, her emotions right there on her face. Then I showed her some mugs of these guys, real heavies, murderers all. She studied them. Then I tossed out some pictures that we'd gotten just a few weeks earlier. They showed the torture and murder of an LNF gangster who had betrayed his boss to La Eme. A big guy, young and strong. The brutality of what they did to him was inconceivable. Unimaginable. They injected him with lidocaine to keep his heart beating every time it looked like he'd die. They kept him alive for three days of that. Three days. They'd sent the video to La Eme as a warning."

Frankie stopped and looked at him. Stromsoe lightly took her arm and they crossed the street.

"What did she do?"

"Exactly what we hoped she'd do. I drove her back to La Jolla. Took my time, let the pressure build. We'd made the arrangements with the Tijuana police ahead of time so they were ready if Ofelia blew into the Colonia to tell Mike that La Nuestra Familia was after her, which is exactly what she did. TJ police tracked her to a Colonia apartment that night. It was a new one, one we didn't even know about. It wasn't even furnished yet. Tavarez was there. It turned into a western. Good

cops and dirty cops and Mike's private army of pistoleros. A mess. Six dead in less than five minutes. Ofelia
was one of them. Tavarez got away."

Frankie stopped again. "The LNF wasn't watching
Mike and Ofelia at all."

"No."

"Mike blamed you for Ofelia because you were the
one who frightened her into doing what she did."

"Correct. My clever plan."

"And he tried to blow you off the earth," she said
softly. "But got Hallie and Billy instead."

They continued up the avenue. Frankie held his arm
now and he saw that she walked with her head down.
He felt primitive and misshapen for having brought her
into his world.

"In your line of work," she said. "You have to figure
that things like that will happen. Things like that *have*
to happen. Don't you accept that when you accept the
badge?"

"I did. It helps. But I also know that if I had been
smarter, more patient, and luckier, my wife and son
would be alive right now."

"That's a heavy load for one little soul to bear."

"I don't mean to complain. I don't want sympathy."

"What do you want?"

"To be seen clearly by you. That's all."

STROMSOE FOLLOWED HER home, gunning his truck to keep up with Frankie's Mustang on the freeways. But when they got near Fallbrook she took the country roads more slowly and Stromsoe fell in behind her on the curves. He lowered his windows and the smells came rushing in as they always did in Fallbrook— oranges and lemons and acres of flowers and the not-too-distant ring of wild sage and chaparral.

He killed the engine and walked her to her door. She let the dogs out.

Then she moved into Stromsoe's arms and they shared a good long kiss. He sensed consequences and swiftly ignored them. His jaw ached and he forced himself not to flinch. He was tired of being a human shipwreck.

Frankie broke off and whistled up the dogs. They came in a blur of tails and tongues.

She let them into the house then turned to look at Stromsoe. "My heart's pounding."

"Mine too."

"I forgot about your jaw. Sorry. But I won't forget that kiss as long as I live."

"I've got more."

"I'll bet you do, gumshoe. Good night."

"Good night, Frankie."

She smiled. "See you tomorrow. And for whatever tiny thing it's worth, your clever plan with Ofelia didn't fail—it worked too well. That's what happened to Great-Great-Grandpa Charley in San Diego. He promised rain and made too much. The city flooded and they ran him out. You got run out too. But now you're back, and I'm glad you are."

STROMSOE HAD JUST pulled up at his guesthouse when Birch called.

"We got a call on the hotline about five minutes ago. Stand by."

"Birch Security Solutions, may I have your name and telephone number?"

"They're going to get the weather lady and the PI."

"Your name and number, please."

Click.

"Run it by me again, Dan."

Birch played it again.

Stromsoe didn't recognize the voice. It was a young woman. The recording was clear.

"What number did she call?"

"Main number," said Birch. "She got the menu and used the urgent-message option. Our watch coordinator picked up."

"They," said Stromsoe.

"They," said Birch. "DWP?"

"Maybe."

"Choat punched you, maybe figures he softened you up."

"For the new friends of the DWP?"

"Sure," said Birch. "Maybe they've replaced Cedros with someone a little more formidable."

"I could believe that. You know what bothers me most about that call?"

"Her tone of voice," said Birch. "She sounds scared shitless. I think she's scared for you and more scared for herself, for making the call."

Stromsoe said nothing for a moment because Birch had read his mind so accurately. "Who knows that she's a weather lady and I'm a PI?"

"Choat, Choat's bosses, Cedros, some of the people at Frankie's work, some of us here. The old guy—Ted? Then there's the San Diego sheriffs, the judges, marshals, and clerks. The courtroom is open to the public. Calls and messages get listened to. Mail and e-mail gets opened. People talk; people hear. It's worse with a celebrity. Everybody's interested and word travels fast. Has Frankie told anyone she's being stalked?"

"I don't know."

"Ask her."

"I will."

"Look," said Birch. "It's early Friday morning right now. She's got one more shift of work for the week, then Saturday and Sunday off. I'll send you two Birch people to help out with Frankie—one man and one woman, both clear to carry. I'll send them in a Birch patrol car, for good measure, and you can use them twenty-four/seven for the weekend. Tell Frankie about the call if you want. If this call is good, we've got people where we need them. If it's just more cheap harassment, then Frankie's only out another twelve hundred bucks. She can afford it. Monday, we'll see where we stand."

"Good."

"I'll need some time to get Janet and Alex down there."

"I'll cover until they get here."

"Eight sharp, then."

"We'll be here."

"Keep her safe and warm, Matt."

"Mind your own business, Dan."

Birch laughed softly, nothing prurient in it that Stromsoe could hear.

Stromsoe parked in front of his house. Inside he got the same blanket they'd shared the other night, and put into a plastic bag a bottle of water and some crackers, his car cell-phone charger, and an extra magazine of .380 loads for the Colt.

A few minutes later he coasted without lights to a stop on Frankie's driveway, hopefully far enough away not to wake her up. At the last second he steered the truck left and brought it to a stop in the middle of the narrow drive with a good view of the house.

He got the blanket behind his head for a pillow and sank back, feeling the throb of his jaw and the metallic ping of blood pulsing in his ear.

24

Lejas sat in a big avocado tree watching the changing of the guard at Frankie Hatfield's house. The tree was thick with young fruit and brown-tipped leaves and it protected Lejas as it might a raccoon or a hawk. Through his binoculars Lejas saw the PI in the yellow truck shake hands with two uniformed rent-a-cops in a Birch Security Solutions cruiser—a red-haired man and a blond woman—both young and armed.

Lejas had driven down from Riverside in the dark. When he rolled into Fallbrook the sun was just rising and now, two hours later, the Friday morning was still cool and the sky that odd shade of white that meant rain coming in from the Pacific. He'd easily found a good place to hide his car and climb into a good, tall tree.

Now the weather lady came from the house, two dogs bouncing out ahead of her like kicked rocks. They looked neither aware nor protective. The woman was very tall and dark-haired and Lejas could see by the way she smiled and shook the PI's hand that there was something between them. Fine. Distraction. She shook hands with the uniforms and was taller than both of them.

He watched the four people walk inside, followed by the dogs. Stromsoe turned and looked in Lejas's direction, then closed the door behind them. Lejas slowly let the binoculars down to dangle from the strap around his neck.

He pulled a handful of black licorice twists from the pocket of his blue plaid shirt, picked one out, and stuffed the others back in. The tree was comfortable as far as trees went. He relaxed, balanced in the crook of the trunk and a big branch.

He looked down at his car. It was a five-year-old Ford Crown Victoria Law Enforcement Edition, with a strong V-8, good brakes, and a blotch of gray primer where the Grizzly Security Patrol shields had been sanded off each door. The black-and-white paint job was still decent. The big, hand-levered searchlights were still attached and operable. The light bar on the roof was gone but Lejas bought a used one from a chop-shop friend, welded up some brackets, wired it into the old toggle, put in new fuses, and replaced the missing bulbs. The shortwave radio and siren had been removed too, but he didn't need those anyway. He'd put new tires on it. The odometer read 223,738 miles. He'd bought it at auction in San Bernardino two days ago using fake ID and real cash—$2,150. Lejas had estimated nine miles per gallon down from San Berdoo. Still, it was the perfect car for the job.

At eight-thirty Stromsoe came from the house, got into his truck, and drove away. A few minutes later Red Hair ambled from the house and got into the security car. He was thin and lanky and looked athletic. Red Hair drove the car about a hundred feet down the drive away from the house and parked it crosswise to take up as much of the drive as possible. He got out, leaned against the side facing away from the house, and made a call on a cell phone.

The weather lady would be tough, Lejas thought, but he could do it. It would take some patience, but because Sunday night was his new deadline, it was going to take balls and luck too. The private soldiers were no doubt competent but all he needed was a moment of disorganization or inattention and he could get it done. The hard part would be having Stromsoe there to witness it. That meant Lejas would have at least one, and maybe as many as three defenders to deal with. He thought of running back up to Riverside to collect two amigos to balance the power but that would mean a lot of guns, and splitting the money. Mainly Lejas liked to work alone, figuring the movements and planning the surprise and getaway, then making it happen and vanishing. When something like this went right it was simple and sudden and final. He was a solitary man and always had been.

Red Hair went around and got in the driver's side, still talking on his phone. He left the door open. It was a good day to watch from a vehicle, Lejas thought—cool and cloudy and still.

Lejas could see the top of Red Hair's head. He wondered what type of person worked as a security guard or private investigator. Were they failed police? Did they have a physical or mental defect that kept them from getting hired as law enforcers? He knew they didn't make much money, so it couldn't be that.

More importantly, though, how ready were these people? What were they expecting? Men with guns meant nothing if they weren't ready to use them instantly. Look how often cops got shot with their own weapons. Weather Lady would leave for work around noon. According to the notes from John Cedros, Stromsoe would follow her, shadow her from location to location as she did her reports, then follow her home. It would be nice to be waiting in the hedge by her garage. He could easily disable the automatic garage door opener. Then he could shoot the woman when she stepped out of her car, blast Stromsoe's truck to keep him busy, then run down the hillside through the avocado orchard to his car waiting on the dirt service road. Stromsoe would attend the woman, no doubt— that much was certain by the way he looked at her as they shook hands. The trouble was Red Hair and Gun Girl because the security cruiser would almost certainly lead the way up the drive, followed by Frankie Hatfield, then the PI. Lejas could still spring out and make the shots—one in the chest, one in the head—but that left Red Hair and Gun Girl to chase him down the hillside. If they were really smart, one could drive the cruiser back down and have a reasonable chance of intercepting him on the road. And there was always the chance that Red Hair or Gun Girl would stay behind to patrol Frankie's home and prevent just such a thing.

Crowded. Loud. Too many ifs. And too far to run to his car.

No. He dug out another piece of licorice. Separation, he thought. If he could just get everyone separated for a moment. Maybe they would separate themselves for him. When? Why? Well, when they were in their cars going and coming from the weather lady's work, for one. Lejas pictured it: the security cruiser in the lead. Then Weather Lady. Then the Big Swine. Three separable units. On the road, other cars would naturally get between the three. It wouldn't be a perfect formation. There was a funny push-pull to the geometry too, because ideally Red Hair and Gun Girl would be far out of the picture, but the PI would be close enough to Frankie to see very clearly what happened to her. *Make the PI watch.* Push-pull, thought Lejas. Push two away and pull two up close. For some reason he thought of his sister teaching him to rub his tummy and pat his head at the same time. Anna had laughed heartily at his failed first attempts but Lejas did what he had always done with a problem that interested him—he stuck with it until he solved it.

He finished the licorice and set his forehead against a branch for support. Push, pull. He was tiring of the tree. But until the tall weather lady left her house this was where he would stay. He watched a trail of ants climb up and down the tree, wondered why they traveled so close together, two adjacent columns going opposite ways, like commuters backed up on the 91. Except no traffic jams here, no, the ants scurried right along at functional speeds, getting where they needed to go without honk-ing or rage. He also watched a bright redheaded wood-pecker as it tap-tap-tapped on a palm down the road. They hid food in the holes, he knew, then came back in the hot dry summer to collect it. A hummingbird landed just a few feet away from him, pointed his long beak at Lejas's face, then was gone with a brief thrum.

A minute later Lejas carefully climbed down the branches and jumped the last five feet to the ground. His legs were stiff and sore and he had a good kink in his back. He crunched through the fallen leaves and relieved himself under a tree, then fetched a soft drink from the trunk of his car.

He loosened his belt a notch and slipped the can between it and his stiff back, roughly opposite the trim .22 autoloader that rested behind his belt in front. Then he climbed back into the tree, pulled the soda can free, and settled back in.

Apparently he hadn't missed a thing. Red Hair was still visible in the security cruiser, probably listening to the radio or even napping. Weather Lady and Gun Girl were still inside, probably talking about men, children, or clothes.

Slowly an idea came to Lejas and he pictured it. First it was an image of ants, then the ants became cars, then lights and flares and cops. He imagined it from several different angles and every time it seemed to be simple, sudden, and final.

Ants going up. Ants coming down.

Push, pull.

Lejas saw that he could employ this peaceful little village of Fallbrook as a coconspirator. He could use its dark hills and its sparse traffic and the few cops on its country roads as allies in his work.

And it seemed like such a nice place. Pretty and trusting and fragrant. Overflowing with fruit and flowers, birds and squirrels and rabbits.

He sipped the drink, watched and waited.

At 12:35, the PI came up the drive in his yellow pickup truck, just as Cedros's notes said he would. He stopped, got out, and talked to Red Hair. A minute later Weather Lady, all dressed up for TV, came from her house with Gun Girl, who got into the security cruiser. The cruiser led the way down the drive, followed by Weather Lady's beautiful red Mustang, then the investigator.

When they were out of sight Lejas climbed from the tree. He got into his car and spread the San Diego County map across his lap, rechecking Weather Lady's route to and from work, as established by Cedros.

By one he was driving along the route. He drove it all the way to the freeway and back. Fortunately, there was only one way to her house for the last five miles or so, so that left him plenty of road along which to find the ideal place to position his car, and to have a good view of the road in the direction she would be coming.

Lejas figured that the road leading past Frankie's driveway was too small. Mission Road, the main artery in, was too broad and too busy on a Friday.

He found his spot on Trumpet Vine, a midsize street that Frankie would have to take to get to her house. For a while he stood up on the little ridge that afforded the long view down the road, breathing in the aroma of the poisonous trumpet vines that grew in profusion along the road.

The smell of the trumpet-vine flowers was the most emotional smell that Lejas had ever experienced. It took him back to his boyhood days in Casa Blanca, a section of Riverside legendary for its family feuds and gang violence but containing a wall along Madison that was completely overgrown with the vine. Lejas's Casa Blanca smelled of the rich, narcotic flowers that dangled like white trumpets in the branches.

One June night his big brother, Ernest, had been blown into that wall by a hurricane of bullets fired from a car by four Corona Varrio Locos. They had come venturing off their nearby turf and onto Madison for vengeance. Ernest was clicked up with Casa Blanca but he was known as a timid and funny boy. He was fourteen. As soon as Lejas found the courage to crawl from his hiding place in the vines, he had rushed and held Ernest but his brother could do nothing but stare up at him in terror, tremble briefly, then die. It was inconceivable that his brother, once a warm and living thing, had been reduced in a matter of seconds to a lifeless bag of bleeding holes. Lejas was ten years old. He killed the car's driver two weeks later, after hiding in the bushes for seven hours outside his girlfriend's door. By the time he was twelve he'd killed two other CVLs he was pretty sure were in the gunship that night. A bicycle and darkness were his best allies. Those, and an unbelievably heavy .40-caliber revolver he'd bought off Tubby Jackson by hawking nickel bags of Mexican brown heroin to yuppies in expensive cars lined up weekend nights on Casa Blanca Street. The fourth gunman had vanished and never been heard from. His name was Rinny Macado and he was still number one on Lejas's list.

As Lejas took a moment and smelled the trumpet flowers and remembered Ernest and his goofy bucktoothed smile, the same can-do coldness that he'd first felt that night by the wall came back to him again. He had never lost it. He could bring it out and put it away whenever he wanted, a tool of the trade, a skill.

BY EVENING LEJAS had parked in the shadows of an oak forest off a remote dirt road not far from Trumpet Vine. The trees were alive with woodpeckers, who paid him almost no attention. There were lovers' initials inside hearts carved into the huge old tree trunks, and when Lejas looked up into the branches they were so thick the failing sun seemed to be caught in them.

Here, he roughly sketched and taped off the shape of a San Diego County Sheriff Department emblem on both sides of his former Grizzly Security Patrol Cruiser. Then he sprayed on the paint. He knew that most law enforcement emblems were a difficult-to-match shade of brown gold, so Lejas had had to settle on a brighter, showier color with more orange in it. He tossed the can into the bushes and waited.

An hour later he stenciled on the words:

**SAN DIEGO SHERIFF'S DEPARTMENT
HONOR, INTERGITY, SERVICE**

The spelling error made him smile and shake his head but it was too late to correct it. If someone noticed it he would probably be dead by then anyway.

But when Lejas finally untaped the emblem template from the doors, he was pleased to see that in the diminishing twilight his car was convincingly official. Just to make sure, he used a handkerchief to wipe clean the door handles, headlight housings, and spotlights.

He stood back fifty feet and saw that his car was believable. At thirty feet, the same.

Even up close it looked pretty good.

Lejas imagined it parked at an angle in the right lane and shoulder of Trumpet Vine, preceded by five triangle reflector flares to slow and funnel the traffic down to one lane, its yellow warning lights pulsing from the roof while a crisply dressed San Diego County Sheriff's deputy with a flashlight waved the Birch Security cruiser through but raised a hand and commanded the driver of the red Mustang to stop.

Push, pull.

HE TOOK HIS time putting on the uniform in the darkness beneath the oaks. He'd purchased it at a military clothing store in Oceanside shortly after getting the original information from Ampostela and the assignment from El Jefe. Military uniforms were not exactly like law enforcement uniforms but this one was close enough—long-sleeved, summer-weight cotton/poly in tan. Matching trousers, plain front, hemmed not cuffed. They were an inch or two too long, like the cops in Mexico wore them.

He'd bought the police belt and holster from a Riverside leather smith he'd known for years. It was stiff, functional, reasonably priced, and provided a nice fit for the heavy .357 Magnum revolver.

His badge was from the police department in Fort Kent, Maine, and he'd bought it at a gun show in Ontario, California; the name-plate he'd found there too: SGT.LITTLETON.

He already owned a pair of black steel-toed construction boots and he had polished them for nearly an hour back home to bring out an impressive luster.

The cuffs were toys; the radio was nothing but a defunct walkie-talkie; the flashlight was a good four-battery Maglite he'd had for years.

He added a fake mustache that he'd bought at a costume store, which had a terrific selection with Halloween just a couple of weeks away. He'd chosen a brown one, full but neat, just like American cops wore.

Lejas stood in the darkness listening to the light crackle of the oak leaves in the breeze, and gathered his thoughts.

The weather lady's last report was just before eight o'clock each week night, and Lejas knew from Cedros's notes that she usually got home between 8:45 and 10:30.

He also knew it would be foolish to drive this counterfeit Sheriff cruiser any more than absolutely necessary—it was only a matter of time before a real deputy spotted him.

Lejas waited until 8:35 before he pulled his car onto the street and headed toward Trumpet Vine. It would take just three or four minutes to drive there, a minute to park and turn on the warning lights, set out the reflector flares, hop out of sight to the top of the embankment, and use his binoculars to spot them in the occasional oncoming traffic.

And when he spotted them, it would take just a few minutes more. Wave the security car through. Stop the Mustang. One in her heart and one in her head, then two shots into the grille of the yellow truck to put the fear of God into the Big Swine.

Then five steps back to his car, a U-turn and the brights heading back past the yellow truck, out of Fallbrook, and onto Interstate 15 for the short ride down to Escondido, where his ex-brother-in-law was waiting with an empty garage and friends who would scrap the Crown Victoria for parts in less than half a day.

The road unwound before him. The moon was low and stifled in the damp clouds, like a bulb covered by lint. The big Crown Vic swerved and swayed through the curves of the road. Lejas hadn't noticed what a sloppy ride the car had until now, like he was riding on gelatin instead of steel-reinforced rubber.

He made the turn onto Trumpet Vine, went southeast for a mile to the spot he'd found earlier. He'd marked it with a boulder just off the road. He pulled onto the shoulder then reversed, leaving his car at a half-on, half-off angle in the right lane.

Lejas stepped from the car, shoulders back and head erect. He was law enforcement now. He turned on the yellow flashing lights on the light bar, then set out the triangle reflectors to slow the traffic. Then he stepped up the embankment, moved out of sight from the road below, tucked the Maglite under his left arm, and raised his night-vision binoculars with his right.

The night turned green, a muted but somehow light-filled color. The road was a pale ribbon, both blanched and detailed, winding back into the Fallbrook hills. The trumpet vines were darker patches along the embankments but the flowers themselves were dangling swatches of cool white.

A minivan approached, slowing when the driver saw the flashing lights and the reflectors. Lejas killed his light and moved to the edge and peeked over a fragrant trumpet vine. The van picked its way past the reflectors, stopped inquisitively at the flashing law enforcement car, then swung around it and accelerated on its way.

A station wagon followed a minute later. Then a motorcycle, then a battered old pickup truck.

Then Lejas saw through his nightscope the Birch Security cruiser slowly winding its way toward him.

He stepped down the embankment, tossed the binoculars into his car, turned on the flashlight, and assumed his stance on the road between his car and the reflectors.

The security cruiser dipped out of sight for a second and after this, Lejas knew, would quickly be upon him.

He glanced at his car, just one last check of the scene to make sure it was right.

But the cruiser didn't look right at all.

It slouched noticeably toward the road. He'd seen this before, dozens of times in his life. It was always bad news but this was not just bad news—it was impossible news.

His eyes went quickly to the new left rear tire, which was flat. The rubber drooled onto the asphalt like something melted.

"Son of the fucked," he muttered.

All he could do was turn his official attention to the oncoming security cruiser and use his flashlight to wave it through. He used the steady, almost bored motion of law enforcers everywhere. He didn't look at Red Hair or Gun Girl but he didn't look away either—just gave them the same noncommittal but alert gaze that a thousand cops and guards had used on him in his lifetime.

Then the Mustang.

Then the yellow pickup truck.

Then their exhaust reached his nose and their lights proceeded away and Lejas stood for a moment in the flashing light of his own fake cop car, staring at the flat tire and shaking his head.

He walked up closer, used the flashlight, and saw the shiny nail head flush against the sidewall.

Son of the fucked.

He collected the reflectors, set them in the trunk, then got in and killed the warning lights. He slammed the door. Then he angrily fishtailed a U-turn in the loose shoulder gravel, throwing up a spray of dust and dirt.

He limped back to the grove of oaks off the dirt road, cursing his luck and the God that made him, but also working on a plan for tomorrow.

25

Late Saturday afternoon the rain began to fall. It was light, just sprinkling the windshield of the pickup as Stromsoe headed out of Fallbrook toward the Bonsall barn.

Frankie was behind him in her Mustang, with Alex and Janet bringing up the rear in the cruiser. Stromsoe led the way because they'd never been to the barn. He had decided to keep the three-car formation because he liked the mobility and the general heft of a column.

If they're going to get the weather lady and the PI, he thought, they'll have four people and three cars to deal with. Plus Ted, who would be waiting for them at the barn. Another body, another truck.

He still didn't like the sound of that caller's voice. You could hear the truth and fear in it. It didn't sound familiar to him in any way. Choat's receptionist came to mind. She had looked like a decent sort, someone who wouldn't approve of things like this, but you couldn't tell for sure. Cedros's wife came to mind too. It was possible that Cedros told her such things, or that she had found out accidentally somehow. Why warn him now? No one had warned anybody before. Maybe Choat had escalated things, as Birch had said.

He pulled to the side of the dirt road and held open the gate. Frankie came through and pulled over too, then Janet brought the cruiser across and continued up the road to where Stromsoe was pointing.

Frankie waited for the cruiser to top the rise then got out of her car, crunched across the road, and kissed Stromsoe unquestioningly. Her hat fell off. The kiss went longer than he thought it should.

"What's wrong?" she asked.

"Nothing at all."

"If they're going to get the PI, they'll have to get through me to do it."

"Let's not make light of things."

"I'm not—I've got the gun. The revolver I can't hit much with."

He handed her the hat and she got back into her car.

Ted met them with good cheer and coffee. They loaded Ted's white truck as they had the week before. Ace and Sadie chased each other through the damp brush then fought it out in the dirt by the barn. Alex and Janet, still dressed in their Birch Security uniforms, sat in their car out of the drizzle, but they kept hitting the windshield wipers to see what was going on.

Twenty minutes later they were parked by tower one. Ted climbed up to check the instruments and when he was ready Stromsoe handed up the drums of unactivated potion. Again he smelled the copper-chlorine aroma of the solution.

Then Frankie dispatched Ted to stand up close to the Birch cruiser, between the window and tower one, so she could climb the tower and work her magic on the formula. Stromsoe wondered what Alex and Janet could have possibly seen through a window dripping with water.

Up on the tower now, Frankie set down her heavy red toolbox and made a little orbit with her finger.

He turned his back to her, smiling.

Again he heard the sound of liquid hitting liquid, of something hard sloshing through the containers, hitting their sides. Then the click of the propane lighter.

Then he heard tools clanging back into the red toolbox, the lid coming into place, the latches snapping shut. A moment later the same faint, ethereal odor as before wafted down to him.

When he heard Frankie's feet on the ladder he finally turned to see the gentle blue glow at the tops of the two drums. Vapor rose into the sky.

She walked by him and put her hand on his shoulder for just a second and looked at him through the rain dripping off her hat.

Thirty-five minutes later they finished up at tower four, then they unfolded their beach chairs in the bed of Ted's truck and waited for the drizzle to turn to rain.

Ted produced the Scoresby and took an inaugural swig. Frankie sipped. Stromsoe passed. The dogs, again wearing the plastic rain ponchos that Frankie had tailored for them, lay on the pickup bed panting lightly, arguably alert. Alex and Janet sat in the idling cruiser with the wipers cycling occasionally and the defroster on to keep down the condensation.

Stromsoe, Frankie, and Ted sat with the uneasy contentment of teammates with a small lead at the half. Stromsoe accepted a smoke from Ted, which got him poked in the ribs by Frankie. This briefly interested Ace. Frankie pinged the back of a fingernail against the Scoresby bottle but didn't drink.

The drizzle stopped.

Stromsoe saw it decelerate and heard the slowing patter of it on the brim of his hat, then it simply ended with a puff of cold wind out of the northwest.

Ted took a long thoughtful look up into the sky. "Stars," he said. "Not what I wanted to see."

Frankie was looking up too.

Stromsoe saw the clouds thinning and the pinprick clarity of stars against a clear black sky.

"It's blowing through," said Ted.

"Damn," said Frankie. "Damn. All my calcs had half an inch. Weather Service, NOAA, everybody agreed."

"Hills make pockets," Ted said uncertainly.

The driver's window of the Birch cruiser went down.

They gave it an hour but the system kept moving through. In its wake blew a cold north wind that riled the sage and chaparral and filled the air with their clean green smell. The stars twinkled in the newly scrubbed sky.

"Let's do what athletes do," said Ted.

"They make adjustments," said Frankie.

"Always makes me think of knobs," said Ted. "They go back home, sit on the couch, lift their shirts, and adjust the knobs on their stomachs."

"Wish I had one," said Frankie. "I'd make some adjustments. All right. Okay. Not the end of the world."

"Maybe this is the exception that proves the rule," said Ted.

"I never understood that sentence," said Frankie. "I never liked it. Let's go. I'm cold." They drove back to the barn, unloaded the drums and ladder, tools and chairs.

"This doesn't mean anything about the formula or the mode of delivery," said Ted. "There wasn't anything for our stuff to hold on to. You can't accelerate what isn't up there to start with."

"I understand that," said Frankie. "But I wonder if our catalytic matter is too dense. If it couldn't rise through the moisture."

"It rose last time."

"I'm thinking. I'm thinking."

THEY CARAVANNED OUT with the Birch cruiser in the lead, then Frankie in her Mustang, followed by Stromsoe. Ted stayed behind to pull the weather stats off the Santa Margarita Web site and see what happened elsewhere in the area.

Stromsoe never thought he'd feel so bad about rain not falling. Never thought of rain at all until he'd met

Frankie Hatfield, and her passion had gotten into him. So had her disappointment tonight.

The blacktop road was wet but not dripping. Stromsoe saw the tight fans of water kicked up by the Mustang's rear tires. The breeze swayed the roadside oaks and their leaf-held rain dropped onto his windshield.

When Stromsoe turned onto Trumpet Vine he saw the disturbance half a mile ahead, the yellow lights flashing. He went around a curve and they disappeared from his sight.

He thought of the Sheriff cruiser he'd seen in roughly the same place the night before, wondered again what exactly the deputy was doing there except slowing traffic and waving the motorists along. Last night, from a distance, he'd figured a sobriety checkpoint, but the deputy had been sleepily efficient and never even talked to the drivers. Then he thought a registration or safety check of some kind, but the guy didn't check anything. Then Stromsoe had figured a fugitive alert, or maybe the cool end of a hot pursuit. Maybe even something with INS or Border Patrol—Fallbrook was filled with illegals doing cheap labor.

Regardless, somebody was at it again. He didn't think that CHP, sheriffs, and cops would set up checkpoints or speed traps the same place two nights running.

INS? Who knew.

Stromsoe thought it telling that a Mexican-American Sheriff's deputy, like the guy who had waved him through last night, would be out there looking for illegal Mexicans.

He followed Frankie's Mustang out of the curve. The Birch cruiser was a hundred yards ahead of Frankie, just now heading into the dip before the straight that would lead to the flashing lights.

The cruiser slowed, then headed up the little grade and over. The Mustang followed a moment later, then Stromsoe was cresting the rise that Frankie had just made and he saw clearly the black-and-white patrol car and the lights and I'll be damned, he thought, it looks like the same guy as last night.

He braked, gave Frankie some room to slow. He saw the security cruiser slow and bend slightly into the left lane, following the red reflectors. The cop stepped out, took a look at Janet at the wheel, then swung his flashlight in the same desultory arc as the night before. The brake lights on the Birch cruiser darkened.

Frankie, no doubt upset about the rain, punched the Mustang quickly to the reflectors, then braked and crept forward.

Stromsoe closed the distance as the deputy walked around to the driver's side of her car. Stromsoe saw something that at first seemed funny: the guy had the same baggy too-long trousers he was wearing the night before. The funny part was that cops down in Mexico often wore their pants this way because their uniforms weren't cut like ours and this guy was a Mexican-American, so he looked just like some of the *policía municipal* guys the task force had used to stake out Mike Tavarez's apartments in the Colonia.

Funny.

But the kicker was, he also looked just like the *policía municipal* cops who were *guarding* Mike's apartments in the Colonia.

Good guys, bad guys. Bad guys, good guys.

All mixed up.

Stromsoe got a charge of adrenaline he wasn't expecting. It hit him everywhere at once: suddenly his vision was extra clear and things were happening more slowly than usual, his muscles were tight and ready, and his breath was coming fast.

The deputy shuffled to Frankie's window and Stromsoe saw the glass go down.

Stromsoe pulled up tight on the Mustang's tail and the deputy shined the flashlight in his face. Stromsoe's one good eye fought the light but before he had to squint away he got a good look at the man.

Skinny face, fat mustache.

Pants pooling down over his boots.

A brand-new duty belt, and not a Sam Browne, but a shiny, showy knockoff.

A big revolver that deputies never carried anymore.

Alone—a checkpoint with one deputy.

Stromsoe's vision returned as the deputy turned his light and attention back to Frankie.

The deputy said something and popped his holster strap free.

He drew the big revolver and in an instant Stromsoe understood that Frankie was about to get shot. He also understood that he could never get out of his truck and draw his weapon in time to help her. He was trapped.

Instinct told him to lift his right foot off the brake and that is what he did, coming down hard on the gas and lining up the side of his truck with the deputy, who turned at the shriek of rubber and tried to lean back against the Mustang for space. His head vanished in an explosion of glass when the big side mirror hit him.

Stromsoe slammed the brakes and threw the shifter into park and was out in a second with his .380 up.

Frankie rounded the front of the Mustang, her own weapon wobbling in her hand, but at least she had it out in front of her like it should be and she was plainly terrified but not screaming.

"Down!" Stromsoe yelled. *"Get down!"*

Frankie dropped and Stromsoe scrambled around his truck, charging the unconscious deputy, who lay flat out on the road. The revolver had landed eight feet away and Stromsoe put himself between it and the man down. Alex burst through the flashing yellow lights, holstered his gun, pulled the deputy over, and put a knee to his back. Janet cuffed him, rolled him onto his back, and got two fingers up to his carotid. The man's head was bleeding and his jaw was clenched and his eyes were closed.

Frankie came around the front of her car, one hand on the hood for support, her gun shaking in her other outstretched hand. Stromsoe took it.

"I'll call," said Janet.

"Wait," said Stromsoe. "What's that?" he asked, pointing at the revolver.

"His gun," said Alex.

"Frankie, Janet—what is that?" Stromsoe asked again. His hands were shaking and his legs felt flimsy and his heart was pounding in his throat.

"His gun."

"His gun, Matt."

"You're damn right that's what it is," said Stromsoe. "Make the call, Janet. Good job, people. Really good job."

He looked down on the unmoving deputy, saw the man and his gun and the scene chopped into frames by the flashing lights.

"Frankie," he said. "The police will want to interview you at home. You and Janet can leave now if you want, get yourself together. It's going to be a long night."

"What am I going to tell the police?"

"Everything you know."

"I'll stay here. I'm with you."

Stromsoe went to the bogus sheriff's cruiser and turned off the flashing lights.

"Hey, look at this guy," called Alex. He was standing over the deputy, holding up the man's cuffed arms at a painful-looking angle. Alex had pulled down the right sleeve of the duty shirt.

In the headlights from the Birch cruiser Stromsoe could see the totem pole of black prison tattoos climbing from wrist to biceps and beyond. Alex let go and the arms slapped back into place. The man still didn't stir.

"Deputy, my ass," Alex said. "Isn't the 'M-13' La Eme?"

A bright and terrible light suddenly went on in Stromsoe's head. He walked over to where the man lay and looked first at his face, then at the tattoos.

He didn't recognize the face but the tats were all La Eme.

Stromsoe pulled the man's wallet from his trouser pocket, then stepped away from the cars and used his cell phone to wake up Dan Birch at home.

"We just had a close one," he said.

"I'm listening."

He told Birch what had happened, patiently repeating several of the details out of deference to friendship and Birch's training as a law enforcement officer. He heard a keyboard tapping as he talked. He wondered if Birch slept with it next to his bed or if he'd quietly wandered into the den.

Stromsoe assured his boss that Frankie was fine, everyone had performed well, and that Birch had been smart to assign the extra manpower. They'd probably saved her life.

Then Stromsoe asked Birch to get a jacket on Ariel Lejas of Riverside, California. He read Lejas's numbers off the driver's license in the wallet. He saw some cash, not much.

"And I want a list of all visitors seen by Mike Tavarez at Pelican Bay Prison over the last two weeks," he said.

Birch paused. "A little time and I can do that. Who are we hoping to find on it?"

"John Cedros or Marcus Ampostela."

"Our stalker and our gangster."

"I'm smelling Mike Tavarez, Dan. He's all over this."

Again Birch paused a beat. "Let's see what we get. If this was Tavarez, it'll happen again. And again, until he gets what he wants. He's got endless time and plenty of money."

"I'm pretty damned clear on that, Dan."

Stromsoe went back to the island of lights, worked the wallet back into Lejas's pants, then joined Frankie leaning against her Mustang.

He put his arm around her and felt her body stiff and trembling under her clothes. He held her firmly but not too tight.

"Stand up straight and take a deep breath," he said quietly. "Don't want to scratch the paint."

"No," she whispered. "Not that."

She stood straight and took a deep breath but the shivers didn't stop and her eyes looked glassy and empty.

"I see Lacerta, Pegasus, and Delphinus," he said. "And Capricornus, Fomalhaut, and Lyra."

"I don't see anything but that."

He followed her gaze to the big revolver lying on Trumpet Vine.

26

Back at Frankie's house the cops separated them. Frankie got her living room and Stromsoe the dining room. Alex took a bedroom and Janet the room containing Frankie's bottled rivers.

Stromsoe's interviewer was Davis, a stocky young detective, early thirties, with doubtful lines in his face and thinning dark hair combed straight back. Davis didn't show the usual cop disrespect for private detectives. He told Stromsoe he had been fortunate. He also didn't place Stromsoe as the narcotics deputy whose family was killed by the bomb two years ago in Newport Beach.

Stromsoe said nothing about that or Mike Tavarez. He would cross that bridge when he knew more about Ariel Lejas and had seen the Pelican Bay visitors' log.

Lead Detective White told Frankie how much he enjoyed her weather reports although he usually watched a different channel. He declined coffee and pointed her to a living-room couch.

Stromsoe watched a uniformed sergeant broodingly shuttle back and forth between Alex and Janet, his holster and cuff case squeaking on his Sam Browne, eyes down, notebook in hand. He seemed preoccupied with something thousands of miles away.

Ace and Sadie wandered from interview to interview with airs of good-natured obligation.

By two o'clock everyone was gone but Frankie and Stromsoe, who sat not close together on one of her living-room couches. The dogs slept at their feet.

"La Eme?" asked Frankie. "Tavarez?"

"I think so."

"In league with Choat? Impossible."

"Don't be naive, Frankie."

"But why would Tavarez help Choat?"

He looked at her a moment before he spoke. "If it's Tavarez, it's personal. It's about me."

She looked back at Stromsoe, shaking her head in gathering disbelief. "So he'll try again and again. He can just sit back in prison and send people here until one of them manages to kill me."

"I won't let that happen."

"It already happened. I was lucky. So were you."

She was right. Stromsoe could barely stand the sound of his own voice as he spoke those words. *I won't let that happen.* How could he promise to her what he hadn't been able to provide for his own wife and son?

How could he not?

He stood and went to the big sliding-glass door, saw the stars in the storm-cleared sky, the tops of the avocado trees tilting silver in the breeze.

"What are my options, Matt?"

"I'll make him see the light."

"What power do you have over a man doing life without parole in the worst prison in the country? In the weirdest of ways, he's totally free. What can you take from him? What can you offer him? He didn't do this because he wants something. He did this because he hates you."

Stromsoe, a man with nothing to offer his enemy and nothing to hurt him with, looked out at the faintly glistening orchard. There were no colors in the night, only black and white and shades of gray. Then the trees gave way to Frankie's reflection and he watched her without her knowing. She sat on the couch with her knees apart and her elbows on them, leaning forward, looking at her hands. Her hair fell down around her face so that only the curve of her forehead and the tips of her nose and chin caught any light.

He remembered the night the kids had thrown the rocks at the marching band and Mike had helped him chase them down. Back then Stromsoe had felt a great affection for skinny Mike Tavarez—clarinetist, ally, compadre, friend. Now Stromsoe felt the same sense of altered time that he'd experienced five nights ago when he had shown Frankie the pictures of Hallie and Billy. In this new version of time—basic time, pure time, time without watches or calendars or the movements of a solar system upon which watches and calendars are based—one moment Mike was fighting beside him and in the next El Jefe was trying to kill an innocent woman because he hated Stromsoe. And in the new time, Matt Stromsoe, the soft-eyed drum major who had befriended a bandmate and hung out at his house riding bikes and shooting pool and eating his mother's chile verde, hated Mike Tavarez back.

"Matt," she said. "I'm not going to back down. I'm not going on a long vacation. I'm not changing my name, my home, or so much as my hair color for that man. I'm going to keep broadcasting. I'm going to make rain. You've got to figure something out."

"I will."

. . .

STROMSOE WAS ASLEEP in the guest room when Frankie woke him up. She stood in the doorway looking uncertain of whether she was staying or going. She was backlit by the hall light but he could see her hair was down and she was wearing a pink satin robe over something black.

When she offered her hand he smelled complexities of skin and lotion and perfume, and saw the glitter in her eyes.

She led him to her bedroom and locked the door. The windows framed the grainy first light of morning.

"This is a first, Matt."

It took him just a second to get it.

"Don't ask now," she said. "Don't say anything."

"I'm wordless."

"I bought this getup for you, the day after we danced and you showed me Hallie and Billy and the flowers at night."

"I'm extra wordless."

"Then show me the steps to this one too, if you'd like."

PART IV

Pistoleros

27

Birch handed Stromsoe a faxed copy of the Pelican Bay Prison visitors' log for October 18, one week ago.

"Cedros spent thirty-five minutes with Mike Tavarez that afternoon," said Birch. "They talked privately, in the presence of an attorney—no listeners, no recordings."

The worst of Stromsoe's fears brushed up against him like something in deep water: Mike had tried to have Frankie Hatfield murdered. It was outrageously logical. It was how he did his business.

But with Frankie now tossed into this violent river—a psychopath's notion of poetic vengeance—Stromsoe replaced the word "business" with the word "evil." Tavarez was evil. Stromsoe hoped this knowledge might be reassuring but it wasn't. It put Mike in a dark league and gave him invisible allies and powers, as if the tangible legions of La Eme weren't enough.

"We have to tell the cops," said Birch. "It will take them weeks to get to this. They're not looking at Pelican Bay."

Stromsoe thought. "Let me talk to Cedros first. I want to hear what he's got to say."

Birch nodded.

"How come the lawyer isn't on this list?" asked Stromsoe.

"Different list. Here."

Birch pushed another sheet toward Stromsoe, *Professional Visits*. Halfway down the page was the only professional visitor that Mike Tavarez had that day, Taylor Hite of Taylor Hite, LLC, Laguna Beach, California.

"He's a dope lawyer," said Birch. "Doing okay for himself. He's twenty-eight, lives in a modest three-million-dollar home in Three Arch Bay. I've got nothing on him. He'll send us packing."

"Did Marcus Ampostela show up at Pelican Bay too?"

"No Ampostela. My guess is he's Tavarez's bagman. They probably communicate through e-mail or kites. And maybe even through Hite. Stranger things have happened."

Stromsoe thought for a moment. "Cedros must have offered Tavarez something substantial. Wouldn't you love to find a pile of DWP cash in one of El Jefe's accounts?"

Birch shrugged. "I'd love to find anything at all in an El Jefe account. Remember?"

"Yeah—El Jefe gets busted with a total of six grand in a checking account at B of A. Everything else was Miriam's and even that wasn't much. He hid the rest."

Birch tapped on his keyboard and a printer started to whir. "When the cops grill Cedros about the attempted murder of the woman he's charged with stalking, he might be ready to cooperate with them."

Something caught in Stromsoe's mind. "Tavarez will see it that way too. He knows we can get these logs. That might put Cedros in a ditch off the freeway with a couple of bullets in his head."

Birch considered. "Naw, Cedros isn't worth it. He's just the messenger. His visit to Tavarez proves nothing and Tavarez knows that. There's no recording, no witness. They've already agreed on a bullshit line if they're questioned—you can be sure of that. Mike can't … well, he can't kill everybody who breathes the same air he does."

Stromsoe wondered about that. "I think it was Cedros's wife, Marianna, who warned us. Maybe he put her up to it. Either way, I couldn't come up with anyone who knew both sides of this—DWP and Tavarez—until now."

"Warn him, then. Return the favor."

Stromsoe used his cell and dialed the Cedros home number. He pictured the pregnant young woman in the Mexican restaurant uniform loading her boy out of the battered old car. He got a recording and hung up. An idea came to him.

"Can you cue up that warning call, Dan?"

Birch fiddled with his keyboard and mouse, then played the call to Birch Security from the unidentified female.

They're going to get the weather lady and the PI.

Stromsoe pulled Birch's desk phone over, redialed the Cedros number, then punched on the speaker mode.

You have reached the Cedros family—John, Marianna, and Anthony. If you leave your number we'll call you back.

Birch played the warning again.

Stromsoe dialed the Cedros number for the third time and they both listened.

Birch was smiling.

Stromsoe nodded.

"You should have been one of the good guys," said Birch.

"You too."

"How is Lejas?" asked Stromsoe.

"He's serious, but stable—broken bones in his face. How's your mirror?"

Stromsoe smiled, looked out the window at the clear morning. Saddleback Peak, the highest point in Orange County, sat in perfect clarity, its top bristling with antennas and communications clutter.

"Frankie won't back down," he said. "She won't hide out or move away."

Birch rolled back in his chair and locked his fingers behind his head. "I didn't think so. A woman who photographs her stalker has some courage. Got a little something for her, don't you?"

"Yeah."

"You don't look like that guy who sat here two weeks ago. She's lovely."

"I'm trying to keep her that way."

Birch nodded briefly but said nothing and Stromsoe understood that Birch had wanted this to happen.

"How long do you think it will take Tavarez to organize another try?" Birch asked.

"A day or two," said Stromsoe.

"Then you've got a day or two to find a way to change his mind."

"I need a way into his head, Dan."

"Personally, I don't want to go there, but I know what you mean."

Years ago Stromsoe had searched for a way to manipulate El Jefe Tavarez, and he had found it.

Ofelia had died, but he had found it.

Who does he love now? Stromsoe wondered. What does he fear now? What does he want?

CEDROS MET HIM at Olvera Street, a tourist *mercado* not far from the DWP headquarters. He looked smaller than Stromsoe had remembered, and more nervous.

They walked past the bright serapes and the leather sandals, the colorful pots and plates, the hats and maracas and marionettes.

Stromsoe told him about Lejas, the fake cop car, the tattooed arm of La Eme. Cedros stared ahead as they walked but Stromsoe could tell he was listening to every word.

"So I decided to work from the top down and guess what?"

"What?"

"You talked to Mike Tavarez at Pelican Bay Prison on October eighteenth. For over half an hour."

"We're relatives. Goddamned distant relatives is all we are." Cedros spit out the words but didn't look at Stromsoe.

"What did you talk about?"

"Family."

"I wondered if you might have taken Tavarez an offer from Choat. It makes sense—you got popped by me, and Choat sends you to make a deal with El Jefe."

Cedros looked at him now, anger in his eyes. "Family is all we talked about."

"You're beginning to make sense to me," said Stromsoe. "If you wouldn't roll over on Choat, you won't roll over on Mike. The trouble for you is, Lejas almost killed Frankie, so it looks like someone contracted with Tavarez for murder. Who's the link between El Jefe and Frankie? You."

Cedros glared at him as they rounded one of the Olvera Street alleys and started down the next. He reminded Stromsoe of a cat he used to have as a boy, a big tom named Deerfoot who used to look at him as if to say, *If I were a little bit bigger I'd kill and eat you.* Same thing now with Cedros, his little man's rage boiling inside.

"I have to give the cops the visitors' log for October eighteenth," said Stromsoe.

"It was just family stuff, man. I'm telling you."

"Tell the cops that."

"I'll make you a deal."

"You can try."

"Get the rain lady to drop the stalking charges and I'll tell you what Tavarez and I talked about."

Stromsoe saw that Cedros was in much hotter water than stalking charges, though he wasn't sure that Cedros saw it.

"I think she'll go for that," he said. He didn't say that the D.A. might prosecute Cedros anyway.

Cedros sped up his walk, out of Olvera Street and onto Cesar Chavez Avenue. Stromsoe was a step behind when Cedros wheeled and grabbed his arm.

"Choat wanted Frankie to stop making rain, and he wanted you off the case. He wanted her formula. That was the whole deal. I presented it to Tavarez. Nobody was supposed to get killed, Stromsoe. Ever. I swear to God. That was not the deal."

"I believe you."

"*Fuck.* Shit. Man, I can't believe this is happening."

"Did you tell Tavarez that I was Frankie's body-guard?"

Cedros looked up at Stromsoe, squinting in the mid-day sun. "No. Choat said it was important that he see the pictures of Frankie with you in them."

"I thought they confiscated those down at the Sheriff's station."

"I had more."

So Choat knew, thought Stromsoe. He'd probably read the articles and seen the pictures. He knew Tavarez would jump at the chance to mess with me again.

"You're a good employee, John. You just choose the wrong bosses."

"Don't I know it, man."

"How much did Choat offer for the intimidation?"

Cedros slowly shook his head. "Two hundred Gs."

"Christ Almighty. Next time tell him to offer about a quarter of that. You gave it to the big guy, Ampostela, right?"

Cedros looked at the ground, then slowly nodded.

"Now that the job is botched, Tavarez will try to kill you," said Stromsoe. "You're the only one who can finger him for Frankie. He'll probably use Marcus. It could be tonight. It could be next week or next month. It might be good to leave town for a while."

"Yeah? Quit my job and run away? Go where? Do what? Change my name and get plastic surgery? I got a thousand dollars in the bank and a baby on the way."

"Get a motel up in Ventura or something. Your life is worth sixty bucks a day, isn't it?"

"I'll just be dead in Ventura. He's the Jefe. He's a fuckin' killer."

Stromsoe knew that Cedros had the score one hundred percent correct. In his years of war against Mike Tavarez and La Eme he had seen the innocent killed and the guilty walk away. He'd seen the good die and the evil flourish. The cops couldn't protect; they could only sweep up.

Hadn't he promised protection to Frankie just a few hours ago?

I'm going to keep broadcasting. I'm going to make rain. You've got to figure something out.

It angered Stromsoe that he couldn't offer this decent man any protection at all. It was an old anger but it was still alive and fresh as when he'd been young. It came from the same conviction that had brought him to this life in the beginning—that you had the law and the scoffers, us and them, good and bad.

"Do you have a gun?" he asked.

Cedros, walking fast again, looked straight ahead and didn't answer.

"Did you have your wife make that call to Birch Security? About them coming to get us?"

"So what if I did?"

"Thanks. Look, Cedros—I can't stop Tavarez or Ampostela. But I can protect you from Choat. Interested?"

Cedros stopped and glared at Stromsoe. "Hell yes."

"Let's walk through the bazaar one more time. I've got an idea."

AN HOUR LATER, Stromsoe was driving back down to Fallbrook when he asked himself again the important questions about Mike Tavarez: Who does he love? What does he want? What does he fear?

And this time an answer came to him from El Jefe himself, delivered across the years in his own clear and reasonable voice.

God put them there for reasons we don't understand. You'll burn in hell for them.

Hell would be better than this. It's bad, isn't it, living without the ones you love?

He called Birch, who called his California assemblyman, to whom he had donated generously for reelection. Later, Birch said they had had a long talk. The assemblyman called a state senator who had recently enlisted his support in getting a gun-control bill into committee to die. The senator was a friend of Warden Gerry Gyle of Pelican Bay State Prison and a big fan of Frankie Hatfield on Fox.

Warden Gyle took Stromsoe's call just before one o'clock.

• • •

SEVEN HOURS LATER Stromsoe met Pelican Bay investigator Ken McCann in the Denny's restaurant near his Crescent City Travelodge room. The night was cold and the lights of the city blurred intermittently in gusts of fog and slanting drizzle. The restaurant smelled of pine-based cleansers and flat-grilled beef. It was almost empty.

McCann had the V shape of a weight lifter, a small head with flat silver hair, and small eyes set in bursts of wrinkles. He said he was sixty. He'd seen action in Hue, buried one wife and married another, loved his grandchildren, and thought Mike Tavarez was the scum of the earth. He bit into his sandwich, chewed with one side of his mouth, and spoke out the other. He told Stromsoe about the 'Nam, about coming back in '70 and feeling so jumpy and weird. Doctors called him hypervigilant, which was a pretty darned

good word for sleeping with a carbine in the bed next to you and a pistol under the pillow, if you could even call it sleeping. So nervous even the dogs got tired of him and ran off. His wife had a heart attack at the age of thirty, which McCann believed was a direct transfer of his own monstrous fears and worries. He met up with Ellen ten years later, when most of the vigilance had worked its way out, and he finished the psychology degree first in his class and went to work for Corrections.

He described his children and grandchildren.

He ate every bit of food on his plate and ordered peach pie with ice cream.

Stromsoe listened with all of his considerable patience and empathy, then told him what he needed: a way to call Tavarez off a murder-for-hire contract that Stromsoe could not prove he was a part of.

"You can't prove anything with guys like that," said McCann, swallowing. "I read two hundred letters a week, either by him or to him—and I don't know a damn thing about what he's doing. Little bits of English. Little bits of Spanish. Little bits of Nahuatl. Whole bunches of bullshit lines and coded instructions. Sentences that mean nothing. Sentences that mean something different than what they say. Numbers and more numbers. They won't talk. You finally get somebody to talk and they torture him, murder him, and post the pictures on the Web. Tavarez? He's calling shots. I promise you that."

"I believe you. I don't need proof. I don't want it."

"What do you want, then?"

"I want to save the life of a woman he's trying to kill."

McCann looked at him. "The old Eme didn't pull that friends-and-family shit. You and Mike go way back, don't you?"

"Way back."

"I think he's got some COs on the payroll. Two young guys—Post and Lunce—I'm sure they got their family problems and need the extra money. I don't know what they do for him, if it's just kites, or maybe a phone or some Internet time. Mike isn't interested in getting high. Doesn't smoke or drink. There's also a situations man, Cartwright, and I think he's dirty too, but I'm not sure who he's down with. I think Gyle could rock Mike's world just by reassigning the guards. Mikey's little treats would go away."

Stromsoe considered. With this information, he could blow some whistles, shut down Mike's contact with the crooked guards, maybe piss him off some.

"It's not enough," he said. "But I had the thought, and this is why Warden Gyle wanted me to talk to you, that Mike didn't do too well in the SHU."

McCann smiled and peered at him, eyes twinkling in their nests of wrinkles. "Who would? Mike came out of SHU looking like a half-drowned rat. The inmates, they don't call it the SHU. To them it's the X. They hate the X. The X was hard on Mike. The smarter the guy, the harder it is on him. But that's not my area. I can't get Tavarez reassigned."

"You can tell the Prison Board what you told me— Mike is communicating with the outside through coded letters."

McCann colored slightly, but he held Stromsoe's gaze. "That's my watch. I'd be cutting my own throat."

"You read two hundred letters a week just to and from Mike. You're understaffed. You're the kid with his finger in the dike. I know that."

"And I know it."

"Well, Gyle knows it too," said Stromsoe. "He says he'll recommend SHU for Tavarez if you'll establish that he's in touch with criminal associates."

"That's the trouble," said McCann. "I can't really actually one hundred percent establish it. Which, when you flip it over, is why I got a raise this year for doing my job so well."

"Gyle wants you for lead investigator when Davenport retires," said Stromsoe.

"Oh?"

Gyle had volunteered the promotion to his friend State Senator Bob Billiter, as a way of enlisting McCann, and Billiter had offered it back up the pipeline to the assemblyman, who passed it along to Birch. Stromsoe had been impressed that politics could be played so fast. And that three men who had never so much as met Frankie Hatfield would stick out their necks a little for her.

McCann stared hard at him now, set his fork on the pie plate in the last suds of ice cream.

"Why?"

"Because you're good."

"No, why did Gyle tell you that?"

"Senator Billiter made a good case to him for the woman that Mike is trying to kill. It shouldn't have been hard. She's innocent, good-hearted, bright. One of Mike's pistoleros was bringing his gun to her head last night when luck intervened."

McCann looked at him doubtfully. "How?"

"I ran over him with my pickup truck."

McCann smiled. "I like that."

"I was too rattled to enjoy it at the time."

McCann smiled again. "So, you want me to speak to the Prison Board if Tavarez won't stand down."

"Only if he won't stand down. Either way, Gyle wants you in for Davenport."

"When does the PB meet ne—"

"A week from Thursday," said Stromsoe.

"When are you seeing Tavarez?"

"Tomorrow morning. Gyle arranged it."

"You got this timed out."

"I got lucky. I hope it works."

McCann shook his head. "Don't worry. He'll change his mind about the lady. He won't go back to the SHU. It drives most people completely crazy. It ruins them. Then we hospitalize them and they scream all day and night in the ding wing. It's like nothing you've ever heard. Even the state doctors know what the SHU does to people. They tried to close it but the courts let it stay open. It's hell."

28

John Cedros looked through the peephole of his Azusa home. Marcus Ampostela's tremendous head filled up the narrowed field of view. He looked listless and tired.

Cedros opened the door before he could ring the bell again.

"Homes," said the big man. "What are you doing?"

"What are *you* doing?"

Marianna came from Tony's room and Ampostela smiled. "Hey, *coneja*. Looking right, aren't you?"

"Keep your voice down," she said. "Tony's sleeping."

"Anybody got a beer?"

"I'll get it," said Marianna.

Ampostela watched her cross the small living room and go through the rounded doorway into the kitchen. Cedros wished she weren't wearing the cutoff jeans that made her legs look so good, even with the sixth-month stomach building over her waist like a thunderhead.

"What the fuck do you want?" whispered Cedros. "The cops are all over me at work because of you guys and the weather lady. That was not the deal, Marcus. Now you show up at my house. I can't believe you people."

Ampostela's anger flashed through his slow bigness and into his eyes. His bulk seemed to tighten. "You owe me twenty-five."

"For that?"

"For that. And you and I have some work tonight. I heard from El Jefe this morning. He has a job for us."

"What?"

"You'll come home with some money, is all you need to know."

Marianna came back with the beers. Ampostela took his with both hands and a smile. He swayed a little and Cedros saw that he was drunk or high or both.

"I'm takin' your husband out for a drink," he said.

"Not tonight," she said.

"Yeah, tonight. Tonight is what it is. I'll bring him home before it's too late. That's the deal."

Cedros's heart beat wildly, as if it were veering off course, then straightened out and beat evenly again.

Marianna looked at her husband, shook her head, and walked past both men, down the hallway and into Tony's room.

"Let's go," said Ampostela.

"I'm finishing my beer." His hand was shaking so badly he could hardly get the can to his face, so he turned away from Ampostela and drank it as fast as he could.

"Drink it on the road. We'll take my car. We don't have all night."

"I have to get the money, take a piss, say good night to my boy."

"Hurry up."

Cedros didn't hurry at all. He used the bathroom then put on a light windbreaker, arranged things, and said good-bye to Marianna. He took the envelope of DWP cash from a bowl of fruit on top of the refrigerator.

When they finally got in the car Ampostela drove them around the corner to El Matador restaurant, where the dog had eaten from the table.

Cedros used the bathroom again, then he was led by Ampostela to the same back room where the women and the drowsy gunman had been. They were there tonight too. The dog was up where he'd sat last time, a clean white plate before him.

"Money," said Ampostela.

Cedros gave him the envelope and stood there while Ampostela counted it.

"Sit," said Ampostela. "Wait here. Come back outside to the car in twenty minutes."

Then he left.

Twenty wordless minutes later Cedros rose from the big empty booth, went to the bathroom once again, then walked outside. It took him a minute to spot the big shiny station wagon because it wasn't in the parking lot but across the street in the faint light of a purple streetlamp.

He got in and it roared onto the avenue.

Ampostela drove them up Highway 39 into the San Gabriel Mountains. Rain had puddled on the roadside from last night's storm and the stars were bright flickers over the tall mountains. Ampostela studied his rearview mirror. Cedros looked in the passenger sideview but saw nothing behind them.

The last time he had been up this road was with the PI Stromsoe, Cedros thought. When he came *that* close to just telling him what he knew already—that scarfaced Choat had drafted him into harassing the weather lady in a completely useless attempt to chase her out of the rainmaking business.

"Where are we going?" asked Cedros. "There's nothing up here."

"We're meeting some people at that restaurant over the river."

"It's been closed for years."

"That's why. Be cool, man. So the cops asked you some questions. Don't tell them nothing except you didn't do it. You got a good lawyer?"

"For which charge? I can't keep track of my own crimes anymore."

"That's what lawyers are for."

They passed the last housing tract, one that was built over the riverbed. You had to use a bridge to get home. Which is why Cedros had looked into buying a place there. The houses were nice and it wasn't the barrio but they were too expensive.

Now he caught a glimpse of the San Gabriel River, swollen with rain, surging down from the mountains. Some of the guys at DWP talked about a place up there that got five, eight, sometimes ten times the rain that fell down here in the city. He'd heard stories of fifty inches falling in a night, streams swelling, trees falling, Forest Service roads buried by tons of running water— and most of it ending up in the San Gabriel, which would then cascade downhill, race toward Azusa, widen and slow by the time it hit civilization, then be forcibly escorted to the ocean in a concrete chute.

Cedros looked down at the river. It was scarcely visible until it passed the houses, then the neighborhood streetlights revealed its speed and volume. It ran at the bottom of a steep gorge.

How many cubic feet per second were barreling their way to the ocean right now—twelve hundred, two thousand? Why didn't they capture it? Why were the reservoirs chronically low? Why was Southern California in perpetual drought when even the humble San Gabriel lost so much good wild water after even a small fall rainstorm like the one last night? For that matter, why try to stop a lady who thinks she can make more rain?

Whatever, thought Cedros. He knew the answer and was tired of it by now. The whole thing was crazy.

Because, John, only abundance can ruin us.

It was all really hard to care about right now, sitting next to a giant who was taking him out to kill him. He finally figured out why they'd gone to El Matador first. It was Ampostela's alibi: he had dropped off Cedros and driven away and they hadn't seen him again that night. Cedros had wandered off twenty minutes later. Ampostela had three witnesses for all of that. And not one who'd seen Cedros get into Ampostela's car, tucked back in the darkness as it was.

Cedros felt the looseness in his bowels, the tightness in his chest, and the sharp discomfort of his stomach, right at the belt line.

He looked in the sideview mirror again and saw nothing but darkness behind them.

"The cops said Lejas tried to shoot her," he said.

"I don't know nothin' about that," said Ampostela. "This is just this. What we're doing is just this."

"Yeah," Cedros said quietly. "This is just this."

"What's the baby's name gonna be?"

Cedros couldn't believe that Ampostela would ask that question on the way to killing the baby's father. But Cedros understood that his disbelief meant nothing so he answered. Instinctively, he lied.

"Maria."

"Cool."

"We got her some little outfits already. Jammies and stuff."

"I got two boys and a girl with their mother up in Fresno. I hate that fuckin' place."

"Never been."

"Don't bother. Where's Marianna work?"

"Dos Amigos."

"Which one?"

"Monrovia."

"We're not stopping at the restaurant I told you about. We're meeting these people up a little further."

"Okay. Whatever you say."

They wound up into the mountains. Ampostela's Magnum was a big bad-looking station wagon that hauled ass and held the corners well. He told Cedros it was the most powerful production car in the world for under $30K. It had looked to Cedros like a fat gangster's ride but he had to confess, he'd love to have one himself. Let Marianna drive it, actually, with the soon-to-be two children in tow.

Ampostela checked the rearview again, then slowed, pulled into a turnout, and stopped. There was no other car in sight. He killed the lights and engine. He leaned across Cedros and pulled something from the glove compartment.

"What's the gun for?"

"Peace of mind, homeboy. They're coming. Get out. I'll talk and you do what I say. Only way it works."

Cedros got out and stood on shaky legs. He watched the big man come around the front of the car. Ampostela had stuffed the handgun into his pants between the shirttails, not even bothering to cover it.

They stood looking down at the black canyon and the whitecapped river barely lit by the moon.

"The river," Ampostela said.

Cedros heard the roar of the water and he tried to back up imperceptibly in order to keep Ampostela in his vision without looking directly at him.

In the very bottom of his field of focus Cedros registered the protrusion of belly and one shirttail barely covering the dully luminous handle of the automatic.

He wouldn't take his eye off the gun.

He couldn't.

To see the gun was to live.

"They'll be here," said Ampostela. "Don't worry about it."

"I won't worry."

"Everything's gonna be good. This is just this. I'm gonna take care of everything."

"Sure you are."

They stood awhile. The river sounded against its banks of rock. Not a single car came up the road or down it.

Far off in his mind Cedros was aware of Ampostela wanting to say something else but not being able to find the right words. Cedros said nothing. It was a matter of self-respect. Ampostela could struggle all he wanted. Cedros pulled his attention away from the big man and directed all of it to the gun.

In his lower vision Cedros saw Ampostela's hand drift upward. It came up slowly and in its wake the gun had vanished from the waistband.

Cedros fired four shots from the pocket of the windbreaker, angling the barrel of the .22 up into the big man's chest. Then he brought out the semi and shot Ampostela three more times in the head. The big face shifted and collapsed oddly. Cedros felt the hot mist hit his skin.

The big man dropped to his knees then fell on his face in the gravel.

Cedros staggered into the bushes, where he vomited and barely got his pants down before he lost control of his bowels. Then, talking to himself in a voice that he hardly recognized, he staggered back to the car and braced his feet against a front tire and managed to roll Ampostela's great body to the edge of the canyon and over. He suddenly remembered the $25K and didn't care one bit about it. He heard rocks sliding, then the body huffing against something very hard, then silence. Cedros stood and watched as Ampostela rolled off the last outcropping and was swallowed by the roaring darkness.

He threw Ampostela's gun into the canyon. He had to backtrack to where he'd gotten sick to find Marianna's .22 then come back and throw it into the river too.

He was shivering in the dirt with his back against the car when Marianna drove up minutes later, her headlights out of alignment and the dust rising into her almost crossed beams, which suddenly died.

He heard her get out and crunch toward him and he felt her arms spread over him and her sweet soft face press against the reek and blood and trembling of his own.

"Oh, baby," she said. "Oh, baby, my baby."

"It's okay. I'm okay. It worked."

"You've got to get up, baby."

"Mom? Dad?"

Through the rising curtain of his wife's hair Cedros saw Anthony's skinny little legs appear on the ground beside the open door of the family car.

"Anthony Mark Cedros, *get back into that car right now."*

"Yes, Mom. Hey, Daddy, what are you doing?"

"Nothing, Tony. I'll be right there."

"Stand, John. Hurry. We've got to get out of here."

29

In the cold northern silence of the Crescent City Travelodge, Stromsoe dreamed that he was back in Newport Beach with Hallie and Billy.

It was a cool March Thursday, a school day. Hallie made them a light breakfast and all three sat at the dining-room table.

"Dad had a dream about driving a car last night," said Billy.

"How do you know that?" asked Hallie.

"Because I was in the backseat."

They laughed and Stromsoe felt limitless love for his son.

But even while dreaming this conversation, he had recognized the terrible portent of it. He awakened and made the in-room coffee and sat at the unsteady table by the window with the curtain drawn and the rain tapping against the glass.

Partly as a way to keep alive people he loved, and partly as a way of getting ready to see Mike Tavarez in a few short hours, Stromsoe now let himself remember that morning a little at a time, sipping the memories.

Because I was in the backseat.

Later he had walked Hallie and Billy outside. The van was parked in the drive because the garage of the old Newport house was too small for anything but Stromsoe's Taurus and a smattering of tools, beach gear, bikes, and boxes of outgrown children's toys.

Stromsoe closed the door behind him and followed them down the short walkway to the drive. Billy led the march, leaning forward against the weight of his backpack. Hallie followed him in jeans and a flannel shirt and a pair of shearling boots sized for a moonwalk. Stromsoe watched the shape of her and thought it was good. As if knowing this, she turned and smiled at him just as they got to the driveway.

Hallie pressed the key fob and the door locks popped up with a single clunk. Billy slid open the side door. He slung his pack in ahead of him and climbed into the seat. Stromsoe helped pull the seat belt around his son and Billy snapped it shut.

"Have a great day, Billy."

"Okay."

"Be nice to Mrs. Winston."

"Okay."

"I love you."

"Okay. I mean, I love you too."

Stromsoe kissed the top of his son's head, slid the door shut, and stepped back.

Hallie tried to start the van but the battery was so weak it couldn't turn the starter.

She threw open the door. "I hate this van."

"Let me try."

Stromsoe got in and tried but even the small charge was gone and his turning of the key made nothing but a mortal clicking sound.

He opened the hood and looked but the battery terminals were clean and the clamps were tight and little else in the compartment made sense to him. He got back in the cab and tried the radio, which was dead.

"Just take my car," he said. "I'll call Auto Club, get a jump, and take this thing down to Pete's."

"Ah, can't you come with us?" she asked.

"I'll just be that much later to work."

"Dad! Can't you just come with us?"

Stromsoe sighed, then reached up to the van's sun visor and clicked on the automatic garage door opener. The motor groaned and the door lifted open. The tightly packed contents of the garage came into view.

"All right, Dad!" hollered Billy.

"All right, Dad!" hollered Hallie.

As Stromsoe followed them into the garage he had one of those epiphanies common to the family man—that he was blessed to have Hallie and Billy, that he should be more thankful for them and kinder to them, that he should slow down and enjoy the little things like taking your boy to school when the van battery goes dead. And if you're an hour late to work, who cares?

This happiness hooked another happiness from many years ago when he had led the marching band in "When the Saints Go Marching In" for probably the ten millionth time. It had hit him in an instant back then—just how wonderful and singular this moment was, and now Stromsoe remembered the green grass of the football field in the stadium lights, the thunder of the bass drums and the trills of the piccolos, the heft and rhythm of the mace in his right hand, the weight of the shako hat with its strap snug around his chin.

For a moment the joyful, many-footed song played again in his head.

He was whistling along with it to himself as he stood in his garage and dug the key fob from his pocket.

Billy was just about to veer to the right side of the Taurus because he liked to sit behind his mom. However, there was a bug of some kind on the trunk lid and he had to stop to inspect it. Behind him Hallie went up on her toes in the way that faster adults stuck behind slower children will do. Stromsoe had slowed too, ready to head for the driver's seat when they got out of his way.

Lord, how I want to be in that number...

He pressed the unlock button and the locks came up. One second later he and his family were blown to rags.

30

Tavarez was waiting in the visitation room when Stromsoe was escorted in. He looked pale but fit, freshly shaved. He stared as Stromsoe sat in the immovable chair and picked up the telephone. Stromsoe stared back.

Mike was not handcuffed but his ankle irons were in place and a guard stood outside the inmate entrance looking in through the perforated steel door. The visitation room was empty now because only weekends were for visits unless Warden Gyle himself made other arrangements.

Tavarez picked up his black telephone, wiped the mouthpiece on the sleeve of his orange jumpsuit, then put the phone to his head.

"You look the same as always, Matt," he said.

"You've gained weight."

"Workouts. Good food."

"I'll bet."

"You don't limp. There are scars on your neck and face and a missing finger. I heard that you have steel pins in your legs."

"Plenty of them, Mike. They tighten up in cold weather. I carry a document for boarding airplanes. I run even slower than I ran before. The list of my improvements goes on and on."

"The eye is realistic."

Stromsoe looked at Mike and for just a moment he appreciated the humor of mad-dogging with only one good eye, figured it was to his advantage to have the glass one staring along blindly like some fearless German sidekick.

He nodded.

Tavarez smiled. "A cold glass eye. Not fair."

Stromsoe listened to the hum of the great "supermax" prison around him. For the worst of the worst, he thought. The most expensive, efficient, and punishing incarceration yet devised by man. A model for prisons for years to come.

"I dreamed about them last night," he said. "They were whole and perfect and alive. That's how they'll always be for me, Mike."

"They should be. The bomb was for you."

Tavarez had not acknowledged this since that very first phone call to Stromsoe on the night he almost burned his house down. In court, Tavarez's attorneys had fought hard to lay the blame on La Nuestra Familia. In fact, they'd made the beginnings of a good case because Stromsoe and the task force had had as many dealings with LNF as they'd had with La Eme. Stromsoe's name had appeared in numerous Familia communications. But in the end they couldn't produce a witness to contradict the low-level La Eme soldier who had turned state's witness after his life was threatened. The soldier had heard El Jefe discussing the bomb. He had heard the name Stromsoe. He had purchased the nails at Home Depot. He had succumbed to a task force offer to drop murder charges and relocate him and his family after the trial.

"And Frankie Hatfield? Was she going to be for me too?"

"Frankie who?"

"More punishment for Ofelia? Because Hallie and Billy weren't enough?"

Mike studied him. "What the fuck are you talking about?"

"We got the visitation logs. We've talked to a lot of people, including Lejas and Ampostela. They were all helpful. Here's the story line: Cedros wanted to keep Frankie from her experiments. He harassed her. He photographed her. When that didn't work he came to you—a distant relative, a man who can get things done. You saw the pictures of her. I was in some of them. A little miracle for you, some more of the good luck you always thought you had. You figured you'd kill her and let me live with her on my conscience, along with my wife and son. Lejas got close. I got lucky. But there are more out there like him. Which is why I'm here."

Tavarez said nothing.

Stromsoe turned his attention from Mike to the pale yellow walls of the visitation room, then to the guard behind the steel door, then to the video cameras in each corner of the long, rectangular room.

"They're going to send you back to the X for the rest of your life," said Stromsoe.

Tavarez smiled lazily. "You can't do that. You don't have the power."

"I had a lot of help," said Stromsoe. "A senator, an assemblyman. Judges, lawyers, doctors. Others. One week from Thursday is the Prison Board meeting. By the time it's over you'll be reassigned to the X. It's a done deal. Only you can undo it, Mike. Only you."

Tavarez tried to bring a stony disbelief to his face but Stromsoe could see the anger in his eyes.

"How?"

"It's Frankie for the X, Mike. Her safety for your life in the general population. You promise me she'll be left alone and you can stay right where you are. You can keep getting your little favors from Post and Lunce. But if she's touched, you go to the X for the rest of your life. If she's harassed on the phone, you go to the X for the rest of your life. If she gets a cold or trips on a sidewalk or sprains her ankle working out at the gym, you go to the X. And the only way you'll get out of the X will be on a stretcher or on a pass to the psych ward. I heard them screaming on the way here. Hard to picture you in a straitjacket, Mike. The madman El Jefe, bellowing his life away in the ding wing."

Tavarez sat back and gave Stromsoe a skeptical look. He furrowed his brow and shook his head as if in amazement.

"You thought of this?"

"After I saw Lejas up close I knew the score."

"You must like this woman with the man's name."

"I hardly know her."

"Dig her as much as Hallie?"

"She's young and innocent."

"Hallie was young but not innocent."

"No. She was guilty of trusting you."

Tavarez shrugged.

"This isn't Frankie Hatfield's world, Mike. You're wrong to throw her into it. Cut her loose. You can't bring Ofelia back. Keep yourself here in the pop where you belong. You don't need the X."

Stromsoe watched the bemused expression drop from Tavarez's face to reveal his murder-one stare. It was a flat look that somehow diffused the light in his eyes and made him look both feral and focused, and ready to act. It was the look that Tavarez had given Stromsoe in court, the look he used on the street, in his business, in prison. It was a look that promised pounds of violence and not an ounce of mercy.

"Your woman is absolutely safe," said Tavarez. "That's a promise. And here's another promise, old friend—the day I see the inside of the X again is the day you both die."

Tavarez stood, then turned and short-stepped toward the door, chain dragging between his legs.

HE ARRANGED TO have his lunch served in his cell that afternoon.

When Jason Post had slid the food tray through the bean chute, Tavarez approached the door to collect it.

"Mystery meat," said Tavarez.

"You eat better than a lot of poor people," said Post.

"I need to use the library Thursday night. And I want my family visit on Sunday because I wasn't able to have it yesterday."

"Why didn't you? You're the one who called it off."

"I was busy."

"That's funny. Those two favors are gonna cost you."

"I'll have the usual transfer made."

"Double it, or no deal."

"Eight hundred dollars for one hour of library time, and a family visit?"

"Lunce told me she was a real cutie last week. So it's double or nothing."

"It has to happen just like I told you, Jason. There's no room for a mistake on this one. Library Thursday night, and my family visit on Sunday."

"What's the hurry?"

"There is no hurry."

"You sound like there's a schedule."

Tavarez looked up and shrugged. "All I have in this hellhole is a schedule."

Post eyed him with his usual latent hostility. "I don't control this place. Things come up. I'll do what I can."

"You will."

"Hey, they transferred Packtor out of the SHU this morning."

Post never missed a chance to bring up the X because he knew Tavarez hated the place beyond words. He looked at Tavarez with contempt, and with an uplifting of the chin that hinted at knowledge.

"Why?"

"How would I know? Maybe because he went insane. Or maybe to make room for someone else. But I thought you'd want to know—so you can make your reservations."

Tavarez looked up from his mystery meat.

"Just kiddin' you, Heffie."

STROMSOE TOUCHED DOWN in San Diego four hours after leaving Pelican Bay, made Frankie's five o'clock broadcast from outside the Wild Animal Park. The day was cooling and the eucalyptus trees drooped fragrantly and he could hear the cries of monkeys and birds from inside the park as he walked up to the Fox News van.

Ted was wearing a black leather cowboy hat and a black canvas duster. From within the right side pocket he let go of something to shake Stromsoe's hand.

"You really strapped, Ted?"

"I'm really strapped, Matt."

"That's illegal, you know."

"So's murder."

"Frankie okay?"

Ted jammed his hand back in the pocket. "She's coming out now."

Stromsoe watched her step out of the van, mike in hand. She saw him immediately and waved. Her smile made his heart beat harder but in a way that told him all his good fortune with her was borrowed and due back soon.

They were shooting up by the ticket booths at the main entrance and the crowd gathered quickly as they recognized her. She tried her best to autograph a stuffed condor chick and a rubber spear. She knelt to talk to a little girl. She posed for a picture with two blushing soldiers.

Stromsoe saw again how open and good and beautiful she was. And as long as she did her job, how essentially unprotectable she was from Mike Tavarez. It could happen any minute, any day, anywhere.

A moment, then forever.

That night, after her sign-off eight o'clock story, he drove her home to Fallbrook, Ted trailing them in his truck.

"Do you believe Tavarez, Matt? Do you believe I'm safe?"

"I can't believe him."

"I'm going to live my life. I'm not hiding. I'm going to keep on forecasting and broadcasting, and making rain."

"That's the way it has to be. I'll do everything in my power to protect you, Frankie."

"Until our thirty days are up?"

"For as long as it takes."

She took his hand and they were quiet for a while as Stromsoe's pickup truck curved through the dark back roads of the north county.

"I'm sorry for all this, Frankie. If it wasn't for me, he'd have no reason to hurt you."

"Maybe he'd do it for the money."

Stromsoe heard the doubt in her voice and, once again, felt the old wave of helplessness and frustration that always rose in him when he thought about Mike Tavarez. It angered him that all his years in pursuit of El Jefe, all of the effort and pain and bloodshed and loss had only brought him and this woman to a place in time where more was sure to happen. There was no real solution, he thought—not even the death of Tavarez— because the strong can reach beyond the grave and the wicked delight in it. Mike was both.

"Will you move in? Stay close for a while?" she asked.

"Sure I will, Frankie."

They bumped along quietly for a moment.

"I don't know if it's because I don't want to die or because I'm in love with you," she said.

"Hmmm."

Another pause.

Their laughter started at the same time, soft and tentative but unsuccessfully hidden. Within a few seconds Stromsoe's had the better of him. He felt the big swooning stomach and chest spasms he used to get as a kid. He touched the brakes because his eyes were watering.

Frankie's head was thrown back against the window and her hand was over her mouth. Tears jumped from her eyes. She whinnied then snorted dismayingly.

"I don't know if it's because I don't want to die or because I'm in love with you!" she choked out. "But either way, since I can't decide, I'm moving you right in like a piece of rented furniture."

"Furniture with a *gun*," Stromsoe added.

"Yeah," she said. "So just forget Mike and his bad guys because you're going to kill them *all*. Every homicidal moron he can come up with!"

"I'll hang their bodies in your avocado trees as warning."

"I'll broadcast with their bodies swinging in the background!"

"They'll ask you for autographs," said Stromsoe. "And you'll do it because it's part of your job."

"I'll sign their foreheads. 'Love ya, babe, but fuck off and die—from Frankie Hatfield at Fox News!'"

Ted passed them on a long straightaway, looking across at them from the cab of his own truck with a doubtful expression on his face.

31

Choat stepped in front of the maître d' to guide John and Marianna Cedros into a corner booth. The Madison Club dining room on Third Street was walnut-paneled and windowless, with high ceilings and crown moldings and a stamped aluminum ceiling. The walls were hung with sconces that gave warm orange light, portraits of once-powerful men and fair-faced women, and bucolic plein air paintings of Southern California.

Cedros slid into the booth, amazed that just a few yards away from where they sat, the downtown traffic of Third Street was whizzing along both invisible and inaudible here in this century-old gentlemen's club. He knew that Choat was occasionally entertained here by his masters on the Water Board. He never dreamed that he would see the inside of it unless he was hired here as a busboy.

Already seated was Joan Choat, the director's wife. She was a thin woman with dramatic cheekbones, long brown hair, and a pleasant expression on her face.

She smiled meltingly as Marianna guided her growing body into the booth, and reached across Cedros to lay a hand on her belly.

"Ohhhh … I'm so happy for you. Patrick and I could never achieve this. Another Rob Roy, please."

The maître d' nodded and handed out the leather menu books.

Choat ordered a double martini up with a twist. Marianna got lemonade and Cedros a German beer.

When the drinks came Choat lifted his glass to John. The women joined in and Cedros held his mug toward them.

"To your service to DWP," he said. "No general has ever had a better soldier."

Cedros felt himself blush, less with pride than with annoyance at Choat's pomposity. He looked at Marianna, who offered Choat a fixed smile.

"Thank you, sir," he said.

"To dropped charges, a new assignment, and a home in the Owens Gorge," said Choat.

Earlier in the day, in the privacy of his office, Choat had told Cedros that Frankie almost getting her head blown off was actually a good thing. If that wasn't enough to dissuade her from making rain, then she simply had no common sense. And the PI? Well, he could loiter around Frankie all he wanted now, so far as Choat was concerned. They could garden together, learn a foreign language.

Choat had also said that the San Diego Sheriff's investigators had asked him about his connection to Cedros's visit to Mike El Jefe Tavarez at Pelican Bay. Choat had, of course, denied knowing anything about it. Mike who? They seemed to believe him because what would a ranking DWP executive need with a prison gangster? Choat told them that a private investigator by the name of Stromsoe had come to his office last week, full of some dumb-ass theory about the DWP harassing a weather lady down in San Diego, and speculated that Stromsoe had pointed the detectives his way as reverse harassment. The detectives had shrugged off the idea.

Cedros had then reassured Choat—for what, the twentieth time?—that he and Tavarez had talked family and family only. Choat had listened closely to this story he already knew, as if to hear in it any falsehood that the police might have heard. Cedros told him that the cops had been suspicious but largely convinced. They had not asked about money passing hands. Cedros told him *again* that the untraceable cash had gone to Ampostela and he had not seen it since. And again, that days later Ampostela had taken him out for a drink at a restaurant in Azusa, but the big man had rudely walked out and that was the last Cedros had seen of him.

You are all that stands between DWP and catastrophe, John, Choat had said. *You are the bridge between here and tomorrow.*

"To a strong and healthy child," said Joan.

"With the courage of the Mexican and the cleverness of the Italian," said Choat. "Have you named her?"

Cedros's scalp crawled, remembering the last time he'd heard that question.

"Cathy," said Marianna. "We like that name."

"It's fabulous," said Joan.

Cedros watched the sweat roll down the sides of his mug and imagined their cabin in the gorge.

Just a few short days ago it had seemed impossible. Now, with Frankie Hatfield asking the San Diego D.A. to drop the stalking charges, and Marcus Ampostela no longer looming over them, and Choat suddenly doing all the things he'd promised to do, Cedros was having trouble recognizing his own life. His new job assignment was approved. He'd already met the director of

maintenance operations and two of his assistant directors. The paperwork for company housing, a company
truck—a new Ford F-250—a company cell phone, and
the hazardous-duty pay bonus was on its way.

Success was different from failure.

The home in the gorge.

He and Marianna and Tony were set to leave the
next morning and drive up to the Owens Valley and see
it. And also see the Gorge Transmission Line, which
Choat wanted to personally show him. Choat had spent
some years tending this "baby" himself as a ditch rider,
and it was more to him than just a steel pipe with a river
inside it. He'd shown Cedros an impressive book of
photographs documenting the project. It had taken ten
years to build the entire system. Men from all over the
world had come to work there. Loss of life had been
minor.

They would then all go to dinner and overnight in
Bishop, just a few miles from the gorge, at a nice motel
with a trout-filled creek running right through it. Tony
would like that. On the way home the next day Choat
wanted to show them a photography gallery that would
impress him and Marianna "mightily." He'd said that
he and Joan would send John and Marianna home with
something special from it.

The roast-beef lunch was the best Cedros had ever had. Since Ampostela, he'd been tremendously hungry, and he ate everything on his plates, three rolls, then dessert.

Choat had another double and talked about the clever but "clearly legal" way that the DWP had deceived the citizens of the Owens Valley back in the early 1900s and "redirected" almost all of their water south to develop small, sleepy, dirty Los Angeles. He talked about the vision of Eaton, who had envisioned the aqueducts, and the gumption of Mulholland, who had built them, and the sacrifice of Lippincott, who had acted as a double agent to make the whole thing work. He talked about the greatness of our current president, and about God and terror and "spine." He mentioned that Joan was "barren," and went on to fondly describe a fistfight he'd won against "two men in matching reindeer sweaters." Joan smiled dreamily through her third Rob Roy. Marianna was unusually quiet. Cedros's mind kept alternating between images of their new home in the mountains and of Ampostela's collapsing face.

AT EIGHT THE next morning Cedros was at the wheel of his gold sedan, Marianna beside him and Tony locked snugly into his car seat in the back.

They followed the Choats' black Lincoln town car up Highway 395 to the eastern side of the state.

Cedros looked out at all the new houses being built in the desert north of Los Angeles, suddenly proud that some hardworking agency such as his own DWP was providing the water to build cities amid the cactus. He had begun to understand Choat's godlike ego. He had begun to consider himself—John Cedros—one of the men who bring the water. *The men who bring the water.* As he looked out at the development rising from the sands of the desert he thought of Frankie Hatfield and wondered if she'd ever really make rain. What if she had found a way to accelerate moisture, like her great-great-grandfather Charles Hatfield? *Extra rain.* When Choat first told him about Frankie Hatfield, Cedros had secretly hoped she would make rain—lots of it. She could bring relief to a thirsty world, turn deserts into rich farmland and sunbaked savannahs into thriving suburbs. But now he wasn't so sure about the value of more rain. Weren't things working pretty damned well the way they were? Abundance really might be our enemy. A strange shudder issued from his stomach up through his body. He'd never felt anything like it: half hope, half dread, all excitement.

Marianna dozed with her head against the window, the sun warming her beautiful skin and shiny black hair. Cedros saw the pale flesh inside her thighs vibrating with the car, and the gentle, slower rhythm of her breasts, and the solid ball of Cathy riding midway in between.

He put his hand on a sun-warmed leg and glanced back at sleeping Tony, lost in shoulder straps, head forward like a reconnoitering paratrooper.

I've been blessed, thought Cedros. I'm a fuckup but God has blessed me anyway.

They pulled into Randsburg, once a gold-mining town and now the smallest and most humble of tourist stops. There was a two-cell jail you could visit, a display of glass bottles turned blue and purple by decades in the desert sun, and an interesting sculpture made of hubcaps and license plates.

At a saloon-turned-diner three young men fretted intensely over the making of milk shakes, which Marianna and Joan found touching but Choat groused about under his stiff broom of a mustache. Tony drank his whole shake and fell asleep in the chair with his head on Marianna's lap. Choat laid his right hand on the boy's beautiful little head. The hand was still bruised from the surprise slugging of the PI. Cedros was relieved when the food came and he took it off.

The rest of the drive to Bishop was the most beautiful that Cedros had ever taken. He'd been to Las Vegas,

Tijuana, and Oregon, and even up here once before, but today's vast tan October desert and blue sky were singular and priceless, and the stretch of 395 where to your left the snowcapped Sierra Nevada Mountains cut their jagged way into the heavens while to your right the White Mountains stood in parched, hulking magnificence, well, Cedros was sure you couldn't run into scenery like that just anywhere. The aspen trees sprouting in the gorges looked like red-orange dabs from a painter's brush.

They passed the old Owens Lake bed, just miles of dry white broken by an occasional silver pool. Cedros knew that the DWP had been sued for lakebed dust pollution and been forced to let just enough water back into the lake to turn the dust to a shallow sludge that no wind could lift and carry.

Farther up the highway he finally saw the last of the Owens River bleeding into the tiny remnant of the lake, depleted of its volume far upstream by the DWP transmission lines and aqueducts that were soon to become his responsibility.

He looked out at the pretty blue ribbon of river winding through a stand of bright yellow cottonwoods and wondered what it must have looked like a short century ago.

"I don't trust him," said Marianna. "Choat wants something."

Cedros looked at Tony in the back, deep asleep again, a teddy bear on his lap.

"He's afraid you'll tell the cops he sent you to Tavarez," said Marianna.

"Why would I do that?"

"To save yourself from prosecution."

"But they're not prosecuting me."

"Not for stalking. But you don't know what they're doing with regards to attempted murder, do you? Choat doesn't either. That's the variable. He has to plan ahead. How good was your story to the detectives?"

"Cops are hard to fool."

"What will Tavarez tell them?"

"Nothing he doesn't want to. He's doing life. San Diego Sheriff's can't touch him."

"And you believe your secret is safe with him?"

"Yes, I do."

"What if Choat doesn't?"

"I spent three hours lying awake last night, thinking about that," he said. "And three more hours thinking about all the good things that are happening. I'm scared, Marianna. But I'm happy too."

She reached over and rested her hand on his shoulder.

"Marianna, let me take this one step at a time," he said. "I can't see more than one step ahead."

"Hmmm," she said doubtfully. "He's going to ask you for one more thing. It'll be a whopper."

Cedros knew that his wife's nose for intrigue was keen and her eyesight for betrayal and conspiracy was better than 20/20. She always solved the mystery novels she read long before they were over, always knew who was getting voted off the island next, always seemed to smell their friends' affairs and divorces before they happened. And her suspicious nature had a practical side. The gun was her doing and she had saved his life. Stromsoe had put the idea in his head, and Cedros had put it in hers, but Marianna had dug the weapon from the upper closet, showed him how the slide and safety worked, told him to hide it in his windbreaker pocket just in case, and instructed him to "empty it" the second Ampostela showed his own killing device—just shoot right through the jacket to save time. An old boyfriend had given her the gun, and hopefully most of the know-how. Cedros had never asked about him.

She had scared him in that moment, and not for the first time in their marriage. Besides her innate cunning, Marianna's temper was ferocious once it got the better of her. It was a blinding and irrational thing, though she much preferred peace and quiet. She worked very hard for her family. She put them first. Left to her own, she was lazy and horny as a cat.

"We'll get through this," said Cedros.

"I wish there was something more I could do," said Marianna. "Choat scares me because he's selfish and cruel and he uses people. He'll do anything in the name of his precious DWP. But the worst part of him is, he's smart."

"Let's trust the PI."

"So far, I do trust the PI," said Marianna. "He's better than the law in some ways."

Cedros nodded. "Yeah, he's got no reason to throw me in jail."

"But notice how the risk always falls on you."

"Things will be different when we're up here, honey. We'll be hundreds of miles from Choat. I'll be out tending to the water. He'll be back in L.A. in his dark office. No more favors. No more rainmakers."

"Yeah," she said quietly, lost in thought. "One more thing. A whopper."

"No more waiting tables for you, honey."

"Something to do with the rain lady."

"They say the schools up here are good."

"What more can he do to her?"

"No bangers, no dope on the streets, no 'hood, no mad dogs, no dissin', no smog."

"You have to be careful, John."

"I've only been sleeping two hours a night I'm so alert. I'm ready. I'm so ready."

"Are you thinking clearly?"

"I'm happy and afraid."

"Maybe that's as good as it gets for now."

"I love you. Through all this shit, I love you, Marianna."

"I love you too, John. You're my man."

LATE THAT AFTERNOON they left the women and Tony back at the motel and drove up Highway 395 in Choat's silent, powerful Lincoln.

Choat was dressed like an Australian adventurer, in shorts and a heavily pocketed shirt, dark socks and chukka boots. His legs were preposterously muscular and white. He wore aviator shades and smoked a big cigar while Cedros drove, the cracked window sucking out the billows of smoke and the air conditioner blasting cold clean air back in.

"I love it up here," said Choat. "Miss it."

"I'm lucky."

"Damned straight. Turn where it says Owens Gorge/ Power Plant."

Cedros caught a glimpse of the little village where he and his family would soon be living. It was nestled between the gorge walls, down by the river, shaded by cottonwoods ablaze in the advancing fall. The power-plant towers and transformers rose high into the air above the village, looking to him like something from Dr. Frankenstein's lab—all curls and spikes and dire labyrinths of cable and steel. He could picture lightning arcing from one coiled spire to another, giving life to something contained within. Giving power to the city, was more like it, he thought. Power to the city all those hundreds of miles away. It's not about the water, it's about the power.

But Choat ordered him to turn away from the power plant and follow the dirt road along the gorge, paralleling the big pipe through which the Owens River was guided into the power-plant turbines.

"Almost a century ago we brought the water," said Choat. "Wasn't easy. We built two hundred and fifteen miles of road. And two hundred and thirty miles of pipeline. We built two hundred and eighteen miles of power line and three hundred and seventy-seven miles of telegraph and telephone line. We had fifty-seven work camps for our guys. There were *three thousand nine hundred* of them and they came from all over the world to work for us—Bulgarians, Greeks, Serbs, Montenegrins, Swiss, Mexicans. We gave them medical for a dollar a month if they made more than forty dollars a month in pay. If they made less, it was fifty cents. Down in the tunnels it hit a hundred and thirty degrees in summer. These guys didn't just work. They set records.

The Board of Engineers estimated we could build about eight feet of tunnel per day—that's four feet a day at each end. We averaged twenty-two feet. At one point they said it would take five years to finish up the last tunnels and get the water to L.A. We came in_ *twenty months* ahead of that schedule. And we killed a lot less people than they did constructing the New York aqueduct, which was built about the same time. They killed a man a week. We killed less than one a month. One was permanently injured. Accidents of a trivial nature totaled one thousand two hundred and eighty-two."

Choat turned and looked at Cedros as if predicting which category he'd fall into.

"It's humbling," said Cedros.

"You know what the DWP's William Mulholland said at the dedication ceremony on November fifth, 1913? I quote: 'This rude platform is an altar, and on it we are here consecrating this water supply and dedicating the aqueduct to you and your children and your children's children for all time.' I think that's beautiful. It rivals the Gettysburg Address, in my opinion."

Choat got out, used a key to open a gate, and Cedros drove the Lincoln through. Choat stood by Aqueduct One holding the gate open and Cedros saw that his head was not nearly as high as the pipe containing the river— it looked close to seven feet tall, not including the short powerful legs on which it was raised. Cedros smiled to himself: the big barrel of Choat's gut and chest mimicked the curved wall of the pipe behind him, and the bulging calves that supported the man looked something like the staunch legs that held up the aqueduct.

No wonder he loves the damned thing so much, thought Cedros—it looks like his own father, or the child he never had.

As Choat opened the passenger door he gave Cedros the only genuine smile that Cedros had ever seen on the man. Even obscured by cigar and mustache, it was an unmistakable expression of a moment's happiness that was gone by the time he sat and slammed the door.

Down the dirt road he drove, gravel popping under the carriage like butter in a pan and dust rising behind. The sun was a simple orange ball high in the west but already lowering toward the sharp tips of the Sierra Nevada.

They trundled down the road in silence for nearly half an hour, following the great pale green pipe.

Finally the pipe was replaced by the river itself and Choat told Cedros to pull over.

Cedros cut the engine and got out. He crunched across the desert and looked down to see the Owens River as it blasted into a wide chute, dropped a few feet in elevation into a narrower chute, then charged in a swirling riot against a grate that looked like the bars of a prison cell before being devoured by the huge intake pipe.

It was not so much loud as vibrational, a subwoofing thrum that he felt in his nerves.

"Where the river meets man," said Choat.

"Impressive."

"More than impressive. Eight decades of growth for the greatest city on Earth began right exactly here. Movies, television, musical recording, aerospace, the Dodgers, the Lakers, the Philharmonic, the '84 Olympics—none of them would have happened in Los Angeles without this pipe. History was created by it. The future begins with it. View it. Not many people have."

Cedros obediently looked down into the rush of water. The river, where it left the earth for concrete, was almost black and it burst into a white boil of protest as it left its bed to be channeled down into the first chute. Then, gathering deeper, it dropped again into the smaller channel and burst into wild, wobbling, glassy shards that slammed against the steel grate and fled down. Cedros wondered how many cubic feet per second were charging through that pipe. He felt the vibrations through the soles of his shoes.

An elevated platform straddled the second intake chute, accessible by metal stairs on either side of the water. The platform had railings to keep anyone from falling to what would be certain death in the water below.

"Let's go up," said Choat. "Get a good look at her. You first."

Cedros looked at his boss. "Okay."

He led the way up the eight steps. Through the hum of water he couldn't hear his shoes hitting the stairs, or tell if the gate leading to the platform creaked when he swung it forward and stepped onto the iron-mesh deck. The deck was rusted smooth in the way that only a desert can rust metal.

Cedros walked to the edge of the platform and looked into the swirl. He held on to the railing. He could feel the power of the water all the way up here, miles away from the place where it would formally create power by turning the gorge turbines. Here, the river's power was invisible—it came off the raging surface as a kind of force field, like when the same polarities of two powerful magnets push stubbornly against each other. Like if you tossed a quarter into this river, thought Cedros, it would float above the water on an impenetrable mattress of pure energy.

Choat moved up close to him. Cedros noted his burly hands on the railing. Cedros had never known that Choat's calves were three times the size of his own. He thought of Ampostela.

"Right here it's only seven hundred cubic feet per second," yelled Choat. His voice seemed unnaturally loud and strong, booming out of him like something amplified. "October, always low. By May, June—one thousand cfs. That's why we built the power plant and the Pleasant Valley Reservoir. So we can break this reckless mule of a river, make it work for us."

"I can feel the power coming off it."

"I want you to burn down Frankie Hatfield's barn with all her rainmaking stuff in it," ordered Choat. "Right to the ground. Totally *hasta la vista*. That will be my good-bye to Miss Hatfield. Do it at night. Use a ton of gas or lighter fluid. Do it quickly and get out fast. Then move up here and do your job. Bone your wife and raise your brats. You'll be free."

Cedros looked down at Choat's hands on the railing. He thought of looking down on Ampostela's as he waited for the man to draw his gun. He realized that he was in almost as much danger here but he had a choice. Choat was giving him a chance to earn his life whereas Ampostela had valued it at less than nothing.

Cedros looked up at the director. Through the wavering cigar smoke, Choat's clear gray eyes and forward-tilted head told a clear and believable story: *My God, my God. John lost his footing on the platform and the intake chute took him.* Cedros saw himself fastened by the river to the grate like a stain on a wall, permanent and unmoving. They'd have to dam the river upstream just to scrape him off.

"Every time I do something for you I have to do something else worse to cover it up," he said.

"Tavarez made fools of us. We're done with him. The fire in the barn ends our concern with the rain bitch. You and I go our separate ways. We bear our secrets as gentlemen do. We'll be judged by God and history, not the changing laws of a squeamish democracy. It's time for you to demonstrate ultimate spine."

"Okay."

"Good. Good, John."

They stood for a moment and watched the river rage in the chute.

"I love this place," said Choat. "Some of the happiest years of my life were spent here. I loved being a ditch rider. But Joan hated the cold and much prefers the Madison Club to the Gorge Transmission Line. A happy wife is a clear conscience."

"It's special up here. I want to learn how to ride a horse and fish."

"The simple dreams of a simple man. I hear that cocktail shaker all the way back in Bishop, don't you?"

"Can we drive by the cabin in the gorge?"

"We can do whatever the hell we want, John. I thought you knew that by now."

WHEN HE GOT back to the motel, Marianna, already in her little black dinner dress and black heels, pulled the curtains and took John into the spacious bathroom where she untaped the recorder from the small of her husband's back. They played the conversation on the platform and Cedros was relieved to hear Choat intoning over the deep groan of the captured river. His voice sounded distant, threatened by chaos, but clear.

I want you to burn down...

Marianna then wound up the tiny microphone wire that had ridden up his chest and into his shirt pocket. She put everything into the padded FedEx envelope with the PI's Birch Security Solutions address and account number on the air bill.

She turned and kissed him hard and deep. He was surprised but in a good way.

Marianna peeked from the bathroom to see Tony still watching TV then quietly locked the door and faced the counter. She flicked off the heels and hiked the black dress to present herself to her husband, leaning forward on the counter with one hand, the other supporting the bulge of Cathy. Marianna pleasurably watched in the mirror as her husband did his thing. They smiled at each other though each was actually looking straight ahead. Then John's smile went crooked and his eyes fogged up like a beer mug brought from the freezer. The whole thing was over in less than a minute, as she knew it would be. He was never much for endurance when he was terrified, which he had been a lot lately. Get him relaxed, though, and the little bantam could go forever. He was the most generous, thoughtful, and deliciously nasty lover she'd ever had.

A moment later Cedros put on a jacket over his bare trunk, drew open the curtains, cracked a beer, and strode outside. The October trees were a blast of red and orange in the ice-colored sky. The Sierra Nevada Mountains loomed beyond him, snow-dusted and sharp. He smoked a cigarette, which he was doing more frequently the last two weeks. He sucked down the warm smoke and celebrated the fact that he had not only cheated death one more time, but made arrangements so that he would never have to do it again. Plus he'd gotten a nerve-tingling quickie from which his heart was still pounding. He pictured her in the mirror.

He watched the little fish dart away from him in the creek and he engaged Pat and Joan Choat in conversation on their patio as they power-drank cocktails. He glanced back into his room to see Tony smiling at the TV and Marianna with her purse slung over a shoulder, leaving to take the package to the front desk for one-day delivery to Birch Security Solutions.

32

That night Brad Lunce let Tavarez into the library and uncuffed his wrists.

"I heard they're making room for you in the X."

"How good is your information?" asked Tavarez.

"It comes down from the guys who know. I heard there's a senator behind it."

"State or U.S.?"

"They're the same, right?"

"What else did you hear?"

"Gyle was for it. He had to be. He's the warden."

"I've been a model prisoner."

"Except for shit like this."

"Nobody knows, do they, Brad?"

"Not about this they don't. We ain't telling. Me and Post have families. We just need a little help."

Tavarez studied Lunce's unintelligent blue eyes for evidence of betrayal. One word of this and he'd get the X, whether Frankie the weather lady lived or died. He saw nothing in Lunce aside from the usual hostility, resentment, and untargeted meanness.

"You got less than an hour, dude. Enjoy your porn."

Over the next fifteen minutes Tavarez got terrible news from almost every part of the country, every area of his life.

He read the messages—some in code and some not—his eyes hardly moving from the words, his breath slow and shallow, his heart thumping with the frustration of the captive.

Ruben—his old road dog from the Delhi F Troop—had exhausted his last appeal and would now face the spike at the Q. Tavarez thought of Ruben's rough voice and hearty laugh, his unquenchable lust for Darla, whom he had impregnated at age thirteen and married three years later after dropping out of Santa Ana Valley High School. It seemed like just a few months ago, not twenty-two years. Tavarez calculated that he hadn't seen Ruben face-to-face in almost fifteen years. Now he never would.

His mother and father were "okay" according to the men he had assigned to watch over them. Reina cooked constantly, then gave her creations to neighbors, friends, and relatives. She actually socialized very little. Rolando spent most of his time in the garage in a white Naugahyde recliner, watching TV and reading boxing magazines. They missed Mike, and remained angry at his ex-wife, Miriam, for cutting off their visits to the grandchildren. Tavarez's heart beat with pure fury at the mention of Miriam, then with palpable love at the mention of his children.

His Laguna sources told him that Miriam was selling the Laguna home. She was asking $9 million and likely to get it. She was still seeing a Miami-based immigration lawyer and it appeared that she would be relocating herself and her children and her parents to Florida. He was divorcing. She recently had cosmetic surgery on her legs and lips.

His ten-year-old son, John, had been diagnosed with diabetes. Tavarez's heart plummeted as he thought of John's future: daily injections, ill health, impotence, blindness. What had the little boy done to deserve this? Does God never tire of His own ceaseless cruelties?

His second son, four-year-old Peter, had been spending long hours in day care and with nannies, while Miriam shopped and traveled with the lawyer. He was morose.

Isabelle, eight and a half, was making money on the Internet, selling the high-end clothing and electronic discards of her Laguna Beach friends. Her grades were dismal and she called her teachers terrible things in both English and Spanish. Expulsion seemed imminent.

Jennifer had broken her leg at a tae kwon do tournament in Las Vegas.

Tavarez scanned the downloaded e-mails for a note from Isabelle—she was the only one of his children who'd shown the guile and desire to contact him through one of his Laguna men—but she had not written this week. Or the last six weeks, for that matter. Busy making a profit, thought Tavarez. First things first.

Jaime in Modesto had been killed in a shotgun blast Saturday night. La Nuestra Familia, no doubt.

God rest his soul, Tavarez thought. He was a good man—faithful and strong and brave. Mike felt a little more of his own soul crumble, as it always did when one of his brothers or sisters died from violence. Sometimes he believed that the fallen part of his soul grew back strong like scar tissue; sometimes he thought it didn't grow back at all and his soul had been shrunk by the scores of murders that had become as much a part of his life as births, marriages, baptisms, and *quinceaneros*.

Tavarez sighed, opened another e-mail, and learned that in Dallas the Salvadoran gang Mara Salvatrucha had killed two more La Eme soldiers. He did not know them. But he did know that Mara Salvatrucha had the most and the best guns, because of the long United States involvement that had left El Salvador awash in weaponry. He also knew that they loved the rustic pleasures of torture, sodomy, and *machetes*. And there were ten thousand of them in the United States alone, with dozens more flooding up through the borders and recycling through deportation every month. Mara Salvatrucha was smart, thought Tavarez, because they opened their ranks to the thousands of Central and South American criminals that La Eme refused to allow into their own Mexican-American ranks. MS was a pestilence in southern Mexico, of all places. The La Eme soldiers in Dallas were gunned down by a vast mongrel army using weapons they could never afford themselves.

Vermin, thought Tavarez. He bit his lip and closed his eyes in a moment of silence for Jaime and the dead men in Dallas. And he promised to wipe La Nuestra Familia and Mara Salvatrucha off the face of the earth.

Tavarez's next message told him that Ernest in Arizona State Prison had died Monday in his sleep of apparently natural causes. This was doubly disastrous, because not only was Ernest a good man but his ruthless power along the Arizona-Mexico border had been creating tremendous business for La Eme. Now, who would step into Ernest's place? How was he, El Jefe, going to replace a man who had been building his strength along that border for ten long, bloody, profit-crazy years?

He said a prayer for Ernest too.

Then he learned that the Los Angeles green-light gangs—those refusing to pay taxes on drug distribution in the barrios—had come together and formally broken all ties with La Eme. In doing so, they had turned themselves from a scattered legion of fearless adolescents into an organization that Tavarez knew would, in the long run, do more damage to La Eme than LNS, Mara Salvatrucha, and all the death rows of the American prison system combined. They were the future. They were undoing everything he had done. They were loyal to nothing but profit. Someday they would piss on his grave, then hop into their BMWs and speed away. They would hear the *corridos* and explode with laughter.

He learned from one of his Riverside compadres that Ariel Lejas was in stable condition with a broken jaw and an ankle crushed by the rear tire of the PI's new yellow pickup truck. Six of his teeth had been knocked out. He was reported to be in very good spirits and was offering to kill the woman and the PI for free, though he would have to get out of jail first.

Then, more bad news from Los Angeles: Marcus Ampostela had been found in the San Gabriel River, shot seven times. And no word that he had done his job on John Cedros. Were those two facts connected? Tavarez smiled to himself: facts are always connected.

Tavarez looked over at Lunce, who was staring at him drowsily. It never ceased to amaze him that fools like Lunce managed to advance in the system, and what that revealed about the system.

Tavarez sat back and closed his eyes again for a moment. A great silence spread throughout his body. He listened to the blood surging in his eardrums and to the quiet tap where the heartbeat in his chest met his orange prison suit. He listened to the voices of Ruben and Jaime and Ernest and even Miriam. He heard the voices of his children. He pictured Ofelia, her young fingers underscoring the Nahuatl text, her young eyes on his face. He saw Hallie, so free and careless and willing. And Matt, so strong and righteous and preferred.

The silence became a murmur and the murmur became a buzz and the buzz became a roar and the roar became louder and louder. He felt his blood surging faster and his heart beating harder against his prison suit and he understood that the time had come.

Finally.

It had really come. He knew it. From heart to toe, he was sure.

And, as if it were a sign from God, even his last bit of necessary hardware had arrived just days ago, pushed deep into the tight pages of a thick new paperback, delivered by one of his lawyers, undetected by eye and X-ray.

As a miracle, it would do.

He opened his eyes.

He tapped out his e-mails in the Nahuatl code—condolences regarding Jaime and Ernest—but also brief declarations that he would be handling the various other matters personally and very soon. Until then, he asked for patience from Dallas and Los Angeles and along the Arizona border. He named interim replacements for Jaime and Ernest and ordered allegiance to them and respect for their commands. He ordered one of Ampostela's men, Ricky "Dogs," to find out what he could from John Cedros, then put him down. He made sure that Ariel Lejas's family in Riverside received his share of recently earned money to help pay for his defense. He ordered Lejas to leave the PI alone for now, even though Lejas was in the med wing of San Diego County jail. He asked that his salutations and thanks also be passed along to Lejas. As Tavarez typed the code he had the thought that Stromsoe was not only responsible for Lejas but had possibly helped Cedros with Ampostela. What kind of deal might Stromsoe offer a man like Cedros—a small fish, unconnected and caught in the middle of things—in return for talking about his prison visit? Stromsoe, he thought: the curse of a lifetime, but soon to be lifted.

Then Tavarez ordered his Redding and Crescent City people to make the arrangements for his Sunday family visit. Sundays were slightly relaxed. Sundays were slightly festive. Sundays were chapel privileges and a slightly upgraded menu. Sundays, Tavarez knew, were nights that Cartwright always worked. He made a few additional requests regarding that visit, but nothing that couldn't be easily accomplished. It shouldn't be hard to bring bolt cutters instead of a woman.

33

The next evening Stromsoe sat outside Frankie's office at Fox News while she collected weather data and worked up her charts and tables for the night's forecasts. Through the window he watched her download the National Weather Service five-hundredmillibar surface maps and consult the Doppler radar, giving them her usual careful scrutiny.

She looked up at him and mouthed one word: *rain*.

He liked the hustle bustle of the news studio, the good-humored hurry of the people, the smokers' conclaves in the parking lot, the pronounced facial changes of the newscasters when they went on and off camera.

It was Friday, and the fourth day in a row that he had driven Frankie to work, sat outside her office, loitered about the various locations as she broadcast her stories, then driven her home and slept with her. Since Tavarez's promise of safety, Stromsoe had watched her even more closely than before. He watched her at work and at home, during errands, at the barn. At times it felt intrusive. But he knew Mike and he knew that Frankie was many miles from safe. At least that was what he had to believe. He enjoyed being around her, couldn't hide it and didn't try.

The pretty young receptionist called him "Mr. Stormso" and he could feel her eyes inquiringly upon him as he signed the visitors' log each day. The misnomer made him think of the *corrido* in which he played the villain, the evil swine Matt Storm. Three different people had taken him aside to let him know how "happy," "carefree," and "together" Frankie had been lately, plainly implying it had something to do with him. Her producer, Darren, had asked to see his gun. The production staff fetched him coffee for a day, then offered him lunchroom privileges. They told him to always make a new pot if he poured the last cup, and to make it strong. They told him that Janice in makeup was the best coffeemaker, so if he wasn't confident, get her to do it. Stromsoe felt large and out of place but accepted for what he was.

Frankie filed her first weather story of the day—just a more-to-come-later "teaser"—from outside the

Natural History Museum in Balboa Park. The afternoon was chilly with a curt breeze off the Pacific and a pale gray sky above. She wore a tweedy trouser-sweater-and-jacket ensemble, vaguely English, which she had purchased by catalog and received two days ago in the mail. Stromsoe thought that all she needed was a bird gun and a dog to be ready for the hunt.

"Rain Sunday, or will it be Monday? I'm Frankie Hatfield in Balboa Park and I'll have the storm schedule just a little later, right here on Fox."

A few minutes later she delivered her first forecast story of the evening, which was aired live. She predicted rain by late Sunday night, with showers continuing into late Monday morning, followed by a clear, cool, blustery afternoon and evening.

"The National Weather Service is calling for up to one inch of rain for the city of San Diego, coast and valleys, but up to two inches in the local mountains. So it looks like our wet October is about to continue. Stay tuned and stay dry. Or go out and get wet. Either way works for me. I'm Frankie Hatfield, Fox News, and I'll be back from the Gaslamp in less than half an hour."

As Stromsoe drove her to the Gaslamp Quarter downtown, Frankie confessed that she wrote and broadcast only "about three hundred words a night." Looking out the window, she told him that this number equaled approximately thirty Chinese cookie fortunes or "ten long-winded occasional cards." She got a calculator from her purse, tapped away. A moment later she announced that she was paid "about three dollars and fifty cents a word—even for 'a' and 'the.' Am I overpaid?"

"You sign autographs and endorse the paychecks too. That's two more words, per."

"I make a lot of dough for writing fifteen hundred words a week. But I tithe very generously to my Fallbrook church though I almost never attend."

"That's called covering your bets."

"No, no. I believe in Him. I believe in all that. Truly. I just hate standing up in a church and saying, hi, I'm Frankie, then shaking hands with strangers. I didn't go to church to see *them*, did I? Girls need privacy. Tall ones need extra. I wish there were still drive-in churches. I'd gas up the Mustang and go, never roll down the window except to get the speaker box in and out. Am I antisocial?"

"Overpaid and antisocial."

"I knew it."

She seemed to dwell on this. "I need two of me. One can broadcast and go to church, the other can stay in bed with you until noon every day, then collect the rivers of the world and work on the rainmaking formula."

"I wouldn't get much done," he said. "If you didn't let me out of bed until noon."

"I know. You've got bad men to catch and people to protect."

Stromsoe guided his truck down Fourth, following the Fox News van into a small parking lot.

"Matt, when you don't work for me anymore, could you live with me anyway? You could take San Diego jobs. There's plenty of bad guys for you to fight. I've got way too many acres for one person and the dogs like you."

"I haven't thought about it."

"I've felt your heart beating next to mine, so I know damned well you've thought about it."

Stromsoe hated this conversation as any man would, even one uncomplicatedly in love. "You're right. I don't know, Frankie. That's too far ahead."

"Bah, humbug, dude. I just asked you to move in with me."

"Let's get through this first."

"I was checking my status with you too."

"Your status with me is off the charts, Frankie."

"Time will tell if that's true."

Stromsoe turned off the engine and looked at her. "You recently lapsed virgins can be difficult."

"I could get pissed off at that."

"I figured you might laugh instead."

She smiled and blushed magnificently.

STROMSOE FLEW THEM to San Francisco later that night, a surprise for which he had only somewhat prepared her.

He thought that a day in a city beyond the immediate reach of Mike Tavarez would be good for Frankie and good for himself. He was tired of guarding and thought she must be tired of being guarded.

Frankie played along with the surprise, pretending to relish the small mysteries of a one-day escape—what city? Warm or cool? Is there a river? When did you think of this? You're a crafty little Mr. Man, aren't you?—until he realized she wasn't pretending. She was happy and playful and in his eyes unconditionally beautiful.

They stayed at the Monaco and ate expansively at the Washington Square Bar and Grill, which was recommended by the concierge. Their room was small and furnished with brightly striped wallpaper, a canopied and lushly pillowed bed, and brass accents and knick-knacks. It was dizzyingly erotic and Frankie didn't pull the "Shhhh…" sign off the outside of their door until noon.

While she showered Stromsoe downloaded to his laptop the audio of Choat and Cedros's conversation up on the Owens River, forwarded by Dan Birch. He took it down to the lobby and sat by the fire and listened to it twice. Good stuff. *I want you to burn down Frankie Hatfield's barn with all her rainmaking stuff in it.* He called Choat's home number—another trophy ferreted out by Birch Security Solutions—and had a brief conversation with the man.

Then he and Frankie took a taxi to Fisherman's Wharf for lunch. Stromsoe was impressed by how much a tall, well-loved woman could eat. They drank Mendocino Zinfandel with the meal and Stromsoe gradually felt at one with the padding of the booth. He felt the desire to drink more but not to oblivion—nothing at all like he'd felt in Miami. His pinned bones hurt slightly in the San Francisco chill, and he was aware of places where nails had been removed, and his legs, in spite of the running he'd done since Miami, ached mightily in unusual places.

Thirty-eight years old and counting, he thought.

You are what you are.

Hi, Billy. Hi, Hal. I love you. I will always love you.

"You look relaxed," she said.

"I could sit here for a week. Like a half-crocked Zen Buddhist."

"Let's. I'm not afraid to be lazy."

She signaled the waiter for another bottle.

That night they had dinner at the restaurant attached to the hotel. Frankie wore a dress that she bought after lunch, a backless black velvet number with a criminally modest neckline above which a string of pearls moved in the candlelight. Stromsoe wore the same new suit he'd worn to Dan Birch's office three weeks ago to be interviewed for a job involving a weather lady, remarking to himself on the great good fortune it had brought him.

After dinner they walked the busy streets around the Monaco. Stromsoe, a product of ordered suburbs, and Frankie, who grew up in languid Fallbrook, liked the way that contradictory things in downtown San Francisco were packed in together—the theaters right there with the massage parlors, the antiquarian bookstore next to the adult arcade, the high-end restaurants and the hole-in-the-wall tobacco and newsstands. They watched as a tide of released theater patrons flooded the bums on the sidewalk, overcoats and scarves overwhelming the knit caps and cardboard signs. The war on poverty, Frankie remarked. The traffic lurched past them in a frantic parade and the woofers pounded from the youngsters' cars and the shrieks of the bellmen's whistles echoed up and down the streets. The city seemed hell-bent, self-important, and wonderful.

They stopped at the Redwood Room for dessert and liqueur. The menu said that the entire room—the bar, floor, walls, ceiling, and columns—had been constructed from the wood of a single redwood tree. Frankie was muttering something against loggers when she read that the tree was actually found in a river, toppled by a ferocious Northern California storm.

"See?" she said. "Behind every good thing there's a river."

"Next time we'll go to a river you haven't captured," said Stromsoe.

"I've never seen the San Joaquin up by Mammoth."

"Neither have I."

"I love you, Stromsoe."

"I love you, Frankie."

"I can't ever be Hallie and Billy."

"I know."

"But maybe...who knows?"

He brushed a dark curl from her forehead. "Yeah. Who really does know?"

34

The sky was bowed with clouds when their jet touched down in San Diego on Sunday, Halloween morning. Frankie had spent most of the hour flight craning her neck at the starboard window to watch the storm front lumbering in from the northwest.

"It's big," she said. "It's awesome."

Stromsoe saw the excitement in her face. She photographed the clouds with the same tiny camera she'd used to shoot John Cedros while he shot her.

When she was finished with the camera Stromsoe scrolled back through the images of Cedros. He was pleased that the young man had shown the courage to wear the wire on Choat. Stromsoe hadn't thought that Choat would be foolish enough to burn down someone's property, but he'd also seen the disregard for consequences in his eyes just before Choat had slugged him in the face. This kind of self-granted privilege was a quality shared by nearly every psychopath and violent felon that Stromsoe had ever met, and by several men he knew who were very powerful and had never done one hour in a jail.

They met Ted at the barn. He wore a twelve-gauge shotgun over his shoulder in a sling improvised from leather belts and plastic ties. At his side was a western holster with a prodigious revolver in it. The holster tip was tied to his thigh like a gunfighter's.

"You kinda scare me," said Frankie.

"I know what I'm doing."

She hugged him, the shotgun protruding crosswise between them. "Ted, you're a true sweetheart," Frankie said.

"They can't fool me twice."

Stromsoe said nothing but in all his years of law enforcement he had never seen anything good happen to a civilian carrying two guns.

He heated cans of stew while Frankie and Ted— shotgun unslung and propped by the door—huddled over surface maps and the real-time weather-station feed coming in from the San Margarita Reserve. NOAA radio babbled on in a stream of static out of San Diego, the meteorologist calling Lindbergh Field *Line*bergh

Field while the Weather Channel played silently from a TV atop one of the refrigerators in which Frankie stored her secret potions.

AN HOUR LATER they set off in Ted's pickup truck, Ace and Sadie whining with excitement and a sprinkle of rain hatching the scents of sagebrush and wild buckwheat from the hillsides around them. Stromsoe noted that they now carried twelve five-gallon canisters rather than the usual eight. Ted had installed a gun rack against the rear cab window which now cradled the shotgun and its cobbled strap. Frankie gripped Stromsoe's knee with a strong hand.

"It's going to take," she said. "It's going to take this time."

"Did you tighten up the suspension ratios?" asked Ted.

"Yes," said Frankie. "But that's all I can say."

"That's all I need to know," said Ted.

At tower one Stromsoe helped Ted get the three heavy canisters onto the platform so that Frankie could activate the solutions. The copper-chlorine smell was clear but not overly strong. This time, it was Stromsoe who climbed the towers and hauled up the containers. Ted wanted both feet on the ground, he said, and Stromsoe noted with respect that Ted never stopped looking around, scanning the bushes and the dirt roads and the hillsides for any sign of Mike Tavarez's hired killers. Stromsoe's .380 was on his waist, secured by the Clipdraw, exactly where it had been nearly every waking moment for the last three weeks.

Then Stromsoe climbed down and Frankie climbed up. He handed her the heavy red toolbox, which clunked to the platform with a rattle of steel.

"I think the world of you, you big lug," said Frankie. "But you know the drill."

Stromsoe walked nearly to the truck and turned his back while Frankie tended her formula. He heard the clicking sound of a lighter, then the soft ignition of propane. Ted stood guard on the road, the shotgun sling resting over his shoulder.

As before, Stromsoe heard the sound of liquid hitting liquid then the banging of a hard object side to side inside the canisters as she stirred the brew. The copper-chlorine smell weakened.

But unlike before, Stromsoe not quite accidentally wandered to a position that framed Frankie perfectly in the side mirror of Ted's truck. The second time in a week, he thought, that a side mirror had come in more than handy.

So he watched her stir and add small amounts of something from a shiny chrome can that she kept in the red toolbox. She measured the liquid in a standard kitchen measuring cup, and made some kind of entry with a stylus on a small silver keypad. Then she stirred again. After working on a thick, black rubber glove, she then lowered a small object into the canister and brought it back out. The object looked like the chlorine tester that his neighbor used on his swimming pool back in Santa Ana when he was a kid. He watched Frankie add something from a dropper, then shake the tester, then bring it up to her face for a reading.

She poured more liquid from the chrome can into the measuring cup, poured a little bit back out, held the cup at eye level, then emptied it into the canister.

The blue light almost instantly appeared above the top of the big can. It cast a blue tint on her face as she put on the glove again and stirred. Wisps of pale blue gas began to rise and the altered smell, ethereal and indescribable, came to Stromsoe's nose in a moment. He watched Frankie watch the smoke, the blue light playing off her throat, her head back and her face to the sky as if to measure its rate of climb.

"Three canisters per tower now?" Stromsoe called back over his shoulder.

"Lucky number," said Frankie. "We're going to build another tower starting next week. If we want consistent results we need to cover some sky."

"I can't ID that smell," he said.

"No one can. This stuff hasn't been named yet."

BY FOUR O'CLOCK they'd finished up at tower four and by five-thirty the rain was falling harder. They sat in the back of the pickup and passed around Ted's mostly gone bottle of Scoresby. Frankie wore the old fedora, which Stromsoe had seen her spraying with a waterproofer before setting out, and now the water ran in undeterred streams off the brim of it and bounced off her legs in silver comets.

Stromsoe heard and felt the rain accelerate, something like the sound of a jet revving, followed by an ambient heaviness as the volume of water increased until it was roaring against the truck and churning up the ground around them in multitudes of small explosions.

Though outfitted in their tailored raincoats, the dogs looked woefully at Frankie and tried to bend their heads away from the direction of the onslaught but it was coming down almost straight.

Ted pulled at his slicker, trying to get it to stay in place over his holster and revolver. He wore a waxed canvas cowboy hat with a tightly rolled brim that funneled the runoff wherever he was looking, in this case at the gun. He gave up on the slicker and squinted up the road in the direction they had come.

"Take a walk with me, Stromsoe," said Frankie. "Pardon us just a minute, Ted. We're okay."

Frankie splashed out of the truck bed. The dogs followed without enthusiasm. Frankie led the way down the road then up a hillock from the top of which they could see all the way back down the valley to the barn. The air was gray around them and gray above, no difference in shade whatsoever. We are the rain cloud, she said. Then she took off her hat and faced the pouring sky. Stromsoe did too. He closed his eyes and thought a prayer for Hallie and Billy and Frankie as he listened to the rain pounding his face and shoulders and he also heard the higher-pitched slapping sound it made on the dogs' modified plastic ponchos. He opened his eyes to see Ted in the distance not quite looking on, shotgun in hand and the rain jetting off his hat.

"We should get back," he said, watching her eyes open and come back into focus.

"I know."

They trudged back with Ted and decided to sit in the truck a little longer but they only had time to pass the bottle once when the rain shifted into an even higher gear and the water seemed to be solid around them.

"Jeezy peezy," said Frankie.

They climbed into the cab and set out. The truck tires sank in the mud, so Ted put it in four-wheel and still had to rock it out. It jumped free and the back end came around and the dogs slid across the bed, paws out, through the lake of water and the red toolbox slammed the bed wall. The wipers hacked rapidly back and forth, providing snippets of visibility.

"Eee-haw," said Ted.

"Take 'er easy, cowboy," said Frankie.

Ted tried to straighten the truck but the angle was too sharp and the tires dug in again. Stromsoe could feel the vehicle lower. He jumped back with the dogs to improve the weight distribution but the tires sank deeper. He got Frankie to help him push on the tailgate, the two of them working side by side and away from the spinning tires, but the mud still blasted into them while they grunted and heaved and the truck finally climbed out. They clambered back into the cab looking like minstrels in blackface. Halfway to the barn they watched a section of earth detach from an adjacent slope and, sagebrush and lemonade-berry bush and boulders still in place, slide to a stop on the road in front of them. It was four feet high.

"Shit, guys," said Ted.

"Use the brush off to the right," said Stromsoe.

But from the dead stop the tires dug into the mud again, and again Stromsoe and Frankie got out and pushed while the truck threw mud back at them. Then, without warning, Ted put the truck into reverse and Stromsoe pulled Frankie out of the way just a second before the truck leaped backward out of the rut and landed left tire then right tire, hard, which launched the dogs in a poncho-wrapped blur. They hit with yipes. Ted emerged from the cab cussing and apologizing.

Stromsoe drove from there, using the roadside brush for lift and keeping the truck way down in first gear. He ground up a rise, made the crest, then looked down at a low spot in the road that was nothing but a red muddy river now, frothing with gravel and plants and sticks.

He could make out the barn by then, a quarter mile out, blurred to a basic barnlike shape by the downpour.

"Let's just walk it," said Ted. "Leave the truck here on high ground."

"The flash flood is too strong," said Stromsoe.

"I agree," said Frankie.

"We got to get somewhere," said Ted.

"This is it," said Stromsoe.

"No guts, no sausage," said Ted. "That barn is warm and dry."

"Don't you even think of wading that river," said Frankie. "When the rain lets up we can cross. These things end as fast as they start."

"I lived in Tucson for five years," said Ted, seemingly to himself.

Stromsoe put the truck in park, set the brake, and turned the key so the engine went off but the wipers and defroster were still on. The barn blipped into his vision twice per second. Despite the defroster the windshield fogged up, so he wiped it with his hand. They managed to get the dogs into the cab.

"The barn sits near the riverbed," said Frankie. "It's a low spot, and flat."

"Naw," said Ted. "You can't fill the San Luis Rey that fast."

"Look," she said. "There's already standing water."

Impossibly the rain came harder. The water jumped a foot into the air when it hit the truck hood in front of them but Stromsoe couldn't make out a single drop—it was a solid body of water, like something poured from a gigantic bucket. It was deafening.

"Whoa," said Ted.

"Man," said Frankie.

"Maybe should have stayed with two buckets per tower," said Stromsoe.

"Maybe," she said.

In brief flashes of visibility Stromsoe saw the water rising around the barn. One minute it looked four inches deep at the door. A minute later it was a third of the way up to the lock.

Ace shook off and the cab filled with wet dog mist. Sadie shook off next. Stromsoe used his fist to clear the windshield again.

Then he saw the barn quiver, as if hit by a bullet. Then the roof buckled and some of the side boards splintered outward. The old building looked as if it were trying to shrug something off. Suddenly it lit up inside as if a single large orange bulb had been turned on.

"No," said Frankie.

Stromsoe saw what happened next in staggered images separated by the wiper: a dull *whuuumph*, a burst of black lumber, the roof gone, the flaming guts inside, an orange inferno, a shower of black rubble and books and paper and furniture and a TV falling back to earth, the fire pausing as the rain cascaded down, the fire struggling, the fire low, the fire out except from the chemical containers littered about like wounded dragons belching flames and smoke against the rain.

The dogs looked out the window matter-of-factly.

"My things," said Frankie in a soft voice. She sounded far away. "Charley's things."

They watched in silence for a while as the chemicals burned and the rain pounded out the last of the embers in the roofless barn. The explosion had brought waves to the standing water, chopping the surface into little peaks that gradually wobbled back to raindrop-riddled flatness. It seemed to be boiling around the blackened sofa and the facedown TV.

HALF AN HOUR later the rain stopped. Sunlight powered through big cracks in the clouds and they could see the torrents of runoff coming down the gulleys and washes to join up with the swollen San Luis Rey on its way to the ocean.

"That had to be five inches," said Frankie. "I wonder what everybody else got."

"I hope there is an everybody else," said Ted.

"We can sit or walk," said Stromsoe. "But we won't be driving this thing for a while."

They couldn't get close enough to the barn to go through the remains. The water was two feet deep and fast, and gave no sign of abating soon. Frankie stood knee-deep in it, shooting pictures, feet spread for balance as the current shoved against her. She fished a book from the flood, and what looked to Stromsoe like an old album of weather maps. She shook her head and waded unsteadily back to him.

They hiked across the hills, staying to the brushy sides and stable tops, to a dirt road that was just barely passable on foot. Freed from the slickers to keep them dry, the dogs cavorted and rolled in the mud. They made Gopher Canyon Road. A ranch hand in an old red-and-white Chevy pickup truck gave them a ride to Frankie's house. He spoke no English but gave them a hearty smile and wave as he drove away.

Stromsoe saw the tears running down Frankie's cheeks as she dug the keys from her bag.

"It's gone," she said. "Everything he did. Everything I improved on."

"You're not."

She nodded without looking at him, then walked to her front door.

35

At seven that evening Stromsoe waited in the hushed immensity of the Our Lady of the Angels Cathedral in Los Angeles. An ocean of pews stretched out before him toward the distant altar and the small red crucifix.

Choat sat down behind him. He wore a black raincoat over a gray suit, a white shirt with a round collar and pin, a wine-colored necktie.

"Feel safer with God nearby?" he asked.

"Less chance you'll punch me," said Stromsoe. "Let's walk."

"Why the hugger-mugger?"

"You'll see."

Stromsoe led the way down the ambulatory and back out the monumental bronze doors. Outside the air was cold and the wind was steady from the west. They entered the cloister garden, where the storm had pounded the flowers flat and raindrops still clung to the tree leaves.

Stromsoe handed Choat four pictures he'd printed from Frankie's little digital camera, all of the incinerated barn.

Choat's face went bright red.

"What's this to me?" Choat asked. "It's nothing."

"That's not what your face says. You know what it is. It's Frankie's barn."

"I don't care about her barn."

"You used to. Listen to this."

He pulled the player out of his pocket and turned the volume up plenty high.

I want you to burn down Frankie Hatfield's barn with all her rainmaking stuff in it…

Stromsoe watched the doubt, the acceptance, then the anger register on Choat's big scarred face.

"Cedros," muttered Choat. "I don't get it. He tapes me like the little f—pardon me—*fellow* he is, then does the deed anyway?"

"He got tired of being your bad guy, so he wore the wire. He never touched the barn. Mother Nature did the job. But your solicitation stands. Your bosses might like to hear it. The D.A. might. There are some media people who'd love to hear you. I've got ten discs like that one, just waiting to go to loving homes."

They descended the grand staircase toward the lower plaza. Above them the stars blinked deep in the black sky.

"What do you want?" asked Choat.

"No more contact with Frankie. You so much as think her name and I'll ruin you. And no more contact with Cedros either."

They stood on the vast lower plaza, the cathedral towering over them, the palms hissing in the wind.

"What guarantee do—"

"You don't get any goddamned guarantee."

Choat stepped forward and stabbed a finger into Stromsoe's chest.

"Watch your language, security guard. You're on the holy site of the world's third largest cathedral and—"

Stromsoe absorbed Choat's stout finger, and the shift of weight that accompanied it.

Then in one purposeful motion he locked his hands around the big man's forearm, pivoted, squatted, hauled Choat over his back, and slammed him onto the cement. He really got his shoulders into it.

"I was raised Lutheran."

Choat lay there gasping, eyes and mouth wide. His looked up at Stromsoe, his face going pale.

"Do we have a deal, Pat?"

Choat glared up at him, mouth open, but all he could do was swallow great lungfuls of air.

"Sure, fine, think about it. You'll see the light."

36

In the late-night twilight of Pelican Bay Prison, Lunce gave Mike Tavarez his usual perfunctory weapons check. In all of Tavarez's years as an inmate he'd never seen an exit-cell search yield a hidden weapon, as if wagging your tongue or spreading your cheeks and taking five deep breaths would magically send a blade clanging to the floor. The inmates always knew when the exit-cell check was coming. Even the dullest and most furious men found ways to have weapons waiting for them when and where they were needed.

Tavarez put his shoes and clothes back on and backed up to the bean chute for the cuffs.

He followed Lunce down the cell-block walkway, heard the whispers of the men, not his men but the others with which La Eme had détente—the Aryan

Brotherhood and the Black Guerillas and the Crips of the Rollin' 60s and the Eight Trays and Hoover Street—and the scores of lesser gangs that ruled the prisons like the tribes they were.

"X."

"X."

"Who do the SHU? You do the SHU."

He saw a plastic kite bag on a string lilting down from tier three to tier two, graceful as its handler navigated the internal air currents of the great prison to land it at the proper cell below him.

Tavarez said nothing. He padded along in his canvas slip-ons, handcuffed as always, but his senses keen and his heart beating hard. Lunce stood at the door leading to the back side of the east-wing blocks and nodded up at the security camera. A moment later the door groaned open and Tavarez led the way through.

"You're walking fast tonight," said Lunce.

"I enjoy family visits."

"I'll bet you do. Wonder if it'll be the little blonde again."

"I never know what they'll come up with," said Tavarez. He didn't want to talk to Lunce tonight. It was uncomfortable and he didn't want a quirk of speech to arouse Lunce's suspicion. He swallowed a little bit of his own blood.

"Yes, you do. You control everything."

"If I was powerful, I wouldn't be walking around in this freezing prison in nothing but peels and slip-ons."

"With reservations for the SHU."

"Right."

"You should have worn a Halloween mask. Scared the shit out of her. Or maybe turned her on."

"Right."

"My kid went as a werewolf, got sick on the candy, and wouldn't eat his dinner."

Tavarez led the familiar way through the back side of the east wing. The walkway was off-limits to anyone but COs, administrative prison personnel, and escorted suppliers, who could bring their vehicles in only through the double sally ports of the main supply entrance.

When Tavarez stepped outside, the chill hit him like a bucket of ice water down the back. It was a typical poststorm October night in Del Norte County—low forties and damp enough to find your bones. The only good thing was the smell of the great Northern California forest that surrounded them, the aroma of millions of conifers and the square miles of mulch and moss and ferns that made up the forest floor.

They stayed tight to the buildings, stopping midway for Lunce to get the signal from the east perimeter tower—just a flicker of the searchlight—which meant that the electricity to the fence was now turned off and the searchlight would not intrude on Lunce or Tavarez for thirty minutes.

The light winked in conspiracy. Lunce grunted and they struck off as usual across the broad no-man's-land parched by herbicides, headed for the twenty feet of electrified chain-link fence topped by twin rolls of razor ribbon still shiny through the years of rain and sun and dust. The tower searchlights had found their usual points of focus about fifty yards to his left and right, which put Tavarez and Lunce in an uncertain light augmented only slightly by the glow of the waning moon.

Plenty of light, thought Tavarez.

He saw Jimmy's flashlight flick on and off twice in the forest, and approached the fence as usual.

As usual, Lunce came up and stood beside him. As usual, he took his spare handcuffs from his duty belt and tossed them against the fence to make sure the electricity was off.

The cuffs clinked to the ground and Lunce bent to get them without taking his eyes off of Tavarez.

Tavarez stared into the forest. Help me, Mother of Jesus.

Lunce took his usual two small steps backward then turned to walk to his place in the near dark from which he always watched Tavarez and the women.

Tavarez listened to Lunce's footsteps while he worked his tongue against the inside of his cheek. He dislodged the new utility razor blade from its hiding place and clamped it between his teeth, off to the right side, blade out.

Strong and light, Tavarez covered the ground quickly. He gathered himself and leaped high.

Lunce had just begun to turn when Tavarez landed on his back and locked his legs around the big man's waist. Tavarez squeezed hard and pressed his face into the back of Lunce's neck. Lunce staggered forward but stayed up, turning his head back to see his attacker, exposing his throat and its pulsing network of life. Tavarez slashed up and fast and deep, then flung his head back the other direction to cut down and across.

The blood blinded him, so he went by feel: up and away again, down and across again, up and away again as Lunce groped back blindly, so he slashed the hands, felt the blade hiss through the flat meat of the palm then ride up when it hit bone.

Lunce went to his knees with a terrified whimper. Tavarez let go with his legs and rolled off, then sprang from in front of the man, burrowing his face in Lunce's throat, his stainless-steel fang cutting deep and across and again and again. Lunce sprawled backward on the grassless earth, head wobbling loosely, a great wet flapping sound coming faster and faster from the ruins of his neck. Tavarez stood up, eyes wide and bright in a mask of blood, blade still clenched, his breath whistling in and out of his teeth. He threw out his feet and landed butt-first on the guard's stomach. With the fingers of his cuffed hands he searched patiently for the handcuff keys on Lunce's belt.

Tavarez saw little but blood, smelled nothing but blood, felt nothing but blood everywhere he touched. Blood was life. He surrendered to it.

He looked over to see Jimmy and a friend, each working at the chain link with a long-handled bolt cutter. The pop of the steel was better than music. Lunce's breathing was slower now. Tavarez could feel the man's body under his own, laboring for oxygen through the extra weight and the cut supply lines.

He located the universal handcuff key with his fingertips and pulled it out. He stood and tried to look down into Lunce's eyes but couldn't find them through the blood and poor light. He spit the blade to the ground. It took him seconds to get the cuffs off. He dropped them to Lunce's slowing chest, kept the key for a rainy day, then trotted over to the fence and ducked through the hole.

37

Monday morning John and Marianna Cedros were packing for the movers. The little house smelled like coffee and pasteboard boxes and Cedros had to remind himself several times that this was not a dream.

Marianna worked with determined speed. Tony sat in his nearly empty bedroom watching a *Power Rangers* video for probably the thirtieth time.

Cedros, carrying a special box of personal things to his car, angled through the propped-open kitchen door that led to the small garage. The garage smelled of clean laundry and the door was open to let in the good morning light.

Ampostela's gunman from the restaurant, Ricky, was leaning against Marianna's aging sedan.

"What happened to Marcus?" he asked.

"I remember you."

"You ought to."

"Ampostela? Somebody shot him is what the paper said."

Cedros set the box on the dryer. The load was done, so he swung out the front door. His instincts told him to act unworried, maybe even offended.

He got a better look at the gunman now than in the darkened back room of El Matador. The man was pale-skinned and slender, bald, with a big drooping mustache and tan eyes. He hadn't brought his dog, which Cedros found important.

"Who did it?" asked Ricky.

"How would I know?"

"You went outside and got in his car at El Matador. Nobody saw him again."

"I sure as hell did not get into his car. I stood out there like an idiot for half an hour, then I walked home. I didn't see *you* anywhere out there, you stayed in with the girls. So don't tell me I got in his car."

Ricky looked at him but said nothing. His expression was placid but the tan eyes bored into Cedros. He was wearing a baggy black T-shirt over a pair of sharply creased blue trousers but the shirt wasn't baggy enough to hide the bulge at his belt line.

"Sounds like you practiced all that," he said.

Cedros put on a disgusted expression, shook his head slowly, and looked out at Ricky's lowered red Accord parked across the mouth of his driveway as if to keep anyone from getting away.

"Moving?"

"Just a vacation."

"Where to?"

"Vegas."

"With the kid?"

Ricky was looking past Cedros now, through the open door that led to the kitchen.

Cedros turned to see Tony standing in the doorway, brandishing a bright green VHS cassette with yards of tape billowing out.

"Got a problem, Daddy."

"Go back inside. I'll be there in a minute. *Now.*"

Tony turned and walked back in just as Marianna appeared in the same doorway, her face darkly curious.

Cedros held her eye, trying to let his alarm show. Then he looked at Ricky and his fear doubled because he saw not lust in Ricky like he'd seen in Ampostela, but anger. Ricky looked like he wanted to hurt her. He stared at her then smiled, skin wrinkling at the sides of his tan eyes.

"Lena saw you get in Marcus's car," said Ricky. "The Magnum."

"Lena needs glasses."

"El Jefe needs answers," said Ricky.

"El Jefe made two hundred and twenty-five grand without doing what he said he'd do."

"Maybe," said Ricky. "The word is Marcus had twenty-five grand on him."

"I *gave* Marcus twenty-five grand that night. You think I'd go to all the trouble to kill him but not take the money back? How dumb do you think I am?"

For one second Cedros assured himself that Marianna was about to reappear in the doorway with a sawed-off twelve-gauge and either blow or terrify Ricky away. But they had no shotgun and the idea was ridiculous anyway. It was possible she had called 911. All he could think to do was to prolong this conversation, keep Ricky guessing.

"I don't know yet."

"That's right. You don't. Look, man, I'm going on a family vacation. I don't know what happened to Marcus. I thought he was actually kind of a cool guy until he left me sitting there. What was that supposed to be—a joke?"

Cedros thought he saw some kind of uncertainty in the tan eyes. Ricky still hadn't touched his gun, hadn't even gotten a hand close to it.

Just then the cop car drove up and parked along the curb. His heart sped up—he'd never been so happy to see the cops in his life. When he saw who was inside he couldn't believe his astonishing good fortune. It wasn't even the local cops. It was a detective's plainwrap and Cedros recognized the San Diego Sheriff's investigators. He heard them shut the doors and start toward him but he never took his eyes off of Ricky's gun because he figured it was now or never.

"Your lucky day," said Ricky. "I'll be back for this."

He slipped the gun from his waistband and tossed it to Cedros, who caught and dropped it into the dryer with the clean clothes.

"I don't know anything about Ampostela," said Cedros. "I swear it to you and El Jefe."

"Be cool for these guys. You and me are just road dogs."

"You got it."

The investigators were Hodge and Morales, the same two who had questioned him about his visit to Mike Tavarez and his knowledge of a gunman named Ariel Lejas.

They came into the garage and their cops' antennae alerted them to Ricky. They eyed him and both seemed to solve the same equation: *1 gangbanger + 1 relative of El Jefe = 2 gangbangers.*

"We have some more questions for you," said Hodge.

"Me and Mike talked family up in Pelican Bay. That was it. I've told you that a thousand times."

Marianna appeared again in the doorway with a big smile and two cups of coffee. She walked right up to the detectives and delivered the cups, ignoring Ricky. Then she marched over to the dryer, grabbed a load, and went back inside.

"Later, homes," said Ricky.

"Okay, man," said Cedros.

The red Honda roared to life, backed up, and low-rode down the street toward Azusa Avenue, the stinger exhaust bragging more horsepower than the car really had.

"La Eme?" asked Morales.

"Just a friend."

"You being related to El Jefe, that puts you right in the middle of things, doesn't it?"

"I don't know nothing about no La Eme. I'm not so sure it's even real. I think maybe you guys make up gang stuff to keep people afraid and make your budgets fat."

"Let's talk about Ariel Lejas," said Morales.

"Fine. Let's talk. I've never seen him or heard of him until you guys came along."

Marianna appeared in the doorway with a falsely pleasant look on her face, looking for Ricky. When she saw his car was gone her smile became genuine and she got another load of clothes from the dryer.

"You guys might as well come in," she said.

"Thank you, ma'am," said Hodge.

"More coffee in the pot if you want it. Excuse the mess. We're moving. We're getting out of this gang-infested rat hole and we're never coming back."

"What do you know about La Eme, ma'am?" asked Hodge.

"Not much," said Marianna, the load of clothes clutched loosely over bulging belly. "I know they murder and steal. But we can't help it if we have a distant relative who's mixed up with them."

"Well, at least one of you has a grip on reality," said Hodge. "You might need it, because Mike Tavarez escaped from Pelican Bay last night. He sawed a guard's head half off with a one-sided razor blade. Some friends cut a hole in the fence and off he went."

Cedros looked to his wife, then out at the street. It was the same information that Stromsoe had given him two hours ago by phone but it wasn't hard to look unpleasantly surprised.

"Haven't seen him, have you?" asked Morales.

"Why would he come here?" asked Cedros.

"You're blood. You saw him just a few weeks ago up in Pelican Bay."

"We talked family. Nothing else."

The cops shrugged. Cedros followed Marianna back inside, the two detectives close behind.

38

At first light Stromsoe was sitting in Frankie Hat-field's living room, the sun splintering through the avocado trees and the coffeemaker gurgling in the kitchen. Frankie and Ace had slept through the ringing cell phone that woke him half an hour ago. Stromsoe had rolled out of bed and talked to Ken McCann from the dark breakfast nook. Lunce had had a wife and two young children.

Sadie now sat at his feet as Stromsoe loaded Frankie's double-barreled twenty-gauge. It was a heavy Savage Arms side-by with a blond stock and two triggers that could be simultaneously pulled for a double discharge that at close range would blow a hole the size of a softball in a man. Sadie followed him to the foyer, where he stood the gun upright in the right-hand corner, then set four extra shells behind the butt. He looked out the window. She followed him to the kitchen, where he poured a cup of coffee.

"Don't worry," he said to the dog, but the dog looked worried anyway.

Stromsoe walked quietly back to the living room with the coffee, sat on the couch that gave him an easy view of both the front door and the back of Frankie's sprawling farm.

He thought that if he'd been this ready on behalf of Hallie and Billy, he might have prevented what happened, though he wasn't sure exactly how. He could have requested a bomb-sniffing dog and the department would have given him one. He could have requested a wheeled mirror with a long handle to slide under his vehicles each morning and the department would have given him one of those too. But the fact was that La Eme didn't use explosives. It would have been as logical to hire food tasters. The compelling fact was that Stromsoe hadn't believed Mike would try to kill him at all. He'd believed that Mike would see the accident of Ofelia for what it was and that their bond, forged in the friendship of adolescence and finished by the enmity of manhood, would prevent such blunt, mortal action. It seemed almost silly now, because he understood their differences in a way that he hadn't when he was young. Mike's blood was heavier than his own. Mike was Spaniard and Aztec, the conquistador and the warrior. He was the serpent and the eagle. He was Montezuma, who had ruled Tenochtitlán, who offered gold to Cortés and was murdered for his generosity. Mike was the pyramids where thousands of human hearts were cut out and held up beating to the sun; he was the young women thrown into sacrificial cenotes loaded with gold and jewels that took them straight to the green depths, where they were reduced to bones and soon to not even that.

Stromsoe remembered something that Mike had told him years ago, just after Hallie had brought her bruised and broken body back to him.

Keep her. You're the romantic, not me.

Frankie came out in her blue terry robe and sat next to Stromsoe on the couch. He told her about McCann's call.

"How fast could he get here?" she asked quietly.

"Late morning, if he flies."

"But he wouldn't fly, would he? They'll watch the airports up there."

"He probably won't fly. I put your shotgun in the foyer, Frankie. It's loaded and on safe. Either trigger and it fires."

"What if he drives?"

"Early afternoon."

"Is he going to come after me, Matt?"

"He will."

"He won't just hire it out like before?"

"I doubt it."

She nodded and bit her lip, dark hair dangling down.

"Can you take a week off?" he asked.

She shook her hair back behind her shoulder and looked at him. "I will not take a week off. I don't budge."

"He could come today, Frankie. Or it could be a year from today."

"Which is more likely?"

Stromsoe thought about it. "A year. He'd want us to be afraid."

"Can he stay lost for a year?"

"If he makes it past the first eight hours. All he had on them was about an hour head start."

"But they haven't caught up with him yet, have they?" she asked. "He's been gone since eleven last night? That's eight hours ago, exactly."

"If he makes it past the Mexican border, he can stay lost forever."

"And it's easy to get back in," said Frankie.

"Children do it."

"Oh, man."

"Frankie, you're going to have to stay alert to stay alive. Every second, every minute. You can do it if you stay patient and relaxed. Don't let it hurry you. Eyes open. Mind open. Always thinking. It isn't a bad way to live once you get used to it. I did it for years undercover. You have to understand it's a long run. You have to slow everything down."

"I'm getting my own carry permit."

"You should."

"We'll practice every day at the range, then come home and make loud, explosive, ballistic love."

He smiled.

"I need a cup of coffee," she said. "Hopefully Tavarez isn't waiting for me in the kitchen."

"I checked it out. You're good."

"*You're* good."

Ace arrived on scene, yawned, then stretched out in a bed of sunlight coming through an east window.

"I just had an idea," said Frankie. She was halfway to the kitchen. "What if we get an apartment downtown? But instead of living there, we just sleep there, and spend the rest of our free time rebuilding the barn?"

Stromsoe considered. "You're just as exposed downtown as you are here. It wouldn't take him long to figure out the change of address."

"Right, but we just sleep there. Then, bright and early, we get up and head for the barn. We'll get the gate lock fixed so only we can get in. There's only the one road. And once we're there we can see in every direction, you know? If anyone came walking up or came in off road, we'd see them way early. Ted can stand guard. He'd love to. And we work outside until I have to go to work, we build a new barn and I can set up all the stuff. My formula works, Matt. It *works*."

"I saw it work, Frankie. I can vouch for that."

"We got four and three-sixteenths inches in two hours. Santa Margarita Preserve, right next door, they got *two and three-tenths*. Fallbrook got *two and one-tenth*. San Diego got *two*. Temecula, Valley Center, and Escondido got *two and a quarter*."

"I know, Frankie."

"What I'm saying is I've got the real thing, Matt. The real, actual thing that Charley was almost onto. I'm going to be a genuine, legitimate rainmaker."

"I'm a believer."

"You are?"

"I am."

"Then wait right where you are," she said. "I've got something for you."

She went down the hall and into the river room. He could hear the closet open, then the sound of objects being moved. A few minutes later he heard the closet door slide shut.

She came back with a sheaf of stapled papers in her hand.

"I had to make some small changes after last night. It's all here—the components and where to get them at the best prices, how to make it, how to disperse it. It's everything Charley started and I continued. You might need Ted or a chemist to figure out some of it. Oh, and when you stir the final mix don't get the fumes directly in your face and don't stir too fast. It's not like whipping egg whites—if you go too fast the hydrogen atoms bond up too early with the chlorides and it gets mucky. Watching me in the truck mirror wasn't quite enough for you to learn it right. There's touch involved, and concentration."

She handed the booklet to Stromsoe.

He looked up at her. "I never thought a few sheets of paper would make me feel so honored."

She sat down next to him. "Look, I can probably get the rest of the week off, but they'll need me for tonight. I'll call Darren."

"That's a smart thing, Frankie. It's not surrender."

"I might do some of that. Where shall we go?"

"The mountains. You've never bottled the San Joaquin River."

"I'm there."

Ten minutes later it was set. Darren gave her four days off so long as she could broadcast this evening. And a dog-friendly cabin with a view of Mammoth Mountain was on hold with Stromsoe's credit card.

STROMSOE PACKED A WEEK'S worth of things then talked to Dan Birch, Ken McCann, and Warden Gyle. Tavarez had not been seen. Gyle learned that Lunce had been in El Jefe's pocket and this was not the first time that Lunce had escorted Tavarez outside his cell for "unauthorized activities." Some CO heads would roll, he said—the union be damned. His most trusted situation manager, Cartwright, was a good ear inside the guard union. Gyle was still not sure whether Lunce had uncuffed the prisoner and allowed himself to be surprised by the razor blade, or if Tavarez had concealed and wielded the blade with his mouth, then let himself loose using the guard's key. It was also possible that the second or third parties who had cut the hole in the fence had subdued Lunce. He said it was the bloodiest thing he'd ever seen.

"The guards are going to set up a fund for the family," said Gyle.

"I'll kick in," said Stromsoe.

"I'll let you know when we pick him up."

"I'd appreciate that."

He called John Cedros's cell phone. Cedros said he and Marianna and Tony were already halfway to Bishop. Stromsoe said there was a GPU homing device under the rear bumper of his car, please pull it off and mail it to Birch Security. Stromsoe wished him luck and asked Cedros to give him his home address when he got a chance.

"I'm mailing you the evidence against Choat," said Stromsoe. "I've got copies and so does Birch Security. Choat clearly solicits you to burn down the barn. He roars it out, over the sound of the river. The fact that Mother Nature did it for him doesn't change anything. I doubt he'll ever bother you again."

"Thanks, man. I really mean it."

"Thank Marianna for making that call to Birch. It saved at least one life. Take care of your family."

"*Vaya con Dios, PI.*"

"Always."

Stromsoe sat in the living room for a moment, listening to the hum of water going through the pipes to Frankie's shower. They'd be leaving for her work in less than an hour. The thought of Frankie Hatfield cheered his heart and he looked through the windows. The guns of Pendleton began thundering away in the west.

A faint feeling of relief came to Stromsoe, and he was surprised by how large and welcome it was.

He loaded his bags into the pickup, then Frankie's as she got them packed.

Frankie was in the kitchen packing up some food to take when Stromsoe's cell phone rang.

"Hello, Matt."

"Hello, Mike."

Frankie looked up and her face went pale.

"I'm out."

"I know."

"I didn't think it would feel this good."

"Enjoy it while you can."

"I'm going to come see you sometime soon."

"Let me know when you're in town."

The artillery went off again. Stromsoe heard the concussion of it hit his chest like a bass drum in a marching band.

He also heard it coming through the cell phone into his ear.

He motioned Frankie to the floor. She pulled the gun from her purse and sank down, her back to the refrigerator. The dogs waddled over and Frankie had the presence of mind to reach up and set the gun on the counter then take each animal by its collar.

Think of something. Keep him on.

"I heard you made a real mess up there," said Stromsoe.

"I can't get the smell off."

"The ocean can."

"First things first."

Stromsoe went to the foyer and looked out the windows to the avocado orchard.

"That razor-blade-in-the-mouth trick," said Stromsoe. "I read about it years ago in the *FBI Law Enforcement Bulletin*."

"I did too."

"You going to kill Frankie, or both of us?"

"Frankie."

"Weren't Hallie and Billy enough?"

"Nothing is enough."

The artillery sounded against his body and through the phone. From the corner of the foyer Stromsoe scooped up four shot shells and stuffed them into a pocket. Then he tucked the butt of the blond shotgun under his right arm, slid off the safety, and trotted down the hallway.

"You'd like Frankie," said Stromsoe. "You wouldn't hurt her if you just knew her a little."

"That's very Matt, Matt."

The master bath was damp and still smelled of soap and shampoo from Frankie's shower. There was a sliding-glass door leading outside to a small patio with wooden furniture and a *chimenea*. Beyond the patio was a stand of eucalyptus trees, and beyond them the orchard. Stromsoe believed that Mike was in that orchard, watching the front of the house. He was armed and intended to kill them both when they came out the front door. This was only a guess but a guess informed by the twenty-four years he'd known the boy and the man he became. It was possible that Mike had someone with him but Stromsoe believed he was alone. In his own way, Mike had always been alone. Stromsoe's plan was to get fifty yards into the looming avocado trees without being seen, then come up on Mike from behind.

He quietly slid open the door and stepped outside.

"How many times do I have to tell you that Ofelia was an accident? I wasn't *there*, Mike."

"You created the *there*," said Tavarez. "You made it what it was. At a certain point, the only thing that can happen is what does happen. This is called consequence and it's a simple concept, my old friend."

Stromsoe passed through the eucalyptus and into the fragrant shade of the orchard, balancing the shotgun on the meat of his right arm like a bird hunter, left hand raised to his ear with the cell phone, eyes searching the orchard beyond the drive. His heart was pounding wild and fast.

The cannons boomed through the sky from Pendleton.

And echoed through the speaker of the phone.

"Why don't we make a deal?" asked Stromsoe.

"You don't have anything I want."

"We were friends once, Mike."

"You're not asking for mercy, are you?"

"Haven't you had enough blood?"

The guns of Pendleton thundered and again Stromsoe heard them in his chest and in his ear.

"I mean, you're free now, Mike. Why not just head to Mexico, find Ofelia's ghost, or her sister, marry her, spend your millions?"

"What are your plans? Do you love this tall news lady?"

Stromsoe stayed to the middle of one row, moving deeper into the orchard. The fallen leaves were thick on the ground but they were soaked from the recent storm and allowed him to pass quietly. Led by faith and instinct, Stromsoe made the turn that he hoped would lead him to Mike. He had never missed his left eye like he did now.

"Yes, I do."

"You're very lucky to love twice. You must say your prayers every night, and pay your taxes, and go to church on Sundays."

Stromsoe saw Mike standing beside the trunk of an avocado tree, facing the driveway and the house, his back to Stromsoe, an arm raised to his ear. Alone.

Stromsoe looked down before each step, keeping away from the leaves and on the damp silent earth left by the heavy rain.

"I'm not much of a churchgoer," he said.

"Can she really make it rain?"

"She really can. It's impressive."

"Think how valuable she would be to the deserts of Mexico. Think of the thousands of acres of poppies."

"Bring us down as your guests when you get settled. She'll make some rain. Funny, though—I have the feeling you're already there."

"I went north. Everyone will be looking south."

"That was smart."

"Enjoy your time with the rainmaker. I'll see you when you least expect it. And I'll make you one promise, Stromsoe, for an old friend—I'll never use another bomb."

"Maybe a razor, like the guard?"

"Too wet, even for me."

Stromsoe was seventy feet from Mike now. Mike had on a white dress shirt tucked neatly into his jeans, and cowboy boots. The sun hit him in a shifting pattern allowed by the big-leafed trees. He leaned on one elbow against a low tree limb and he looked like a gentleman farmer sizing up this year's crop.

The artillery thundered again.

Sixty feet.

Mike hummed a few bars of "When the Saints Go Marching In."

Every nerve in Stromsoe's body stood up and listened.

Lord, how I want to be in that number...

Fifty feet.

"Adios," said Mike. "Always watch your back, my friend."

"Good-bye," said Stromsoe. "Don't forget to watch your own."

He guessed that Mike had heard him, but Tavarez was still and silent for a moment.

Then Mike wheeled quickly to his left and Stromsoe saw a flash of steel in the sunlight.

Stromsoe swung his left hand up to the gun stock as Mike dropped and rolled and fired.

The double blast took out the limb. The bullet from Mike's handgun screamed past Stromsoe's head. Tavarez zigzagged into the grove, his white shirt flickering amid the tree trunks.

Stromsoe barreled after him, reloading the twenty-gauge without looking at it.

Tavarez scrambled up a hillock, made the top, and whirled around. Stromsoe saw the muzzle flash and heard the wooden knock of the round hitting the tree beside him. Mike was gone by the time he had the shotgun to his shoulder.

Stromsoe thought ambush as he reached the hillock, knew that if he rounded the crest he'd catch a bullet, so he veered out around the rise and tried to do it fast so as to keep Mike at least guessing.

He came around the back with the shotgun held out and two fingers on the two triggers but Mike had already made the road. Stromsoe charged ahead. Through the trees he watched Mike lope across the asphalt into more orchard and he could see the blood on the white shirt.

Mike made straight between the trees now, trying to stretch his lead, but Stromsoe stayed heavy upon him. Bars of shadow and sunlight held Mike as if inside a large cage but Stromsoe knew that if Mike could get out of sight, Mike could surprise and kill him, so he willed his legs to do more.

Then he came up a gentle swale. The grove ended abruptly at a high chain-link fence topped with barbed wire. Beyond the fence were rolling hills of flowers—an ocean of reds and yellows and white stretching all the way back to the blue Fallbrook sky.

Mike ran parallel to the fence but geometry was on Stromsoe's side now and he closed the distance.

Mike fired but Stromsoe could hear only the roar of the two barrels and feel the sharp kick of the butt against his shoulder.

He stepped behind the trunk of an avocado tree, reloaded the side-by, and flicked the safety off. He could see Mike outstretched on the ground. Stromsoe aimed down the barrels as he walked.

Mike's chest was a bloody mess and he was breathing fast. One arm was out and one was trapped beneath him. His legs were spread. His pistol was on the ground by his right boot. Stromsoe lowered the shotgun but kept it pointed at Tavarez's head as he kicked away the handgun. Mike's eyes followed him but he didn't move.

Stromsoe went to his knees beside Mike and looked at his white, blood-splattered face. "Mike."

Mike opened his hand and Stromsoe wondered what he meant by it. It's over? I have nothing? You mean nothing to me?

The eyes stared at him with the same broad mysteries. Stromsoe saw nothing cruel or furious in them, nothing illuminated or forgiving—just the partial understanding that is all a man can have.

"This isn't how I pictured it, Matt."

"Me neither."

Mike stared straight ahead and said nothing for a moment, as if listening to the speed of his own breathing.

He blinked. "We did our best with what we were given."

"We were given everything, Mike. This is what's left of it."

"I never once felt like I had enough. Never."

The breeze stirred Mike's hair and something in his throat rattled and caught.

"It doesn't hurt, Matt."

"Good."

"Come closer. I can't hear you. All I hear is wind."

Stromsoe moved closer.

With a groan Mike freed his hidden fist and swung but Stromsoe caught the wrist and slowly turned it back on itself until the switchblade slipped from Mike's hand.

"Your luck will run out," hissed Tavarez. "And the luck of your pale race and your soulless country. And the devil will then fuck you to death one at a time then all at once."

"Yes. He's practicing on you right now."

"You still believe in the God who ignores you?"

"I believe, yes."

"My faith isn't strong like it used to be."

"Faith doesn't make God."

"Or hell."

"That either," said Stromsoe.

Mike tried to slow his breathing but this made his throat stutter like a truck on a washboard road. He gagged and swallowed loudly. "Tell my children I loved them. Tell my wife I'm waiting in hell for her."

"I'll tell the children. But you'll have to pass along your own curses, Mike. You always find a way."

"You were never as smart as me," said Mike.

"Never. But I'll be here an hour from now and you won't."

"That's an arguable privilege."

"It's not arguable to me at all."

Mike took a series of very shallow breaths, then coughed weakly. His voice was a whisper. "We did have everything, didn't we?"

"Everything."

"I don't have a single regret."

"I've got a million," said Stromsoe.

"Except that I didn't shoot you first."

Mike managed to lift his head off the ground. His eyes searched for the pistol but his head lowered back down to the leaves. Then his fists slowly opened and the light left his eyes.

Stromsoe sat for a long while. He could smell the blood and the rich earth. It was cool in the orchard with the sun streaking the leaves. A painted lady landed on the toe of Mike's right boot, fanned its wings in a spot of sun.

Stromsoe remembered the time Mike had helped him run down the kids who threw the rocks at the marching band, and how surprised he'd been at Mike's ferocity as well as his own. He thought again of the abandon, when every nerve and muscle was needed for that good fight, when he was stronger and faster than he would ever be. What a pure thing, what a rarity as the years had gone by—a moment to be right, and to have a friend there with you.

He looked down at the body and thought of the many people who had died so that he could sit here in this dappled garden. Long ago, standing in the burnished afternoon light of a Southern California cemetery with his father and mother, Stromsoe had understood with a child's simple wonder that some lives end so that others may continue. Later he came to understand that a man's life can be made rich through love as by Hallie and Billy and Frankie, or cursed through hatred as with Tavarez, but it was all their lives that coursed through him now as he reached out and closed Mike's eyes forever.

Author's Note

Fallbrook got record rains that season. The total rain recorded in our area was 34.89 inches, a place that usually gets 12 inches. My rain gauge stands just a few miles from where Charles Hatfield once had his secret laboratory.

T. JEFFERSON PARKER *Fallbrook, California* August 2006

About the Author

T. JEFFERSON PARKER is the author of thirteen previous novels including the *New York Times* bestseller *The Fallen* and the Edgar Award–winning novels *California Girl* and *Silent Joe*. He lives in Fallbrook, California.

www.tjeffersonparker.com

Visit www.AuthorTracker.com for exclusive information on your favorite HarperCollins author.